Foop!

A novel

Chris Genoa

ERASERHEAD PRESS
PORTLAND, OR

This is a work of fiction. Names, characters, places, and incidents are the products of the author's imagination or are used fictitiously. Any resemblance to actual events, locales, or persons, living or dead, is entirely coincidental.

ERASERHEAD PRESS
205 NE BRYANT
PORTLAND, OR 97211

WWW.ERASERHEADPRESS.COM

ISBN: 0-9729598-9-0

Words to original *Livin' in the Sunlight, Lovin' in the Moonlight* by Maurice Chevalier

Printed in the USA.

How's your Lord these days? ....Still worth having? ...
Still lapping it up? ... The passion of our Joe ...Wait till
He starts talking to you ...When you're done with your-
self ...All your dead dead ...Sitting there in your foul
old wrapper ... Silence of the grave without the mag-
gots ...To crown your labours ...Till one night ...'Thou
fool thy soul' ...Put your thugs on that ...Eh Joe? ...Ever
think of that? ...When He starts in on you ...When you're
done with yourself ...If you ever are.

- Samuel Beckett, Eh Joe

Overture

Sung in falsetto with heavy vibrato
Accompanied by ukulele, upright bass, maracas, bongos,
and a child's piano

I'm so happy, ha-ha!
Happy and lucky me!
I just go my way, living every day!
I don't worry, worrying don't agree!
Things that bother you,
never bother me!

Things that bother you never bother me
I feel happy and fine, ha-ha!
Monkeys in the sunlight, goats in the moonlight
Having a wonderful time!

Chasing chimps a lot, I don't need a lot!
I can always eat slime!
Monkeys in the sunlight, goats in the moonlight!
Having a wonderful time!

Just take it from me I'm just free as any robot!
I do what I like, just when I like, and how I love it!

I'm right here to stay, 'til the world gives way
I'll be right in my mind!
Monkeys in the sunlight, goats in the moonlight!
Having a wonderful time!

(Mouth trumpet solo)

Just take it from me I'm just free as any robot!
I do what I like, just when I like, and how I love it!

Oh ho ho!

I'm right here to stay, 'til the world gives way
I'll be right in my mind!
Monkeys in the sunlight, goat in the moonlight!
Having a wonderful time!!!!

Part 1

How

1
Sock-dologizing

I've always thought that the existence of Abraham Lincoln pro-
vided conclusive visual evidence that humans are indeed descended
from apes. I look at apes, and I look at men, even Cro-Magnon man,
and I think, there's gotta be something in between. Where's the link?
The link is Abraham Lincoln. The man looked more ape-like than some
apes do when they're dressed in shorts and suspenders and wearing
sunglasses.

Ape Lincoln. Imagine seeing those Neanderthal cheekbones, bushy
eyebrows, and way-the-hell-deep-set-back eyeballs that constantly remind you of the spooky skull underneath. I'd give him a two percent
chance of being elected in the TV years. People today would lock him
in a cage and throw bananas at him before they locked him in the White
House. And even if he did manage to get elected I imagine people
would still throw bananas at him. At least I would.

He had that same sad expression on his face that all primates have,
especially Koko, that poor gorilla they taught sign language. The sad
eyes and slightly protruding lower lip mirrored that mysterious inner
agony that my dad once compared to the anguish a monkey at the zoo
feels when it looks out into the glorious freedom beyond its cage and

sees a man, its evolutionary superior and only hope for the future of life on earth, wearing a fanny pack.

There's something about that ape—Koko, not Abraham—that always makes me lonely when I think of her. Long dead before I was born, I saw a video about her in high school that gave me nightmares for years after. Koko was the first of many gorillas taught a type of sign language while in captivity. Towards the end of her life, when her own personal zoo ran out of funding, she was released back into what was left of her natural habitat. There she tried to use sign language to chat with the wild apes.

I used to have nightmares that I was Koko, returning home to my family, trying to tell my daddy, using the elaborate hand gestures taught to me since I was a baby, how much I loved him and in return only getting blank stares, confused offerings of bananas, and finally hot fresh feces hurled at me, driving me deep into the forest to a life alone when all I wanted was to tell everybody "Hi! My name is Koko! K! O! K! O!"

Enough. This explains nothing of what happened that night at Ford's Theater.

"Do it or you're fired," my boss told me after I refused to shoot Aperaham Lincoln.

"It's murder," I tried to tell him.

"You can use Booth's gun," he added, as if this perk made it worth it.

"No."

"I'll give you a raise."

"I can't."

"You will."

It isn't easy arguing with my boss, Robert Burk. Born in New Orleans and raised in Texas, the man was as thick as a longhorn. Even though he was pushing sixty, the guy was still physically intimidating. If Lincoln was an ape then Burk is a gorilla—just like Koko. His neck was about the same size as my thigh, and I could probably, in a pinch, take a nap on his chest. He also has these intense green eyes that have a slight flicker of insanity in them, which makes it difficult to look him in the eye for very long without fearing for your life.

"I'll open the curtain, you shoot Abe, and I'll toss Booth over the balcony." He said this with a hint of whatsthebigdealedness in his voice.

"Why can't I toss him?" There were clearly two tasks to be completed, and I didn't see why I had to do the killing. Bosses should delegate, but this was ridiculous.

"You're weak. You'll never be able to pick him up."

"He's a toothpick. I can handle him."

"No, you can't."

Mr. Burk was right. Physically, I'm weak and can barely carry myself around let alone an adult male. In high school I was the skinny dork, not to be confused with the fat dork, who was, I admit, my only friend, but senior year he turned all of that fat into muscle, and I was left with the kid who always wore a long black trench coat as my only friend, and he, I admit, was incredibly annoying.

I looked down at the stage. Act III, Scene II of *Our American Cousin* had come. For the first time in the play there was only one actor on stage, Booth's personal cue to get ready to plug Lincoln. Most of the audience, except for Abe, who was looking his usual somber self, was in hysterics. The play was a laugh riot to people in 1865, a comic farce that played over a thousand performances, but didn't elicit a mere chuckle out of me. The tour group I had been leading didn't get anything out of it either, not that it mattered, as they were there to see an assassination, not dated stage humor.

As I looked across the audience to check on the tour group, I saw John Parker, the man assigned to guard Lincoln that night, sitting in the dress circle, laughing so hard I thought his head would explode. He was supposed to be stationed outside the Presidential Box, but decided to sit elsewhere so he could see the play, apparently preferring the sensation of his head nearly exploding from laughter to the satisfaction of knowing that the President's head would not literally explode.

As I pondered whether I would have made the same choice as John Parker did that night, somehow, without my approval, Mr. Burk's plan was put to a vote, unanimously agreed upon, and put into action.

"On the count of three, we do it." Mr. Burk told me, holding up three fingers in case I needed a visual representation of the concept of three.

"Then what?"

"Then we run like hell."

"Won't the group see you tossing Booth over?"

"I'm going to toss him from here, behind the curtain."

"He is still alive, you know."

"I know. Ready?"

"Absolutely not."

"Good. A-One and a-two and a—"

"Wait! How's Booth gonna yell 'Sic Semper Tyrannis!' if he's unconscious?"

"Does the group even expect him to say that?"

"It's in the brochure."

"OK. Fine. I'll do it for him. I know how to throw my voice."

"Oh please."

"Do you have a better idea?"

"No."

"Right then. A-one and a-two and a-three!"

I stepped through the curtain. The sight of its occupants—Lincoln with perfect posture, looking like a monkey about to be shot into space, his wife next to him, doubled over, laughing manically, Major Rathbone slapping his knee and shaking a finger at the stage, his cute little fiancée, with her fingers over her mouth, her cheeks red—was too much for me. They looked happy. Not O Happy Day happy. *Real* happy.

Neither my BA in History, my teaching certification, my one year teaching US History to hormonally insane teens, nor my stint as a Park Ranger in the nation's capital, prepared me for what I was about to do to keep my current job. So right after pointing Booth's derringer at Abe's head, I did what most people do when they're about to do something physically simple but morally complex—I closed my eyes. Imagining that I was only shooting into the blackness I saw behind my eyelids, I waited for the line in the play that would send the audience into a level of hysterics hitherto unknown at Ford's Theater, the line that Booth used as his cue.

The character left on stage at the end of the act yelled out, "You sock-dologizing old mantrap!" The audience broke into a fit of laughter so intense I expected every one of their heads to explode, one by one, from the pressure. But only one head exploded.

Tick.

That's the sound the gun made. I expected a BOOM! Something that would rattle the whole theater, sending aftershocks through the capital and even out across the Union. But all I got was a tick.

It was enough. The audience immediately screamed. I opened my eyes to see Booth's limp body wiz past me in mid-air and fall the eleven and a half feet to the stage below, culminating in a loud, dense thump, directly followed by two sights. One being Mr. Burk holding his cupped hand to his mouth, yelling in a high-pitched voice that sounded nothing like Booth and everything like a talking mouse, "Sic Semper Tyrannis!" And the other sight being Major Rathbone charging me, looking a tad bit angry.

I closed my eyes again since there wasn't anything pleasant to look at. Then I heard a punch land on what sounded like someone's face, directly followed by the feeling of someone grabbing my arm and dragging me away to what I supposed was the gallows. But the familiar sensation of entering a wormhole, pins and needles all over my body, made me realize that it was Burk who was dragging me away to safety and not Rathbone dragging me to the nearest noose.

All of my visits to the past felt like dreams. Like I was an observer in a world where I could do anything—a world without consequences. And that's because of the Shaved Cat Principal, which will be explained soon enough.

Just as one feels a bit out of sorts on waking up after having had an elaborate dream where you wined and dined your grandmother at a fancy restaurant with the clear and obvious intention of getting her drunk and back to your place, and then succeeding, I felt out of sorts about shooting Lincoln. Not that I thought of it as murder, because the man was supposed to be shot, but as something else, something without a name because it's not something many people do, that is, to go back in time and kill a person who should have been killed by someone else. But I'm certainly not the only person ever to perform an irrational act for the good of his company. History is littered with such suckers. From the guy who hurriedly eats a four-page memo while the Feds search the office next to his, to the chef who hides a dead rat in the soup du jour, the list is long.

But I didn't appreciate being added to that list, or any list, and it was for that reason that I planned to inform Mr. Burk, the very next day, that I would never do such a thing again.

At least not without a raise.

2
Spooky Stuff

"Mr. Burk, I need to talk to you."

I paused in the doorway to his office as I said this, to give me that framed Hollywood style entrance and thereby increase the drama.

He was sitting at his desk, an old oak beast about ten feet long and with not a single piece of paper or office utensil on it. Mr. Burk didn't like clutter. His hands were folded and he rocked back and forth in his chair—which is what he always did in his office. It seemed like he was trying to work out an ultra complex physics calculation in his head, as if there were pages of scrap paper, a pencil, an eraser, a chalkboard, and a calculator all floating around in there.

"Sit down Joe, I need to talk to you," he said, standing up. He then sat back down, demonstrating, I think, how one sits. At least that's the impression I got from the expression on his face.

"I need to talk to you too, sir." I wasn't giving up my framing device until we had settled the matter of just who would be talking to whom.

After a moment, he slowly stood back up again, pushed his chair in, and said, "I need to talk to you Joe."

Matching his slowness, not to be outdone, slowly, I replied, "I need.

To talk. To you."

He blinked once. I blinked twice. We stood there.

We both had something we wanted to tell the other but neither of us wanted to hear what the other had to say, a common problem which usually results in nothing being said and the two parties walking off in opposite directions muttering to themselves what they would have said.

The tension was getting to be too much to bear.

"I have something I'd like to say to you, Joe."

"As do I, Mr. Burk."

He pulled out his chair and sat back down. Head in his hands, his breathing getting heavier, he started to turn red.

"I just need a few minutes of your time sir and then I'll—"

He grabbed the edge of his desk with both hands, threw his head back, and began to scream. His screams came in short intense bursts. Every time he began a new one his head changed position: looking at the ceiling, the floor, then me, and so forth.

"Mr. Burk. Mr. Burk, please don't do this."

His screams became more violent, his body movements matching the new volume. He lunged forward now and the veins in his neck and on his forehead were popping out, ready to explode.

He screamed and lunged at the wall behind me, at the wall in front of me, at his feet, at my feet, at various sections of his desk. Even though the only items in his office were the desk and two chairs, Mr. Burk showed no sign of running out of things at which to scream, since after yelling at his hands, he would later scream at his thumb, and then move in closer to his thumb's fingernail, and then closer to what I can only guess was the cuticle.

Seeing this and fearing that he would continue until he was screaming at individual thumb protons, I gave up and took a seat in front of his desk.

Playing it safe, Mr. Burk screamed three more times after I sat down before stopping completely, catching his breath, and allowing the blood that had collected in his head to leave and return to whatever it had been doing beforehand.

"So we're agreed then?" he asked as he used a handkerchief to wipe the sweat from his forehead.

"Yes."

"Good. I want to talk to you about Lincoln."

We then went over the chain of events that led to me shooting the missing link.

One of our tour group members, a Mr. Sloophauer from Kansas City, had taken it upon himself to knock John Wilkes Booth out cold. He snuck away from the rest of the group while we stood outside the theater, and I related the highlights of Booth's childhood—the over passionate mother, the drunken Shakespearean actor dad—in one of my favorite pre-event lectures.

I was so absorbed in what I was doing—every facial expression, every hand gesture, every knee bend had to be in sync with what I described—that I failed to notice Mr. Sloophauer's sneakiness. He was a round little man, molded much like a meatball, with a disgusting tendency to sweat even when standing still, and I'll admit that I was trying to forget his existence at the time.

I should have known he was planning to do something desperate. Men like him, which is to say men who resemble hunks of ground chuck, have a tendency to fantasize about being the hero, saving the day, stopping the bad guy, scoring the winning goal, and getting the girl who'll let him touch her where nincompoops don't get to touch. And I suppose everyone does so to some extent. But most keep it that way, as something to dream about, not something to act upon.

But this halfwit, this Sloophauer (this Meatball) somehow mustered up enough moxie to actually do something about his dreams. Unfortunately for him, he played the part of the hero a bit too soon, knocking Booth out while the guy was in the bathroom at the pub across the street. Meatball could either think or act, but never both at the same time. Because if he was thinking at all, he would have realized that before Booth killed Lincoln he was a rather popular actor, so knocking

the piss out of him, literally, while he was still in the pub getting ready to make his mark, won't get you much praise. In fact, it'll get your ass kicked right quick.

Just as I was shuffling the group into Ford's Theater, I saw Sloophauer burst out of the pub, pursued by the bartender and three patrons—all pissed in every meaning of the word—with Meatball screaming, "I did it! I did it!" and grinning like an idiot, not realizing that he was about to get tenderized.

Meatball reached the middle of the street, raised his arms in the air as if he had kicked a winning field goal, and proclaimed to the crowd of cheering fans that existed only in his fat head, "I did something!" And he was then immediately punched in the kidney by the bartender.

Following official procedure, I immediately sent a typed message back to the office using my sleek and stylish pocketsize Trasmito-ditto device, invented by Mr. Burk who planned on marketing them to the general public, claiming, accurately and disturbingly, that a person would be able to communicate with himself in the past from the point at which he bought the Transmito-ditto onward. Which would be a novelty at most, something to do on a rainy day, and I imagine many would amuse themselves and their friends by sending cryptic messages back to their past selves that said things such as, "Beware the color orange. It will be your downfall. And while we're at it, the same goes for Magenta."

But it wouldn't be of much value beyond that, since changing past events doesn't do anything to change present situations—once again courtesy of Mr. Burk's famous Shaved Cat Principle. For now, the message I sent that night read as follows:

> I have a problem. This problem of mine is one I would like to make a problem of yours, or failing that, at least a problem of ours. HELP.

One may think that I should have known that Mr. Sloophauer was up to something no good, seeing as that day was his fourth time on the Lincoln tour in less than three months, seeing how he had annoyed me with endless questions on the whereabouts of Booth during every minute up to the shooting, and seeing how he once asked me what I thought a hero was, and my response of "A hero is a sandwich of great courage and fortitude" made him giggle and shake his head side to side like a garden sprinkler. But my job as a guide was to interact with and lead a *group* of people, not to deal with them as individuals. So if the group as a whole had planned to wallop Booth, I surely would have detected and foiled their plan with great flair.

Help was sent in the form of a company security guard and Mr. Burk himself, making a rare personal appearance on a tour. Mr. Burk calmly stepped through the wormhole, walked directly over to the men kicking Sloophauer and stunned them with his electro-zapper. Then he grabbed Meatball—who was yelling out to me through his bloody mouth, "A sandwich of great courage and fortitude!"—and threw him into the wormhole by the seat of his pants. Mr. Burk then went into the pub to see what damage had been done. The security agent and I looked at each other and shrugged our shoulders.

When he came out of the pub, Burk gave orders to the guard to watch over the tour group in the theater and to take them back through the wormhole instantaneously following Lincoln's death. The guard questioned Mr. Burk's use of the word instantaneously, bringing up all sorts of concerns about if one can really define an instant, citing the example of how instant oatmeal takes a few minutes to prepare while instant coffee takes a few seconds. Mr. Burk responded by leaving it up to the guard whether he invoked the oatmeal or the coffee meaning of the word instant, adding that he could give a rat's ass.

The guard took a moment to gather his thoughts. "I guess it'll be oatmeal then."

Mr. Burk then, without even a "Hello, Joe," grabbed me by the arm, dragged me up the balcony level, and the rest is history, but not History.

However, whether it's physically possible for it to become a part of History or not, making history wasn't in my job description

"How do you like your job, Joe?" Mr. Burk asked from behind his desk.

"Oh I love it, sir, I couldn't imagine doing anything else really."

"Any complaints?"

"No, I can't think of any. Well, besides having to shoot historical icons in the back of the head, but I don't see that becoming a regular thing."

"Let's hope not."

I was a tour guide. And as I sit here writing, I still am a tour guide, as no one has gotten round to firing me just yet.

"I've decided to give you a promotion, Joe," said Burk, sliding his arms back and forth across the ample surface space like a fidgety little kid.

"Is that like a raise?" I asked.

"It comes with a raise."

"That sounds nice," I thought that the man was reading my mind, "What's my new job title?"

"Chief of Probes."

"That doesn't sound like it has much to do with guiding tours."

"It doesn't have squat to do with that."

"Then what does it have squat to do with?"

"What does it sound like it has squat to do with?"

"It sounds like it has squat to do with probes."

"Exactly. I want you to probe something for the company...a person's life. Mr. Martini will be the Assistant Prober."

"Martini?"

"What's wrong with Martini?" He asked as if he didn't know, which he did.

"A lot of things."

"Do these things have anything to do with probing?"

"No."

"Then I see no problem."

"Who will we be probing?"

"A man who is in serious danger. Serious, horrible, disgusting, nasty danger—spooky stuff."

"Who is he?"

Mr. Burk slowly stood up. "He is me."

3
The Duo

Even though I was scheduled to lead an afternoon tour on the day after I shot Lincoln—a tour to see Babe Ruth hit his called-shot homerun—I was given the rest of the day off. And even though I was looking forward to eating my own personal bag of those tasty hot peanuts while discussing the finer points of Mr. Ruth's excessive orifice-stuffing lifestyle with the group, I didn't mind the new assignment. It was a chance for me to experience something new at work, to see people walk by and not know their History, such as when they were going to get shot in the back of the head or exactly which pitch they would hit out of the park. Because when you live through a particular day for the first time, every person you see could conceivably get shot in the back of the head someday, even that day or that very moment, and *that* is what makes life so interesting. Unless of course you are the one who gets shot in the back of the head.

On my way out of the office I stopped by the employee lounge to say goodbye to May—the person, not the month—who always did one hundred deep knee bends at 10:15 a.m. every day as part of her routine.

Routines like that turn me on (they make me say oooooo yeah), mainly because I haven't ever been able to establish any of my own, and things that I can't do, when I see them done and done well, make me hot to trot.

It's not because I never tried to get a healthy routine going, because I have, desperately. I've tried everything from drinking a pitcher of water first thing every morning to running in place whenever I shower, but nothing stuck.

If I could have a routine of my own, something like deep knee bends, my life would be easier to explain to people when they asked me what I did, or what I liked to do. I could have told them, "Me? I do deep knee bends." And they would say, "Oh, I do deep knee bends too! Let's talk about deep knee bends, shall we? And then maybe we could do deep knee bends together every Tuesday at sunset, and afterwards we could lie down somewhere and hold each other until the burning in our thighs subsided."

While going through puberty, I recall putting together an impressive streak of consecutive days having violated myself, but the time of day and number of times a day were nowhere near consistent enough for it to be called a routine. And whether that's healthy or not depends on whom you ask.

I wished that it was May and not the depressing mule that is Martini who was working on the probe with me. The man always brought me down, the sound of his voice alone being enough to make many people consider suicide.

But not my May. Ah May, what a gal, what a gal, I'm in love. I've lost count of the number of times I've dreamt of us getting to know each other via verbal back-and-forth and physical in-and-out. But I never could seem to get past her outer May shell, or possibly out of my outer Joe shell, and into the inner May.

"I'm dying, May." I told her for no valid reason except for a lack of anything else to say. What I should have said was, "Come with me, there isn't much time. Let's take to the open road, just you and I, driving in a big car with the top down, headed towards something even bigger, also with its top down."

"Don't say such things, Joe. You frighten me!" She said while I pondered her thighs. I must admit here that I wanted to use them as pillows. I'm not talking about chopping her legs off and making them into pillows like that nut across the river did to his neighbor a few years back. I wanted them still to be attached to May. I wanted them warm, and I wanted them to wiggle and squeeze, not rot.

"I've been reassigned, May. I won't be leading the afternoon tour with you today, or possibly ever again. So I might as well be dead." I told her, sticking my lower lip out while I reconsidered the thigh desire, figuring that thighs, being solid, do not lead to the soul. So I considered a kiss, which concerns the mouth and which is an opening connected to a tunnel. And all tunnels must lead somewhere.

May smacked her hands on her cheeks. "Oh my God, Joe! You've been fired!"

"That's not what I said."

"Oh Joe. Joe, Joe, Joe. What will you do? You'll become a bum. A bum!"

"You're not listening to me."

"What's going on over there, guys?" piped in Dale, the tour guide who was staring at the vending machine in the corner of the lounge, and I suspect that he had been standing there for over fifteen minutes, frozen by the sheer magnitude of choices before him. He was such a man.

May turned her look of horror towards Dale. "Joe's been fired, Dale! He's going to become a bum and he's going to look just like a real bum and he's gonna follow us home one night and do all sorts of horrible wonderful things." May informed him, incorrectly and, might I add, bizarrely.

"A bum?" Dale, shocked out of his stupor, smacked his hands on his cheeks and came sliding over.

I believe that people stopped listening to exactly what other people said at or around the time humans started using words. There's just too many of them, and a lot of them don't really mean anything, so why should people tune in? Before language, when a guy grunted "ooga dooga gabong!" to you, you knew, without having to do any deep thinking, that he was about to bash your head open and make a meal out of your brain goo. Or if a woman came up to you and said "ooooo aha o o a o aha" you knew that she wanted to inform you that she had just invented the wheel. And if she went on to grunt something along the lines of "oopa oopa! gaaaaaazoopa!" you knew she was, in addition to being the Henry Ford of the Stone Age, also, much like Ford, fucking nuts.

I tried to break it down for my coworkers.

"Stop it. I haven't been fired and I'm certainly not going to become a bum. Nor will I do any horrible wonderful things to you. I've been promoted. Promoted to an exciting new department that nobody knows about yet. It's new. It's exciting. And the work being done is incredibly important. But that's really all I can say."

Dale's shock went to awe. "Why's that, Joe?"

"It's all very hush-hush, Dale." I told him and then turned to May as I gravely added, "Spooky stuff."

May shivered. Dale's jaw dropped as he smacked his hand on top of his head.

I casually grabbed Dale's coffee cup out of his hand, took a sip from it, looked into the cup, and said, "That's right." And then looking up into Dale's eyes, "That's right."

Then I left, and that was that. Another chance to get to know May ruined by what I now suspect was a strong sexual desire of hers to have a bumified version of myself follow her home and make love to her. For me it's routines, for her it's bums. To each one's own.

When I walked outside, thousands of people hustled around me. I was reminded of the ant colony I kept as a kid. The difference being that my ants were always working together towards a very clear end, not one of them ever stopping to look at me and say, "Why am I doing this?" as they built another tunnel or gathered more food for the Queen.

Boogedy & Nibbles

And while the people around me also never stopped to look at me and say, "What am I doing?" I would often see a face pass me by with an expression that asked that very question, not to me, but to itself, with the only answer I can imagine being a shrug and, "Don't ask me."

It was almost impossible to not be in a crowd those days, to not have people brushing up against you, pressed against your shoulders, boxing you in. Especially in the city. There were eleven billion people in the world and often it felt like they all lived with me, or were at least always near enough to stop by for a chat.

Living in this mass—rarely physically alone, but always mentally— I was obsessed with intimate contact. Not the sticky, smelly, awkward messy kind with lots of poking around and missing the mark, gases escaping, bad tastes, and odd odors. And not the cattle-drive-to-and-from-work kind. It's the warm glowing kind that I was obsessed with, the kind that perhaps only exists in retrospect, seen through nostalgia-tinted glasses.

As I was bumped and jostled, and as I retaliated with bumping and jostling of my own, I entered into equilibrium with my environment like a dingy in a rough sea, which allowed me to focus on my new mission.

Mr. Burk had given me an envelope (on paper no less!) with instructions that I could not open it within fifteen miles of the office and not until the sun had set. After reading the contents inside I was to destroy (destroy!) everything. I assumed he meant everything inside the envelope and not everything in general, but just to make sure I asked.

"Well," Mr. Burk replied, his face lighting up, "I suppose if you feel up to it you could take a stab at everything in general. It certainly would mean a lot to me."

I told him that I really didn't think I was up to it, and he wholeheartedly agreed, but not without a tinge of disappointment on his face and in the middle finger he flicked me on my way out.

On the subway ride home, the train was overcrowded as usual, even though it was still early in the afternoon. Rather than more seats or extra trains, we needed another earth to spread out into.

By an act of physical dexterity I never knew I was capable of—it involved a squat, a thrust, a spin, and a limbo—I managed to get a seat, squished between two people far too big for their own seat partitions, allowing their overflowing haunches to spill into my God-given area. It was uncomfortable, but it beat the frequent elbows to the gut that came with standing on the subway. I prefer my abuse in the form of mild constant rubbing rather then sporadic wallops of unpredictable power.

In the row of seats on the other side of the train, directly across from me, I could see, between the swaying arms and legs of the people standing in the aisle, a strange old skinny man looking at me. The odd thing was that when I looked at him and saw him looking at me, I turned away, but he did not.

Out of the corner of my eye I could see him still staring, defying social interaction law number ninety-three which states that if you find yourself engaged in the creepy behavior of staring at a stranger, be it a beautiful woman or a deformed child, and that person looks up and sees you staring then you must, for the sake of all that it holy, look away.

This man did not.

He was tall, wearing a tight, faded black suit a couple sizes too small. Even his liver spots were old and faded. His skin looked like rice paper and he was so thin that he looked like a walking skeleton that somehow got his hands on a can of flesh-colored paint and slapped on a coat. His little eyes, one blue and one green, burned through me when he was able to make eye contact, which wasn't easy with the people swaying in front of us as the train lurched about. I felt as if he was trying to see all the way down into my soul. His lips were so red against his white skin that it looked like he had just eaten a cherry popsicle. Maybe he had.

In short, he looked like the type of man who, at any moment, had the potential to jump in front of your face with his tongue flapping wildly, his eyes bulging, and scream, "Boogedy boogedy boo!"

That's why I call him Boogedy.

"He could be out to get me," I thought. "Maybe he has lofty dreams of toppling the Chief of Probes."

I clutched the envelope tightly to my chest for protection as I scanned the train to see if anyone else could be in cahoots with him. People like him normally don't work alone. They prefer having a partner, someone to distract their target while Boogedy creeps up from behind and then jumps out screaming his catchphrase.

I looked up and down the train. No one curious to my right. The left looked good too, with just the usual creeps in their post and pre-work stupors, so I figured I just had Boogedy to worry about. That's when I saw the little man sitting next to him.

You may wonder how I could have missed seeing this man during my initial look about, and I answer by saying that when I say he was a little man I mean he was itty-bitty. No taller than a fire hydrant, he could easily be mistaken for a child or even a doll if he kept still for too long.

He truly looked like a man who was perfectly shrunken down by a voodoo priest. He had thick, curly black hair and he too wore a faded suit, but brown. Even though it looked like he got the suit from a doll, it was still too big for him. I refer to this tiny man as Nibbles only because upon seeing him, the first thought that entered my head was, Please Lord don't let him nibble me. I've always been worried that every small animal I come across—especially rodents, and including children—enjoys nibbling things, anything really, including flesh. I suppose this fear goes back to my childhood, to the time when I awoke one night to find my pet hamster Doodlepot nibbling my pinkie finger.

The itty-bitty man was too much for me. I immediately knew, from the simple fact that they both had freakish appearances, that Boogedy and Nibbles were together—a Duo.

The train kept rocking and the Duo kept bobbing their heads and bodies to keep their eyes on me. Didn't they realize how obvious they were being? I decided to show them just how silly they looked by mimicking them, moving my head this way and that to see them between the shifting passengers, hoping they would make the connection that they were being terribly unstealthy. They didn't.

People with possible plans—plans involving me, regardless of what those plans are—make me more uncomfortable than anything else in this world. Unable to change seats, unwilling to stand up, but needing to do something to get away from those stares, I stopped my bobbing and closed my eyes, blocking out not only the Duo but the world as well—yes, like a fool, but I assumed I was safe with so many people around.

With my eyes shut the world didn't seem like a place where people would bother to harass a guy like me, and I thought that maybe I was being a bit too paranoid and needed to chill out. So I let the rocking train lull me into a light sleep, where I dreamt I lived in a city full of nothing but Boogedies and Nibbleses. Where every corner, window, mailbox, parked car, and door held the strong possibility of a "boogedy! boogedy! boo!" And every change of pants held the high likelihood of a nibbling for the old testes.

After a multitude of such dream encounters I awoke to find that I had missed my stop and that the train was so far out from the center of the city that it was empty except for the Duo and I. So much for chilling out.

They sat in the same seats, looking at me with blank expressions on their faces, giving me nothing to gauge what they were thinking. They were empty. I tried not to make eye contact with them, to occupy my vision with something less offensive, but it was difficult as there was nothing else to look at besides the wall to wall flashing and twirling advertisements, which I had seen almost as many times as I've seen my face in a mirror.

With no people there to at least give me the illusion of safety, I couldn't just close my eyes this time and hope for them to go away. And I couldn't get up and walk to the next train car because if they followed me there would be no doubt they were after me, and the fact that there was still doubt was the only thing keeping me from freaking out. With no sane options, I seriously considered leaping up and down the aisle shrieking like a child in a moon bounce, when someone entered our compartment.

It was a salesman, of sorts.

"Ladies and gentlemen! Hydrogen! Hydrogen here, folks! Only a dollar a squirt!"

It was a homeless hydrogen salesman with a metal tank on his back that was so heavy it made him sway and nearly fall over as he walked. I had seen him on the subway before, trying to sell his low-grade squirt to folks whose various portables had run dry. I always ignored him, looking at my shoes to avoid eye contact, but this time he was my salvation. I turned away from the Duo and looked his way.

"Grade-A Hy-dro-gen, ladies and gentlemen. You can't...you just can't go home without some of my grade-A. Not when it's only a dollar, one dollar! For a squirt! A Grade-A squirt!"

The Duo didn't need any hydrogen that day, in fact, I rarely saw people who needed it on the subway. He must sell enough to get by on, why else would he keep doing it? Maybe it was something to pass the time, so that when people asked him, "What are you doing?" He could answer, confidently, "I'm selling hydrogen. What are *you* doing?"

A ray of hope flashed across his face when he saw me looking at him. I was a potential customer, the first of the day or even the week, the month, hell, his first customer ever perhaps.

He stopped in front of me. "I couldn't help but notice your interest in my grade-A, sir. Now you've seen grade-A in stores for twenty dollars a squirt. But here now, just for you, this day only, for a limited time, don't walk, run, while supplies last, product may settle during shipmen—WHOA!"

I grabbed him by his coat and shoved him down into the seat next to me. A stupid move considering he had a tank of gas under pressure on his back, but I needed him to confirm what I was seeing sitting across from me. I wanted to see his reaction to the Duo so I could react the same way because, as things were, I had nothing. I held him down by his arm as he squirmed to get away.

"Whoa! Crazy man! Help! H-E-E-E-E-E-ELP!"

I whispered into his ear, "Stop it. Look. Look at those two guys across from me. What are they doing? Are they looking at me?"

He karate chopped my arm several times consecutively, but there wasn't much force behind them so I kept my hold. "What two guys?" He asked. "You're crazy. There's just one man over there. Help! Murder!"

"What does the one guy look like?"

"He's tall, skinny. And he sure is looking at you. HELP! CRAZY MAN!"

"What about the short guy?"

"There ain't no short guy."

I immediately released him and looked in front of me to see that Nibbles was indeed gone. Boogedy was still there, but Nibbles had vanished. I looked up at the ceiling, expecting to see him stuck up there like Spiderman, but he wasn't.

I stared at Boogedy, trying to detect any change in his appearance, wondering if Nibbles had somehow combined with him to form a new super being with the terrifying ability to say "Boogedy! Boogedy! Boo!" *and* nibble my testicles at the same time. When I couldn't find any such transformation in Boogedy, I ran through other possibilities. What if Nibbles was a ghost? What if he was Boogedy's pet ghost? What if he was a four dimensional being capable of popping in and out of our dimension? What if he was standing in the aisle at the other end of the train, arms and eyes crossed, still looking at me?

He was.

And by the time I saw him the hydrogen man was trying to sell him a squirt.

Boogedy and Nibbles were obviously trying to divide my attention. Clever. They made their move, a bold one, and it was my turn. So I countered with a move of my own, doing what I feel is the most threatening thing a man can do—I stood up. I took such extreme measures to show them what they were dealing with, what I looked like at my full height, that I wasn't afraid of their superior numbers or superior oddness, that I wasn't the sort of guy who takes things sitting down, and that I wasn't afraid of playing all my cards at once.

Unfortunately, the only person who fully understood my move and was justifiably shocked by it was the salesman, who stopped his sales pitch to Nibbles and pointed at me as if I was the devil.

"Look out! He's standing up! He means business! Help! Help! Stop the train!" He screamed as he beat on the closed train doors, making quite a scene, but not enough to get the Duo's eyes off me.

With the screaming and pounding of the hydrogen man as a backdrop, and as the train finally pulled into a station, my arm, acting alone and without my consent, raised the envelope high above my head, all the way to full extension, and with it rose the eyes of the Duo and the hydrogen man. My move to stand had excited my arm so much it too wanted to do something bold. I only wish that it had consulted with me, and given me some time to work out what I would do next. As it was, I was stuck there with three men staring at me and no idea where I was going with this. I supposed that I needed to say something bold to match my arm, but all I could think to say, as the train stopped and the doors opened, was, "I am!"

After that vague outburst I dashed out the door and sprinted down the platform, with the envelope still above my head.

The train pulled out of the station, traveling in the same direction as I was running, and as the car I had been in passed, I saw Boogedy, Nibbles, and battery man huddled together, looking out a window at me. I continued running as long as I could, that is to say, until I reached the end of the platform. By that time the train had completely left the station.

I briefly considered waiting for the next train headed back towards my stop, but decided against it. Instead I took a cab, quite happy to pay the extra money to ensure a safe ride home.

When the cab stopped at the first of many red lights, a thick horde of people crossed the street in front of me and I was reminded of a school of fish migrating through the ocean. Then I looked up through the window at the evening sky and saw a swarm of planes crisscrossing by, and was reminded that the fish had taken over the sky as well.

I closed my eyes and drifted off to sleep, dreaming I was a fisherman.

4
The Birth of Dactyl

Somehow, over the three years that I lived there, my apartment building turned from just another faceless high-rise in the city into an old folks home. No, that's not what it was. It was less of a home and more of a resort, with the basement turned into a pool (every morning filled with what I often mistook to be numerous floating corpses), hot tub (boiling corpses), sauna room (steamed corpse anyone?) and the first floor converted into a combination bingo hall (never have numbers and letters been put to a better use) and buffet style cafeteria (where men in black socks and sandals hang like vultures over the precariously empty vat of butterscotch pudding).

When I moved in to the twenty-two floor complex the other occupants were the usual mix of single men and single women (some yuppies, some bartenders), young couples (some happy together, some indifferent together), lonely old men (some grumpy, some creepy), lonely old women (some dumpy, some sleepy), ethnic types (some foreign, some domestic), perverts (some shifty, some shiftier), exercise nuts (some healthy, some psychotic), and so on. There was variety.

But gradually, under my nose, all of those people moved out, while nothing but people in the age group known as golden oldies moved in.

Actually, for all I know, the golden oldies may have moved in all at once, en masse, or worse, taken the place over by force and leaving me intact as the token young guy. I can't be sure exactly what happened, I just know that one day I came home to find that there were either short old women popping quarters into slot machines or short old men playing bocce ball on almost every hallway.

I later found out that at some point, by a unanimous tenant vote, my building had changed its name from Astral Apartments to The Smiling Sunset Community. If I don't bother to vote I really can't complain about the state of things.

After the subway incident I entered my apartment, which was on the first floor then, but hadn't always been. I used to live on the ninth floor in a nice little corner unit with no less than two big windows in each room, but was asked to move by another unanimous tenant vote, so they could turn my place into an indoor hydroponic tomato garden. Not willing to put up a fight over something as inanimate as a room, I agreed to move and was given Mr. Pushcatela's place on the first floor just two days after he died. Kind of creepy, but it was worth it for the free tomatoes.

Waiting for me was a postcard, my first mail in months. It was from my older sister, Mary, who I haven't spoken to in years.

Mary and I never got along as kids. We constantly abused each other physically, via stealthy pinching and roundhouse kicks, and verbally, via vicious name calling such as fatso, fatstuff, fatbag, fathead, fatface, fatcheeks, and fatty fatty fatburger, even though neither of us was fat.

As a teenager, Mary abandoned the fisticuffs and turned to the higher calling of making me her personal servant. She incessantly begged me for little favors, and was able to wear me down just enough times to make it worth her while. I even caught her praying one night, asking God to please oh please make me use my allowance to buy her a boy band poster. Remarkably, I did.

As adults, the abuse turned solely emotional, via guilt over my moving away and leaving her with the burden of our aging parents, and in time we stopped talking to each other all together. She still sent me the yearly Christmas card and occasional vacation postcard, this one from Alcatraz Island with an aerial photo of the prison on the front and a message scribbled on the back that read "Wish You Were Here." Very clever on Mary's part, as there was no way for me to determine if she was trying to make amends for years of abuse and neglect and truly wished for me to be there with her and her family to share their vacation bliss, or if it simply meant that she wished I was rotting in prison. I suppose she could have meant something else entirely, on a number of deeper levels, but I'll never know, because at the very least, I'm inept when it comes to these things, and at the very most, I just don't give a shit.

After putting the postcard on the fridge, between two take-out menus from restaurants that went out-of-business years ago, I locked myself in the bathroom, landed my blimp in the porcelain sea, and tore into Burk's envelope. The only things in it were a yellow legal pad, an index card, and a photograph. The card read as follows:

12:14 pm, July 5, 2001, Methodist Hospital,
New Orleans, Louisiana

That meant nothing to me.

Moving on, I took out a photograph of a man who looked like he could be Mr. Burk's younger brother, but it was hard to tell because the fellow in the picture had a gag in his mouth, something stuffed up his nostrils, and a pair of black, as in bruised, eyes. Very curious.

I pulled out the notepad. I don't have it with me now as I write this, but I read it quite a few times and I've remembered it well. So I think it's all there, the main points and voice at least, and anything I've forgotten wasn't very important anyway.

The Position of my Condition:
An Essay for Joe in Four Points
by Dr. Robert Q. Burk

Point One: you suck.

Point Two: I have one scar on my entire body and that scar is located on my right cheek. Did you ever notice it? Do the other employees call me The Scar behind my back? If not, please tell them to do so immediately because I believe that the happiest people in life all have nicknames. Some people are embarrassed by their wounds, both physical and emotional, and they go to great lengths to conceal them. Not I. To me, every wound is an enthralling story waiting to be told and exploited, and the story of my scar goes like this:

I was drunk late one night, tipsy and on my way to being hammered, and I found myself alone, wandering around the Relatively Robust Ion Collider (or RRIC) where I worked at the time. This was many years ago, back when I was first put in charge of the RRIC program. It was the best damn particle smasher in the world at the time. Much better than that piss poor Atlas Collider the idiots across the pond had. The complex that held the RRIC was visible from outer space. So it was big. There I was, alone with the Collider, just sitting there, begging me to fire it up. So I did. And I was drunk. Do you see what's happening here? Great things are being set in motion. I was drinking rusty nails. Do you even know what a rusty nail is? Do you even care? It doesn't matter. I was getting the collider ready to do its thing, all the while spilling my hooch and blowing menthol cigarette smoke all over the machine. This wasn't in the manual, but I was drunk. By the by, I'm leaving some sensitive, top-secret information out for two reasons. One being that I don't want my competitors or those who are out to get me to know my secrets, and two because I feel the need to dumb all this down for you—because you're dumb. So I won't even mention, in detail, what I did to the Tandem Van de Graaf or to the booster synchrotron that night, but I will say that I did some inspired, alcohol induced tinkering. So the thing, the collider, starts humming, which means that it's on and working. That's what humming means. The thing always hummed when it was on. ALWAYS. This is a fact. But that night, the humming got louder. And louder. Until...wait for it...bing! There was a flash of light. This too was new. And it was a bright light, less like a lightning bug passing in the night and more like an infinite number of lightning bugs flying up your nose. And after that dot dot dot nothing. A moment of silence. Nothing happens. And then. Bubbles. Weeeeeeeeee! Little bubbles pop into existence in the air around me. It's like popcorn popping, Joe. First there were only a few at a time, but the rate of popping increased and within a minute the room was full of them. And I was, in my state, skipping around the room trying to catch these bubbles, like some damn girly. They were like soap bubbles, varying in size from a golf ball to a large boulder, and I couldn't see my, or any, reflection in them. But I could see other things. Kooky stuff. Oceans, mountains, stars, toast, cars, cities, fingers... They were floating spherical windows and they were all around me, circling as if they were in orbit. I went from bubble to bubble like people go from painting to painting in a gallery, checking out each one but not thinking much about what I was seeing. Before I could see them all, they began to shrink away back into nothingness, until only one remained. It was the biggest one, and it was moving extremely slow. I walked up to it and looked in. There was an ocean and great black cliffs. In the air around the cliffs were countless brown birds. Big ones. Were they eagles? Hawks? I couldn't tell because they were so far away.

And there were fish in that ocean, black fish jumping out of the water, much bigger than the birds, but again they were too far away for me to make out much detail. I was just about to give the bubble a good poke to see what it was made of when I was knocked down by something big and slimy. On my back, lying on the lab floor, I saw that it was a pterodactyl. Good God! And it was seriously fucking shit up in the lab. I immediately took evasive action and hid under a table. After a good half hour of wailing and making a mess, the bird gave up and perched on a filing cabinet in the corner, looking around the lab and shitting on the floor. I decided to get a closer look, so I came out from the table and walked towards the beast saying soothing, friendly things like, "Nice birdie. Good little bird. Goooooooooooood birdie. Niiiiiiiiiiiiice bird. Hello bird. Hello there guy." Keep in mind that this was all to a dinosaur with teeth bigger than my nose. I have balls, Joe. Great big brass balls. That gives me an idea: maybe you should tell the others to call me Big Brass Balls (or BBB) instead of The Scar. At least consider it, will you? Good. Now, I got up real close to the bird and looked into its empty black eyes, which were fixed on me. It was blinking a lot, enough to annoy me anyway, and its head was cocked to the right. I reached out to touch the thing, to pet it really, as if it was Benji, I was trying to be nice, and the bastard scratched my right cheek. On my face, Joe! What kind of a bird does such a thing? Something had to be done, a response needed to be prepared. So I went into my office next door, leaving the bird blinking on the cabinet, went over to my desk, opened the bottom drawer, brushed aside the gun magazine, grabbed the handgun hidden under it, kissed it, went back into the lab, went back over to the blinking bird, and shot that fucker in its head.

Don't judge me, Joe. Not you.

Anyway, hence the name Dactyl for my company.

Now, to lighten the mood, it's time for a humorous antidote: Why didn't Niels Bohr cross the road? Because he was already there. And there, and there, and there, and there, and there! Bada-bing!

Sorry, that may have been over your thick, dim, misshapen head. The important thing is that now you know why people will one day either call me Big Brass Balls or The Scar behind my back, because of my ONE scar. Remember that. Let's move on.

Point Three: a few days ago I received a picture in the mail. You have a copy of the picture. A copy which I want you to burn before the sun comes up. You read me? The sun, Joe. The sun knows all. The man in the picture is me. Me, Joe. Look at me! It's a younger me, but it's still me. Look closely at the picture, past the hotdogs up my nose. What do you see? You see my face. You see a tear in my eye and a scratch on my cheek. You see the kind of scratch that leads to a...SCAR! But look at me now, boy! Do I have TWO scars on my cheek? NO. BBB has one scar. So what have we learned? We've learned that what you see happening in the photo never happened to me. I should know because I'm me. But here's this picture. What does this tell us? Someone, some psycho, has gone back in time, kicked my ass, took my picture and mailed it to me in the present. Did you comprehend what I just said? Stop for a minute. Think about the young you. Cocksure and full of moxie. Now, imagine finding out that some nut job has gone back in time, going through all that trouble, spending all that money, just to smack you around a bit and take your picture. Regardless of The Shaved Cat, how would that make you feel? I'll tell you how I feel. I'm so mad I can't shit. Not could, CAN'T.

This monster sent me a second picture. Do you know what that picture is of, Joe? It's a photo of a hospital, the hospital I was born in. This is a clear threat to the baby-me. Do you see my problem? Would you say that I am a man in need of assistance? Yes. The final point will address this issue by giving you your nonnegotiable marching orders.

Point Four: go back in time. Visit me as I leave my mother for the first time to see the world. Keep your eyes open. Take notes. Take pictures. Do NOT rough me up. If you see someone attempt to rough baby-me up, STOP THEM. I don't care how, just protect me. Because if I get a photo of the little innocent, defenseless baby-me with so much as a paper cut on him I will fire you Joe, on the spot, and then I will proceed to lock myself in my office, assume the fetal position on top of my desk, and, with the photo two inches from my face, cry and shit my pants for ten days straight.

This is an image that you must keep in mind as you go about your mission.

You have at your disposal all of the resources of Dactyl, Inc. Your own personal worm room is located in the basement of the office and your operator's name is Warren. Don't fuck with him. He knows nothing of the mission, just that you have unlimited access. Keep it that way. Talk to no one. Fuck with no one. Trust no one. Record everything. Be nice. Use a stun gun if necessary. Anyone who tries to hurt me I want to see in my office, stunned, gagged, and hog-tied. So bring some rope.

Understand? Good. Destroy this letter and give the card to

Warren in the morning. The date on the card is my birthday. That is where you will begin. Godspeed, you son-of-a-bitch.

After reading Burk's letter I understandably had mixed feelings. On one hand, I was excited that I was finally getting a chance to go into the past on my own and look for something new and not do the usual, which was to take a group of people back to look at something that had been seen, recorded, written about, and commented on hundreds of times over. But on the other, the whole business of stunning and hog-tying worried me. I don't know if you've ever been asked to hog-tie someone before, but it makes a guy ask all kinds of questions about himself, such as, "Hog tying: is it for me?" and "Hog tying and I: where is this relationship going?" Not willing to lose my job, and with a lifelong inability to not do what I'm told, I was about to find out.

5
Fiddle-de-diddle

That night I dreamt I was at the ballpark with The Bambino. It was one of those dreams I often have where I'm the size of a finger and everyone else is a giant. Most of the time I scurried between people's feet, hid out in women's purses, threw pebbles at hostile rats, and basically tried not to get squished or eaten. There was also a touching moment when, in a rare display of giant altruism, a smiling child bent down and let me lick some strawberry ice cream off her pinkie for sustenance. It was the most delicious thing I ever tasted, and I did a little tap dance for her as a way of saying thanks, which made her giggle with delight. Of course, right after that the girl picked me up and forced me to tongue-kiss her grimy doll, but everything up to that borderline rape was sweet.

And, as is typically the case with my dreams, just as I figured out how to use my size to an advantage, as I put the finishing touches on a tiny catapult I intended to use to launch a peanut up the Babe's nose as he took a full-count swing, my alarm went off and I woke up to the Bert and Monkey morning show on Q 93.3 DM. Monkey was in rare form.

He was screaming. "Bonk! Bonk! Bonk! Ruff! Ruff! Oooooga! Oooooooga!"

Bert's reply was, "Yesssssss sir, mornin' time! Time to hup, hup, hup! And geeeeeeeet up! Good morning, Monkey."

"Good morning, Bert."

"How ya feelin' today, pal?"

Monkey's reply was a long sequence (about 2 minutes) of ape freaking out noises with some conga drumming backing him up. His noises started out extremely high-pitched and frantic and gradually made their way down to soft and slow monkey patter before stopping completely.

"That good, huh?" asked Bert.

"Yes," confirmed Monkey, in his deep baritone. He was supposedly part man and part ape, played up as a genetic experiment gone wrong.

"It's eight after nine, time for weather on the eights with Monkey."

"It's going to be hot today, folks. Hotter than an oooooga booooooga."

"You know what I say to that, Monkey?"

"What's that, Bert?"

"Fiddle-de-diddle!"

"Nonsense!"

"I speak the truth!"

"Your truths are lies, sir!"

"But how could it possibly be hotter than an ooga booga?"

"Don't ask me, I'm only a monkey."

"Prove it."

"Look into my eyes."

"I'm-a lookin'."

"What do you see?"

"I see myself."

"Exactly."

Pause, dead air.

"Fiddle-de-diddle!"

This was followed by the sound of a slide whistle, a spring uncoiling, and a car horn honking three times.

Commercial break.

I had been concerned that the show was slowly killing me, but it was the only thing that would get me out of bed in the mornings.

Waking up five days a week to the Bert and Monkey Show must have been bad for me, causing some kind of cancerous sphere to form somewhere deep in my body, possibly in my loins, because I didn't turn it off after I was out of bed. I needed it on until I was out the door. The show dragged me out of bed, pushed me into the shower and then out, forced me to eat my breakfast quickly, and finally gave me a good kick out the door. If it wasn't for the inspired idiocy of Bert and Monkey, I would have been late to work everyday.

Because of the mandatory staggered work hours, designed to relieve some of the congestion on the roads and subways, I was working from 11am to 7pm, Tuesdays through Saturday, with Sunday and Monday as my weekend. This all shifted twice a year, just to be fair, but I never noticed a difference. Forty hours a week is forty hours a week.

Boarding the subway on my first morning as Chief of Probes, I brushed aside worries of Boogedy and Nibbles being out to get me, figuring that they were just another odd pair of people living in the city. I was more concerned with the hog-tying issue anyway, trying to prepare myself for the possibility of having to lasso a grown man and keep a straight face in the process. And besides, could Boogedy and Nibbles have the financial backing to take me down? Please! Not in those raggedy clothes. And then again *maybe*, because once again they were sitting across from me.

It's a coincidence, I thought. In fact, it's the very definition of a coincidence. A remarkable occurrence of events, ideas, etc., at the same time or in the same way, occurring apparently by mere accident.

Ah, what a happy coincidence for the three of us to be on the same train two times in a row! What a happy, gay day!

They wore the same clothes as the previous night. Maybe they got lucky, hooking up with a couple of equally freakish ladies they met at some dive bar on the south end. But that seemed unlikely seeing as how I hadn't been able to get lucky in over a year, and while I'm no prime rib, I'm not tripe either.

I wondered if the suits were their work uniforms, or if they had been sitting on that train all night, riding it up and down the city, looking for people to spook. Or maybe they were twins of the Duo from the other night, or body doubles. In a world with so many billions of people, there's bound to be someone out there who looks exactly like you.

The train was packed, but I took no comfort in the strength in numbers. To me it just meant more people to watch me die.

The Duo was staring at me again. There was no explaining that away. Two sets of eyes, four balls, all connected to two brains via a cord of optic nerves. What was going on in those brains? What were those bloody sponges doing with the info those eyes sent them? Evolution needs to get to work on telepathy. Of course, then they would have been able to read my thoughts as well, and Boogedy would probably nod his head in agreement as I thought these things, which would have spooked me even more.

Other people came and went from the train. The Duo continued to stare, with Boogedy looking desperately sad and Nibbles looking as if he had a fire raging inside him. I looked around at the other people on the train and no one else seemed to notice these two guys and how strange they were.

I stared back at them this time, trying not to blink and failing, and also trying to look mean but only managing to look like a confused, lost puppy. I'm surprised Boogedy didn't break off his arm to throw me a bone.

After I lost forty-five minutes worth of staring contests, the train finally reached my stop. When I got out, once again, the Duo did not follow me. But their heads did turn to look at me as the train pulled away.

I decided to bring up the Boogedy and Nibbles incidents to Mr. Burk before I left on the day's mission, hoping he would be able to answer those questions, and also to talk him down from hog-tying to handcuffs. But before I did that, I stopped by to see May, who was sitting under her desk crying.

"What's wrong?" I asked, squatting down to get eye level with her.

"We had an incident. It was horrible! Just horrible!" she told me before burying her head between her knees. In that position she reminded me of something I had tried to do unsuccessfully a number of times as a teenager while going through puberty, always a few short inches away from the Promised Land of my crotch.

"When?" I asked, "The Babe tour?"

"Yes!" She screamed into her thighs.

"What happened?"

"Nudity! Nudity! Nudity!"

"Nudity?"

As I tried to figure out just how nudity under any circumstance could be horrible, Dale popped up out of nowhere and squatted down next to me, saying, "She ain't lyin', Joe. I was there. I saw it."

"Saw what?"

"The nudity."

"I don't understand."

"A tourist streaked the field."

"Someone traveled back in time to streak a baseball game?"

Dale nodded. "After we caught him, he said he wanted to be the first person in history to do it. He said, and I quote, 'Like Lewis and Clarke, I did it for the glory of being first.'"

I felt for the guy. At that far-advanced point in History it was hard to be the first to do or even say anything new, considering how many people had came and gone before us, doing all sorts of new things before they left, making and saying all the cool stuff and leaving us the scraps. And there were also eleven billion other people out there at that moment, all competing to do something first, even when there wasn't much left, like hungry dogs fighting to the death over a chicken bone.

I suppose the streaker wanted to be able to look around at the audience and see just what kind of an expression people make when they're seeing something for the first time, even if it was only his pimply naked ass.

May felt that the innocence of the entire crowd had been destroyed—as if no one in the 1920s ever saw a naked man before that—that the children at the game would go home to nightmares of naked men running through the grass, that wild orgies would break out all over New York City, that family values would be ruined decades earlier than before, that streaking, getting such an early start, would grow to become the country's most popular pastime with husbands turning to their wives to say things like, "Hey honey, do you mind if we pop over to my parents house before the movie so we can streak their dinner party real quick?" and she felt it was all her fault.

Some of the tour guides developed a sort of protector mentality when it came to people in the past, as if they were all children, and it was their duty to protect their innocence, but I wonder how man could lose something that it never had.

Even though May was being foolish, I wanted to crawl under the desk to hold her. More specifically, I wanted to take all my clothes off, crawl under the desk, take all her clothes off, and then have her hold me.

I imagine it's difficult to get so upset about nudity when you yourself are nude and even holding another nudie. But I was afraid that a confused and embarrassed Dale would have followed my lead and joined us al fresco under the desk for a trio of awkwardness. So instead I told May that it wasn't her fault, that the crowd would be fine, and then went on my way, leaving Dale squatting there, staring at the spot where I had squatted, and leaving May to take comfort between her knees, wishing I could do the same.

Mr. Burk had his "Sorry, we're closed" sign up on his door which meant that he wasn't in yet, so I had to put off asking about the Duo and assume that the hog-tying was still on.

I went to the employee supply wing of the building to get some essentials for the mission. In order to blend in with the past it was important to have the right merchandise. Within the wing there was a section for each decade, and within each section a room for each year in that decade. I found the 2001 room and loaded up with a backpack, a video camera, a still camera, a fanny pack, a notebook, a small tape recorder, a stun gun, a rope—which I spent an hour trying to make into a lasso and failed repeatedly—a t-shirt that stated that I was a certified muff diver, and some pens.

Strangely, the best way to blend in to New Orleans back then was to look like a tourist. You know a place is in trouble when the tourists, who feel comfortable enough to piss and puke on the streets, look more at home than the locals, who shuffle about trying to block out eighty percent of the things they see happening to and in their town.

And New Orleans certainly was in trouble.

6
Travel Perks

The experience of time travel is a peculiar one. The first thing you notice as you step through a wormhole is the loud fooping noise, which is sort of like a combination of a sucking and popping sound. The second, and most memorable, thing you notice is the unique physical sensation it causes.

It's like having pins and needles run up and down your entire body, like a wave of white noise that starts in your toes and flows over your feet, up through your legs, your privates, your butt, your tummy, your chest, your shoulders, and this is where the static splits into three paths, two heading down your arms and into your fingers while the other shoots up your neck right to the top of your head, where it bounces back down the way it came.

Did I mention that it goes through your privates? It does. A girl once said that I made her feel like that, saying that I produced a wave of pins and needles throughout her body, and for six days I walked the earth as a god, but on the seventh day, just as I was about to engage in the act with the same girl, I found out that I had misunderstood her. The feeling I had evoked was apparently one of numbness, as if her whole body had fallen asleep, hence the pins and needles. Language really is the root of all my troubles.

As for wormholes, the further back into the past you travel, the more intense the wave of white noise is, and the more it will continue bouncing back and forth in your body until dying out. The formula for this is roughly one bounce for every fifty years traveled. On my last trip, the trip to my present location, I had a wave bouncing around my body for about a week. With a wave taking ten seconds to travel from toe to skull, the mathematicians in the audience can take the time to compute when I am. I tried to work out the calculation myself but couldn't even get as far as figuring out how many seconds there are in a day, let alone in a week, the whole thing requiring a level of concentration impossible to attain while in a forest full of shrieking monkeys.

There's something sexy about the ordeal—wormholes, that is. And that something is an erection, which is standard for men going through wormholes, and sometimes, if one is either lucky or particularly desperate, an orgasm will result. We should have charged extra for that. Of course, more than a few tourists have pissed themselves on the way through, the same sensation causing urination in some and climax in others, which gives you an idea of just how difficult it is to name anything as a universal truth.

Climax or urine, the standard outward response was for the women to draw air quickly in through their clenched teeth and for the men to sigh in a voice slightly higher than usual for them. What came out during or after that was their own personal business, and I would rarely point and laugh at them. The tour guides all stopped having such reactions to the sensation after a few weeks on the job, becoming numb to the whole experience, much like that girl who became numb to my touch and I to her words.

I met Warren, my operator. He was one of those short guys with a shiny bald head and thick black glasses.

"I'm Warren."

"Joe."

He blinked. "Don't fuck with me."

"So I've been warned."

"Where you headed?"

"Here."

I handed him the card.

"New Orleans?" He winked at me. "Woo yeah, am I right?"

"It'll be July and about ninety five degrees," I said, "I don't imagine there'll be much woo yeahing going on."

"Are you kidding? That place was home of the perpetual party. My dad once went down there, about five years before it washed away, on a Wednesday, A WEDNESDAY, in the afternoon. He said the place was cuckoo crazy. Girls were puking in the streets, guys *and* girls pissing in the alleys, girls, music blasting out of every joint on Bourbon Street. Man." He paused to savor this image and then said, with reverence, "There must have been filth and bodily fluids everywhere."

He looked at me expectantly.

"Um, well then, I suppose the water it's under now has done the place good," I said, "An enema if you will."

"So...are you gonna?"

"Gonna what?"

"Piss in the street."

"Why would I do that?"

"Why wouldn't you do that?"

"Well...because I really don't want to."

"What's that have to do with anything?"

He had me there. I told him I'd consider pissing in the street, but wouldn't make any promises. He was satisfied with this and, after reminding me not to fuck with him, skipped over to the computer terminal that controlled the generator, humming a New Orleansy sounding song I couldn't name. Once at the terminal he input the date, time, and location of where I was headed and we both put our dark protective glasses on for the initial burst of light when a wormhole opens.

An ion collider, while no longer as big as the one Mr. Burk mentioned in his letter, is still quite a large machine. It's so bulky and ugly that Mr. Burk had the two that he and his corporate sponsors owned built underneath the floors of where the transport rooms were. So all that the tourists saw was a virtually empty room with nothing but a computer and small desk in one corner, a hole in the floor in another corner, and on the floor a thin metal circle that the computer could shrink or expand.

Beneath the floor, twelve feet down, lies the machine encased in a tunnel. What happens—please keep in mind that everything I know about the process comes from Mr. Burk, who, as he said in his letter, dumbs science things down for me because I'm dumb—is that within this tunnel, ions race back and forth at the speed of light until a number of them collide into each other at one point. This creates more energy than multiple nuclear bombs, and is enough to rip a hole in space-time. Which it does, every time.

The energy, instead of blowing us up, with the entire planet, is dissipated into what physicists have determined to be another dimension. Which dimension that is and whether the inhabitants of said dimension like all that radiation coming at them has yet to be determined and yet to cause much concern in this dimension.

Where the hole in space-time leads is controlled by the computer, which varies the intensity and angle of the collisions. There are equations and formulas that explain all of this nicely, but damned if I can make any sense out of them.

The wormhole is created in that hole in the floor, and it really does look like a massive soap bubble floating around the room. But unlike a real soap bubble, the wormhole travels in a perfect circle around the room. The dimensions of its orbit changes with the size of the wormhole, and the computer adjusts the metal circle on the floor to trace this path. As the wormhole moves, little lights on the metal circle light up so that people don't ever have to guess where the thing is.

And that folks, is all I can tell you about that. For more info on wormholes see your local science geek because a scientist I am not, a tour guide I am. My job was to parade small groups of rich couples and families around, throwing interesting tidbits their way, and making sure they didn't do anything idiotic or obscene to ruin the tour for the others or, more specifically, anything that would entitle the other group members to a full or even partial refund. With the costs of running the generators being so high, Mr. Burk, and his sponsors, couldn't afford refunds.

As for high-speed particle physics, or the smashing of the iddy biddy into the iddy biddier, I am as clueless as a sack of dead squirrels. Maybe I, and others, should have taken more interest in what was going on in this regard, the energy being both used and created, but a person can only be interested in so many things at once, and at the time I was at my limit. There just wasn't any more room.

What I did know, and what I was interested in, was that the wormhole was ready.

As I stepped into the bubble, Warren shouted something about "letting it flow," but most of what he said was lost as the foop filled my ears and my focus turned to the tingling in my toes and the fluid-like warping of the space around me.

7
The Art of Getting Pissed On

From its birth until it was a grizzled old man, the Mississippi River enjoyed almost total freedom. It cut through the country, changed course whenever it felt like it, hopped over its banks for the hell of it, and always looked for a quicker way to get to the Gulf of Mexico. I imagine that the critters that lived near the River accepted this, that few complained, and none had the balls to even dream of disciplining the beast. When the River moved, everyone simply packed up their nuts in their cheeks and moved with it.

But then people moved into the area, bringing all sorts of stuff with them (much more than could fit in their cheeks), and since they needed places to store all that stuff and future stuff they may and hoped to acquire, they built houses that grew into towns that grew into cities along the banks of the river, which, if you need an analogy, is similar to a child building a sandcastle too close to the surf.

Bucket and mini shovel in hand, the child, who I'll call Dim Dolly, charges past sunbathers and sunburners to plop down on wet sand just a few feet in from the tide. There she begins to build her castle. She uses a combination of the bucket mold and wet sand drip methods, she becomes oblivious to the goings-on around her, even of the fact that her brother, Chunky Charles, has already eaten both his and her week's allotment of fudgie wudgies and has the gooey chocolate beard to prove it.

The castle gets bigger and more elaborate, smaller castles pop up around the main building, a moat is put in at some point, and just as Dim Dolly begins to use seashell bits to reinforce the walls of her buildings, she realizes that in its current location her sandcastle is fucked. For if the sand she built on is wet, and if there are shells all around her, then the sea must have been there not to long ago. And if it could be there once, then it certainly could, and would, be there again, washing away all her hard work.

It's at this time that Chunky Charles, on his way to the sea, waddles past Dim Dolly, who sees the chocolate lipstick around her brother's face and realizes the full extent of what she's sacrificed to build her castle and, since relocation is out of the question, swears to protect her creation with all her might. Yes indeed.

So while Chunky Charles occupies himself by attempting to bellyflop a seagull, Dim Dolly is hard at work, frantically building a deeper moat and even a buffer moat in front of the main moat, building walls higher than the castle around the moats, a circle of driftwood around the walls, and finally, in an act of desperation, she lays down her body in the sand, between the rising tide and her fortress. She is willing to endure the tide battering her young body, forcing tiny seashell bits into every open orifice, just to prolong the life of her castle made of sand.

But don't cry for Dim Dolly unless you plan on crying for New Orleans as well, because her story is theirs, the only difference being instead of sandcastles they built houses, stores, factories, offices, and roads.

Industries popped up, harbors became essential for trade, millions and then billions of dollars were invested in the city, and it was no longer peaches and Chantilly cream for the river to hopscotch around southern Louisiana.

So the people there began to think up all sorts of kooky ways to keep the Old Man in its place. First, after rubbing their hands together and clapping once, they, using shovels (just like Dolly) and wheel-barrows, relocated a crapload of dirt to the river banks, building levies with the idea that these would contain the water if it should ever try any funny business, which it did. And no, the hills didn't do squat as the river found ways to break through time and time again. And even when, during heavy rain, the water didn't naturally break through, there would almost always be some selfish bastard who'd help it break through a few miles downriver of his home, ruining others to save himself.

Then came the US Army, stroking their chins and walking around with hands on hips, to save the day and become the first army in the world to declare war on a body of water. Their battle plan consisted of setting up bigger and stronger hills, a system of gates, levees, and pumps, all to control the water flow and keep the River as is forever.

This, amazingly, worked—for about a hundred years.

The river stayed its course but the land around it sunk to the point where New Orleans was below the river which looked like an elevated train running through the city.

And then there was Maude. Hurricane Maude. A class five storm born in the Gulf of Mexico, destined for the mouth of the Mississippi River. The odds that a hurricane would exactly follow the path of a river—as if the storm was a pinball and the river its shoot—are super slim, but Maude did just that. She worked her way up Louisiana, stalling twice. Once over New Orleans, where she stood still for three days, dropping a years worth of rain in seventy-two hours, and once over Baton Rouge, where she rested for two more.

The soup bowl that was southern Louisiana filled up as the Mississippi flooded its banks and then changed direction, washing away Baton Rouge and cutting off New Orleans from the rest of the United States by turning it into an island that spent a good part of the year with its head barely above water. The people of New Orleans, the few that stayed, often compared living there to constantly being in a tub with a stopped-up drain.

So many people abandoned the city that it became a city no longer, and those who remained rarely felt like putting on parades, showing their tits, or dancing to zydeco. The only thing left was drinking. People still found plenty of time to do that.

But in 2001 New Orleans was still relatively dry. The Corps of Engineers still had its noose around the River and Maude was decades away. So, soon after I stepped through the wormhole, I had to ask myself, "Why am I wet?"

And soon after that I had to answer myself, "Because a man is peeing on you."

The wormhole came through in a narrow alley in the French Quarter at 10 a.m. and, thanks to the careful planning of Warren, I'm sure, there was a drunken man performing the miracle of making water on my leg. Jesus turned water into wine. This guy was turning cheap beer into urine.

"Stop that," I told him.

I was actually lucky that he was drunk, as a sober man in 2001 would have found it a bit strange for a man to walk through a large soap bubble. That he wore sunglasses was also a big plus as the flash of light preceding the bubble has been known to cause temporary blindness, at least in mice, and at most in cows. Since humans fall somewhere between those extremes, it's safe to assume it would have blinded the guy.

"WOOOOHOO! SAY FELLA! ARE YOU A QUEER?" shouted Mr. Sprinkler as he rocked from foot to foot with his penis out and flopping along with him.

"No."

"NO?! WELL WHAT'S YOUR SHIRT SAY?" He was squinting and running his finger along my shirt to follow the words, "CERTIFIED MUFF DIVER, EH? WHAT'S THAT SUPPOSED TO MEAN?"

"I'm not sure."

"I'LL TELL YOU WHAT IT MEANS! IT MEANS YOU'RE

QUEER!"

"Queers don't muff dive."

"SURE THEY DO! I'VE SEEN EM DO IT! SEEM EM DO IT ALL...THE...TIME. THEY'VE EVEN DONE IT TO ME ONCE!"

I suppose I should have said something along the lines of "Takes one to know one," but his logic was all screwed up, along with his definition of a queer (and a muff), so I didn't get into it with him. I just stared at him. He stared back at first, waiting for something from me he could react to, while twiddling his exposed member in the meantime. But when no words or movements came his way via me, Mr. Sprinkler saw that he would have no chance to display his drunken wit, so he quickly shuffled off, his penis still waving in the wind, to find, as he put it, some snatch.

It was hot and sticky, but it's not the humidity that really gets you. It's the stupidity.

I had been to New Orleans twenty seven times before that for the Mardi Gras tour, so I knew my way around. I made my way through the Quarter with a banana daiquiri in hand and slowly going in stomach, passing Bourbon Street—which was making a halfhearted attempt at cleaning up the mixture of plastic beads, vomit, beer, liquor, and hotdogs from the previous night, working by the motto that a job worth doing is only worth doing until it hits ninety degrees and then to hell with it.

8
My First Kung fu

I walked through the doors into the Methodist Hospital imagining I was an action hero in a movie, walking in slow motion into what would soon be a bloody gunfight that would end with me walking out of the place in slow motion, slowly smoking a cigarette, with a trail of dead bodies behind me and my supposedly tragically dead wife (who, it turns out, really didn't die but had amnesia for five years) waiting for me outside and showing off her new breast implants.

This wasn't because I planned to gun down the various innocent patients, doctors, and nurses milling about, but because I wanted to look confident. No one asks the action hero "Can I help you, sir? You look lost." They get out of his way and let him tend to his shit-kicking business. My stride was confident, my jaw clenched, my eyes narrowed, and I turned my head slowly from side to side, scanning the room for what must have seemed to be a brain-eating alien cyborg run amok, but really was nothing at all.

"Is a Mrs. Burk a patient here?" I figured that asking at the front desk would be easier than knocking out an orderly and stealing his uniform in order to roam the halls freely in search of Robert Burk's womb.

"Yes, are you family?"

"Yes."

"She's in room 118-A but she's just gone into labor. You can wait in the maternity waiting room if you'd like. It's down the hall and on your right."

"Is there a TV in there?"

"Yes."

"Is it on?"

"Yes."

"Then I'll do that."

But then I realized that the only way I would be able to actually see the birth of my boss would be to knock out an orderly and steal his uniform so I could roam the halls freely. So I wandered around the areas of the hospital I wasn't restricted from, keeping up the action hero persona, searching for an orderly of suitable size. I needed someone feeble, a runt, because I couldn't see myself going twelve rounds with someone in good health.

After passing up four orderlies who looked as if they were moonlighting refrigerators, I found the perfect candidate for a bop on the head. He was a good three inches shorter than me, thirty pounds lighter, and he was literally sick, throwing up in a supply closest. I heard his retching from the hallway, stuck my head in to survey the scene, offered him my assistance, had my assistance declined, and then gave him a swift kung fu chop to the back of his neck.

This approach didn't work at all.

"What are you doing?" He blurted out along with various elements of his lunch, or possibly breakfast, or maybe it was just a snack of some kind, or simply bile, who can tell?

"I apologize."

"Get out of here!"

"I'll just go."

"Leave!"

I imagine if he wasn't throwing up so horribly he would have turned me in to the proper authorities or possibly taken a swing at me. I've never been one for violence so it really was silly of me to try something like that. I should stick to what I know, I thought. But what did I know? What skills did I have to accomplish my mission? What tools did I have in my toolbox? Did I even have a toolbox? Or at least a bag of tricks? I sat down in the hallway, partially hidden by a cart of some kind, and tried to figure things out.

After half an hour I decided that I, unfortunately, had and knew nothing. After coming to this conclusion, a stranger, not knowing about my lack of tools and tricks, bent down and asked me a question.

"Excuse me, sir?"

"Are you speaking to me?"

"Do you work here?"

"Just because I have puke all over me doesn't mean I work in a hospital, you asshole."

As you can see I have a tendency to turn vinegary rather quickly and snap at strangers who speak to me. And since statistically speaking the overwhelming majority of people on the planet are strangers to me, I suppose it would be fair to say that I have the ability to snap at anyone. It's nothing against those people, it's just that sometimes, or most of the times, I don't know how else to respond to people besides either snapping or running away at a full sprint. Both seem to accomplish the same thing.

"Don't call me an asshole! I just want to know where the maternity ward is. My sister is having a baby."

Baby? I thought: a Burkish baby?

"What is your sister's last name?" I asked, leaving out the "you prick" I was itching to add.

"Do you work here?"

"Would I have puke all over me if I didn't?"

"I guess not."

"What's the name?"

"Moorse," he said.

Crushed, I turned and walked away from the guy without a word. With no skills to turn to, and now no dumb luck on my side, I was planning to go back to Mr. Burk and admit defeat. "Wait! Wait!" The guy ran after me, arms flailing.

"Wait what?"

"I don't know what I was thinking. She wouldn't be under Moorse. She just got married. Moorse is her maiden name."

"What's her new name?

"Burk."

9
It's a Small Space-Time After all

By sticking close to Moorse I got to see and hear the ooey gooey birth of Robert Burk.

I stood in the corner of the birthing room and observed, well, was *present* for the whole thing, and I must say that this was one baby who had second thoughts about making his postnatal debut.

As I entered the room there was screaming. Then some drugs were given which stopped the screaming and started the heavy breathing and maniacal laughter.

I saw a doctor rub his hands together, a nurse shake her head, and a med student smack himself across the cheek.

Fluids of various hues from clear to black splattered everywhere, followed by splashing sounds (my eyes promptly shut after the fluid rainbow so I can only describe the sounds after that point), some cracking, like when people eat crabs, some suction, a drill, a saw, a plunger unclogging what sounded like a toilet but what must have been something more organic, then the plunging abruptly stopped and a man said, "wait, wait, wait...what are we doing?" which was followed by a brief silence during which, I assume, there was some deep contemplation, a few shoulder shrugs and some finger pointing, followed by the plunging again, promptly joined by the saw, the drill, and the suction. It's amazing how much birth sounds like sex.

I didn't open my eyes again until I heard the crying. Again, it's amazing how much birth sounds like sex.

Shortly after the cord was cut and the purple slug put into the mother's arms, I made my exit. Mr. Burk Baby was safe against his mama's bosom, and I saw no reason to stick around for the inevitable, "Say pal, who the hell are you?" So I headed out to the waiting room to sit down and write up my report.

Official Probe Report #1

Note: If you are not Mr. Burk, stop reading this immediately and go away. Or else.

At 12:14 pm at the Methodist Hospital in New Orleans, LA, Mrs. Emily Burk gave birth to her only son, Robert Joseph Burk. The birthing process seemed standard. In attendance was the father, Mr. George Burk, Mrs. Burk's brother, Edward Moorse, and me, Joe. Dr. Flasto, with the help of a med student, did the honors of inducing and enticing the baby to come forth. Nurse Tuttie did the honors of taking the baby to the baby aquarium.

Neither during nor after the birthing was Baby Burk smacked, slapped, sliced, punched, poked, pushed around, or made fun of in any way.

That seemed to cover everything. I had the setting, the main characters, and the action. No dialogue, but what does that matter? I was, however, going to take one quick trip to the baby room to see if Burk Baby truly was safe and sound for the time being before heading back home.

"Excuse me, Miss? Which way to the baby aquariums?"

"The what?"

"The room where babies are stored in aquariums."

"Second floor."

As I walked up the stairwell, a doctor still wearing his surgical mask rushed past me on his way down. I didn't get a very good look at the guy, but for a second I thought it was Mr. Burk. He had those same intense green eyes, although I didn't notice a flicker of insanity in them. I turned around to get another look at him and noticed, just as he burst through the 1st floor door, that his hair was jet black. Mr. Burk's hair is salt and peppery, so I decided it couldn't be him. Besides, if it was Mr. Burk why would he run by me like that and pass up a golden opportunity to call me names?

In the baby room I expected to see rows upon rows of wrinkly babies. I expected to see family members gathered outside the glass, fogging it up with their goo goo ga'ing. I even half expected to see a nurse walking around sprinkling food flakes into the babies' mouths. What I didn't expect to see was Boogedy and Nibbles.

But I did.

This was no coincidence. This was an incidence. Those guys were clearly up to something and I was going to find out just who in the hell they thought they were, following me around, making it a point to freak me out. I could live with seeing them on the subway everyday, that's fine (the subway is a public place and I do not consider my time on it as "me time"). But this, this following me around at work, this intrusion, this blatant attack on my private life, on my career, on my mission—my probe—this, buddies, shall not pass.

"ENOUGH!" I was raging. Be weird if you like, lead a bizarre life, that's fine. But don't shove it in my face. Don't make me a part of your ridiculous existence.

My exclamation turned a few heads, including the Duo's. They turned their stare from the baby room to me.

How could they follow me through time? As far as I knew, the only wormhole generators on the planet belonged to Burk—well, to the corporation. Had a foreign country discovered how to build their own? If so, why were they using it to follow me? And why did this foreign country choose to send two circus freaks? The Duo had some questions to answer. I pulled out my notebook and clicked open my pen, ready to record their responses which they would either give voluntarily, or after a bop on the head with my stick.

I had no stick.

I advanced on them, full of rage, yes, but also full of fear, because let's face it here, Boogedy could have said, "boo," and I'd be running out of there like a torch bearer. But before I could get close enough to start in with my interrogation, Martini stepped in front of me.

I was under the illusion that I was working alone (a maverick!) and had forgotten that Martini was the Assistant Prober. So his appearance was a bit jarring, or rather more jarring than his appearance normally was. To give you an idea of just how negative this man was I'll say this: when Martini walked into the company Christmas party one year, a few people looked around and asked, "Who just left?"

In the hospital he greeted me with a "hey" that had little emotion besides the emotion of being completely empty, which is an emotion if you count black as a color.

"Why are you here?" I asked, miffed.

"You don't look happy to see me."

He looked bad, but he always did—dark circles, eye boogers, wrinkled clothes, unshaven, mouth hanging open. He wore the classic New Orleans "I fucked your girlfriend" t-shirt, and I could tell from his widening eyes that he was about to make a scene.

I raised a warning finger. "Don't do this, Martini. Just tell me why you're here."

"You wish I wasn't here," he blubbered, "I can tell. I can see it in your eyes. Your eyes betray the truth, Joe."

"I'm busy. I'm about to get some answers and you're in my way."

I could see the Duo over his shoulder. They weren't staring at me any more, they weren't staring at Martini, and they weren't staring at the babies. They were staring at each other.

Martini defiantly put his hands on his hips. "Mr. Burk sent me. He told me to give you a hand, something about hog-tying. I have a right to be here!"

"Well I don't need a hand right now. I can hog-tie just fine by myself, so split."

Now he raised a warning finger. "Maybe I will split. Maybe I will! I'll just split and leave you here alone, by yourself, Joe, not a friendly face in sight, just you and your stupid face, with no one to turn to, no one to exchange a knowing look with, nothing Joe, just you and your fat head, you'll be left with nothing but the abyss, the abyss and the answers to your precious questions, which are more important to you than—"

And he was gone.

And so was the Duo.

When I say gone, I don't mean they all turned and walked away, or even that they ran away, what I mean is they all blipped out of my field of vision. It was as if somebody changed the channel on what I saw, to a new channel showing the same location as before, but with three fewer characters on screen.

I looked behind, below, and above me for signs of them. Nothing. I blinked twice. Nothing. I pinched myself to see if I was dreaming. I wasn't. I finally rubbed my eyes, just for the sake of covering all the bases, and they were still gone.

Poof.

10
To Shave a Cat

"Mr. Burk we have a problem."

"Already?" He asked, not even looking up from his desk. It was difficult to tell from where I stood but it looked like he was doodling.

"I'm afraid so, sir. Two problems in fact: One is creepy, the other is disturbing. Which would you like to hear first?"

"I'll take creepy."

"As I go to and from work and as I go through time I am being followed by a tall elderly gentleman and a near-midget."

Mr. Burk jumped up from his chair onto his desk. "Through time? Good God, Joe! That's a bit much don't you think?"

"It's true. I've seen them twice on the subway, and once today in 2001 New Orleans."

"Maybe you just happened to run into the younger them."

"They looked the same age each time."

"Same, or similar?"

"Same."

He paused to think about this.

"Well, how are they traveling through time? Answer me that, smart guy!" He challenged, pointing down at me.

"I don't know. Maybe they've built their own wormhole generator."

"Oh as if, Joe. AS IF!"

"I'm just reporting what I saw."

"Well in the future," he said, crawling down from the desk, "Please
only report elements from reality, and not from your dream life. OK?"

"Fine."

"Now what's this disturbing news you have for me?"

"Martini has disappeared and I believe that a certain imaginary duo
from my dreams are the cause of his disappearance. I also have reason to believe that they are, as we speak, doing all sorts of odd things to
his feet, elbows, and genitals."

"You need some rest, son."

"I'm serious, sir."

"Why don't you take tomorrow off, sleep in."

"Something's going on out there, sir. I think this Duo has something
to do with your beating photo."

"Wait, when did this become about *me*? I thought they're following
you."

"I suppose that's true."

"Look at me, Joe."

"I'm looking."

"What do you see?"

"I see a man."

"What kind of man?"

I chose my words carefully.

"A man's man."

Burk slapped his knee. "Bingo! Did you know that I was Junior
State Rodeo Champion three years running? I could do anything with a
rope. Lassoing, the flat loop, the Texas skip, the butterfly, hog-tying,
ANYTHING! Is that the kind of man who would hobnob with a near-
midget and his freakishly tall old friend?"

"Well..." I pictured an adolescent Mr. Burk doing something called the Texas skip, which I assumed involved him playing hopscotch while wearing chaps.

"No, Joe. The answer is no. So why would this duo, which couldn't possibly have any history with a man's man like me, want to slap around younger versions of me?"

"Maybe they're trying to change something about the present."

"The present? Joe, you are familiar with the Shaved Cat Principal, right? It is covered on page one of the training manual."

"Right, page *one*. By the time you get to page two hundred ninety-seven, page one is a tad blurry. I know it has something to do with shaving a cat."

"It does. But what does it prove?"

"That you can't change the present by changing the past."

"Good. Shall we sing a song about it?"

"No."

He did.

(To the tune of "Take Me Out To The Ball Game")

Joe, went back
To the old days
Joe, went back
To the past
He shot his mother
And killed his dad
He don't care if
He never gets born

Let him kill, kill, kill
All his fam-ily
If they all die
It's the same
For there's, no way

To change the fact
That you're here to-day!

"That was lovely, sir."

"Thank you. Do you understand now?

"Well...more or less."

"I think you need a demonstration."

Burk and I went down to one of the wormhole rooms, stopping by the supply area to pick up an electric razor and a cat, a nice tabby by the name of Fingerly Doo—at least that's the name I gave him right then and there.

Before we entered the room, Burk opened the door and threw in Fingerly Doo. Apparently the cat needed to be in the room alone for a few minutes for the experiment to work. Checking his watch after five minutes had passed, Mr. Burk and I went in.

The wormhole that was generated went back to only five minutes into the past and to a location just across the room. So when we stepped through, we ended up on the other side of the room, and five minutes in the past. There we found Fingerly Doo alone in the room. We could have opened the door and seen our past selves standing outside, waiting for five minutes to pass, but that would only have made our past selves yell at our present selves to get back to the task at hand.

Burk pulled out the electric razor, grabbed Fingerly Doo by his loose neck skin, and proceeded to shave him rather haphazardly. The end products were a scratched up and slightly bloody Mr. Burk and a not-quite-hairless, but plenty pissed-off, Fingerly Doo.

That done, we went back through the five-minute wormhole, and when we stepped back to the present we observed Fingerly Doo standing where we had left him in the present, with a full coat of hair and a pleasant disposition.

What had been done to the recent-past Fingerly Doo had no effect on the present Fingerly Doo.

Mr. Burk looked proud of himself. "So you see, Joe, changing the past does not affect the present in any way, shape, or form."

"What about mentally?"

"What about it?"

"Well, the cat thing only really proves that you can't change physical things. But what about memories? Does the cat remember being shaved?"

"Nope."

"How do you know?"

"Because when I show him the razor, he doesn't freak out." And indeed, when Burk waved the razor in front of Fingerly Doo's face, the cat only sniffed and licked it.

"How is this possible?"

"Timelines, Joe. Timelines. You can create a new one, but you can never change one that already exists."

"How many timelines are there?"

"I don't know...a lot?"

"That doesn't sound like a very scientific answer."

"I'm a PhD, Joe. The real deal. So this isn't open to discussion unless you want to go back to school for six years."

"But how is that when we travel through time we only travel on our timeline and don't jump from line to line?"

"I don't know. Luck?"

"Luck!"

He shot an accusatory finger at me. "Deal with it, Joe!"

"And how did you decide to shave a cat for this experiment? Why not just paint a piece of wood or something? Does the choice of a living creature have any significance?"

"No. There just happened to be a cat in the lab at the time."

"But why shave him? Why not just tie a ribbon around his neck?"

"Because we didn't have any ribbon, Joe. Duh."

"But you had an electric razor?"

He rolled his eyes. "Yes."

"I find that hard to believe."

"I find *you* hard to believe."

"Oh yeah, well you'd better believe it, baby!"

That ticked him off. He stepped so close to me you could put a piece of paper between our noses, but not much else.

"Just answer one question for me," he said, "Did this Duo try to smack baby me around at all?"

"Not to my knowledge."

"They didn't take a swing at me?" He asked. "No choke holds or anything? What about the soft spot on my skull? Did they tap it?"

"Who would do such a thing to a newborn?"

"Answer the question."

"No, they didn't touch you."

"Good. Now I think you'd better get out of my face, you're making me very uncomfortable."

"Me? You're the one shaving cats."

"This has nothing to do with behavior. It's your body, this one-on-one stuff. I can't stand it for more than 22 minutes at a time. Any longer than that and I break out in hives."

"It sounds like you're making this up."

"Oh yeah? Look."

He pulled up his sleeve and sure enough, there were hives breaking out all over his arm.

"Dear God!"

"That's right. I need crowds or at least groups, Joe. Either that or absolute solitude. Intimacy like this eventually gives me an anxiety attack. First my heart rate shoots up, then the hives come out, followed by hyperventilating (like I'm beginning to do now), and finally I grab the nearest blunt instrument (such as that metal lamp stand over there) and just go to town on everything in my sight, completely forgetting the concept of Right vs. Wrong and inanimate object vs. living creature. By the way, I'm not walking towards the lamp merely to illustrate my point, if you catch my drift."

"I'm leaving."

"Good move."

11
Home, Home, Home

The train home was packed tight like a can of, a can of, well a can of anything really. A string of refrigerated cans, barreling through the searing earth and sometimes over it, briefly emerging for a breath of hot air.

The Duo was nowhere in sight, too busy sucking on Martini's earlobes I assumed, and thankfully leaving me alone.

All those other passengers, all so close to me, smelling me, breathing in what I was breathing out, some even touching me, and I didn't *know* one of them in any sense of the word, especially not in the biblical sense. We were tasting, touching, and smelling each other, but were barely aware of any of it, too concerned with what we heard and saw, which was nothing but ourselves. Oh I noticed quite a few other people, catching an eye here and there, glancing away much more slowly when it was the eye of a lady, but I rarely thought, Oh there's that girl I know, hey there, how about we go catch up, or maybe just hold each other, how's that sound? Instead, at the moment of eye contact, what I thought was, She looks nice, or, He looks nice, and then, quickly, as my eyes turned away, Well, that's that.

That day on the train nobody spoke to anybody else beside themselves, and there were quite a few people doing that. I used this, as I often do, to pass the time, looking around at the various people talking to themselves, focusing on one at a time, imagining that they were talking to me, nodding my head to whatever nonsense they babbled, chuckling when they chuckled, looking outraged when they looked outraged, sharing in their tears—I was there for them. I was their friend from afar who agreed with everything they said, even though I couldn't always hear everything they said. I always listened, even when their lips moved without any sound coming out, I always understood, even when the language wasn't my own, and I never interrupted, not even to introduce myself.

And why would I? A person who talks to himself surely doesn't need me, or anybody else—he has become completely self-contained. Because if someone talks to himself, you can be sure he also violates himself, and a person who violates and talks to himself clearly prefers his own company and is making an obvious statement to the rest of the world: piss off.

I remember a tall gentleman from the South who stood in front of me on the train one night. He looked starchy, fresh from the dry cleaners in his bright white dress shirt, string thin black tie, and pressed black slacks, with closely cropped hair, shiny skin, and pearly whites.

He stared into my eyes, pressed his fists against his chest, and launched into a discussion on God, which was fine by me, as I see discussions as strange, wonderful things, things I'm not sure how to bring about and am always a bit startled and disoriented by at first when I stumble into one. But once I get my bearings, I do enjoy a good back and forth, regardless of the topic.

"As you're going about your daily business," the Southerner began, "whatever foolishness that may be, GAWD may someday poke his head, which is larger than anything you can fathom, through the clouds and say to you, 'Stop there, son, and listen to what I have to say now.' And you will stop your foolishness, you will put down your briefcase, and say, 'Yes GAWD, I'm listening.' And GAWD will ask you, 'Do you know me?' And just what will you say? You will say, 'Yes GAWD, I know you well. You GAWD.' And GAWD will say, 'You know my name, but do you know me?' And you will say, 'I do know you. You GAWD. You my tender friend.' And GAWD will shake his head and say to you, 'Well if you know me, and if you're my friend, where can you find me?' 'That's easy, GAWD, I can find you in the church.' 'Anywhere else?' 'Nope, just in the church.' 'What about under this rock?' 'There ain't no GAWD under that rock.' 'No?' 'No.' 'Why?' 'Because that rock is ugly, and under that rock is nothing but muck.' 'Until you can find me under that rock, and under every rock, and in nothing, you won't know me. And I will make your life, and the lives of all, nothing but pain and solitude until you do.' And then GAWD will pull his colossal head back through the clouds, and you will pick up your briefcase, scratch your fat head, and go back about your own savage foolishness. Amen."

It was during this pause, when the man lowered his head and closed his eyes that I saw my chance to jump in.

"So what you're saying is that God," I said, "or GAWD, is more Old than New Testamenty. That he pops his head out from behind a cloud and has a chat with you as you roam around the desert in search of pita bread and easily combustible bushes. Interesting...because I thought that most people today think of God as being quite dead, or at least retired, and therefore unable to bother with doing things such as speaking."

To which the man responded, as his eyes opened again and peered into mine, "One day you'll have a woman bouncing on your thing, bada boom bada bing, screaming out 'e! e! e!,' and Satan, who also is larger than you can fathom, will pull himself out from under the earth and say to you, 'Do you know me, son?' And your woman will continue her lively act while you wipe the sweat from your face and say, "I know you. You Satan! Now scram, Scratch.' And Satan will smile and say, 'I can't scram.' 'Why?' You will ask as you reach satisfaction. 'Because I have nowhere else to go. I'm already everywhere.' Satan will say this as he runs his fingernail up your woman's back. 'Even under a rock?' You'll ask as you slap Satan's hand away from your woman. 'No, not there.' 'Why not?' 'Because that's nowhere. That's where GAWD is.' And Satan will sink back down into the earth while you stand up to scratch your ass in the moonlight. Amen."

Even though the things he said made little sense to me, and even though other people on the train were staring at us, I smiled as he spoke. He had a personal message about God that he wanted me to know, and that was enough for me. He cared enough to share his ideas with me—Joe.

That's what I thought, that is, until my stop came and I excused myself. As I walked off, the Southern gentleman continued talking. He looked straight ahead at where I had been standing, and went on chattering about God and Satan joining you in the shower, even though there was no longer anyone listening to him. That's when it hit me. He had been talking to himself the entire time, not me. Not Joe. He had no interest in me, no interest in sharing, he was merely working these things out for himself, and by himself. He had no desire to save my soul, nor a need for my presence.

So yes, the tree that falls in the woods when no one is around does make a sound, and we're all fools for ever wondering if it didn't.

Talking to yourself really was becoming the preferred method of communication. I'd say that one out of every four people now talk to themselves to some degree, whether it's quietly muttering or all-out screaming, they clearly have quite a bit to say and choose to say it without bothering to find someone else to listen. And that's strange seeing how there were more people on the Earth to talk to at that time than ever before. Every place I went, from the street to parks, was bursting with people, so it's not that there weren't enough options.

In the city, we all lived in large living complexes together. We all crammed into trains on our way to and from work, walked shoulder to shoulder, and waited in lines. Very rarely, only extremely late at night, did I find myself out of earshot of at least ten other people. So why were there never any messages on my voice mail? I should have left messages for myself, maybe that would have made me happier. At least then I would have known there was at least one person out there interested in how I was doing: me.

But as it stood, there were none, because unlike everyone else I couldn't talk to myself, try as I did. I would always look around while I talked, half worrying that others were staring at me, half hoping that someone was willing to listen.

I stepped out of the train, home from Mr. Burk and his half-assed explanations and into the hot, stale evening air. The four seasons seemed to be downsizing into two: summer and spring.

A woman walking ahead of me had a small dog with her, a silly little hotdog thing, shaved bald. Because of the constant heat, most people gave their dogs haircuts, but few went as far as shaving them bald. The obvious reason being that the difference between a bald dog and a pig are minimal.

The older I got, the more it seemed as if humans, rats, pigeons, and cockroaches were the only free-range living things left on Earth. I mean, plants and vegetation were growing wild out there for sure, but I'm talking about critters, things with peepers and legs. Things that eat, fart, and puke. Where did everybody else go?

Maybe some of them just left. Packed up their shit and got the hell out without bothering to tell us—the ones who wrecked the joint in the first place—just how one goes about getting the hell out. I suppose it's wishful thinking that every extinct species on the planet did get out in time, and now all live communally on some blue dot co-op way out there in the ether, splashing each other in the warm, virgin waters, feeding each other bananas and peaches, washing each other's backs, kissing each other's smooth, soft necks, strutting around naked and spotlessly clean, kissing, heavily petting, doing it like animals in the grass, in the trees, under water, upside down.

That's another thing I thought about as I walked home—the lack of sex in my life. Although I can't say it ever felt like I was walking anywhere. Instead, it felt like I was always in line. I'm not walking down the street to my apartment, I'm in line to get to my apartment. I look across the street to the other sidewalk and as always, the line seems to be moving faster over there. Maybe I should move to that side of the street.

It's the lack of any kind of physical contact really, outside of the constant bumping and pressing against people as I commute from here to there, that I worry about. I don't so much need to fuck or to get fucked, as I need someone warm to hold and hold me. Give me a body. One that is familiar, one that doesn't leave, one that is soft, one that won't push me away, one that fits in with the piece that is me, and I think I'd be content...as long as we roll around naked every now and then.

I got to my building and entered my apartment. No messages. No warm body. No naked rolling. Just my cat, a fat fatty named Mr. Puss. He ran out from the bedroom as I closed the door, as he always did, but he did something different this time. Just as he entered the main room I swore he jumped backward into the bedroom and then ran out again. I didn't think much of it, just that I never knew cats could jump backward.

As I sat at my little table eating my can of soup—and canned goods really were the only safe way to go those days—I knew that there were people all around me. People above, below, and to every side, all just a few feet away. But I still felt alone, and it wasn't because there were thin walls between us. Remove the walls, let them fade away, and I believe I would have felt just the same.

I thought about screaming. Just belting one out and seeing what happened. Maybe someone would knock on my door to ask if I was OK. Maybe more than one would come. That might be too much for me. Maybe someone far away would shout out, "ARE YOU OK IN THERE?" I could shout back, "I'M FINE, THANK YOU. HOW ARE YOU?"

None of that seemed likely though, because if I myself heard a scream I'd probably hide in the shower. So instead of screaming I ate my soup, purposely sipping loudly to add my small part to the constant background noise of my building, which I often thought of as a song and I as part of a human orchestra. It gave my noise purpose. My footsteps were a tom-tom drum, my yawns a saxophone, my heart beat a bass. Even farting was elevated to cymbal crash status, or sometimes a triangle ding. But I do realize that an orchestra with only one musician who thinks of it as an orchestra and with the others who think of it as just farting, and with no conductor, is not an orchestra at all, and that it was really just me, my cat, and I.

Oh yes, and that night, a ghost.

12
Spooky Spook

I saw it, or him, over a spoonful of chunky veggie noodle, the steam rising in front of me, adding to the spookiness of the whole occasion.

It was Mr. Pushcatela, the previous tenant of my apartment. A man who was dead, a man who's body I saw being carried out of the very apartment, a man who's obituary I read in the Metro section, a man who should be a pile of ash by now, or a bunch of scattered ashes, whatever, but for shit sure, a man who should not be taking a shit on my toilet with the door wide open.

At least close the door, you paranormal pigfart!

It was him. Who else would take a shit in here as if he owned the place? Mr. Puss would and does, but even I don't. Primarily because I can't stand it when that cat stares at me as I go to the bathroom, as if the human defecation process continually amazed him.

I was sure it was a ghost because he didn't look fleshy at all. It was more like looking at a projected image or a hologram. If all we really see is light, light reflected off of stuff, whatever that stuff is, then what I was seeing was light reflected off of nothing.

I looked around the room for Mr. Puss. Cats are supposed to have a sixth sense for dead people so I was hoping he could help me out.

"Mr. Puss? Psssst. Mr. Puss?"

He was behind me, doing that jumping backward thing in and out of the bedroom again. Although now he was doing it repeatedly, like he was stuck in some kind of loop. Hell of a time to start exercising, you fat fuck!

I began to think of all the horrible things that happen to people in horror movies when ghosts appear. Bad things. People's souls get sucked out through their ears by cold dead lips, their guts get eaten like pasta by maggot-infested mouths, their eyeballs get licked by bleeding white tongues, their private parts get nibbled on by yellow and black teeth, they get hit over the head by tombstones, locked into coffins, mummified, cremated, turned into stone, and sent to rot in hell—none of those very pleasant experiences.

When the ghost started to pull his pants up I knew I had to do something. Hiding was the first thing that came to mind, but he was too close to my favorite hiding place—the shower—for that to work. Furthermore, this was *my* home, the one place where a man should never have to hide. He's the guest here. He's the one who should be hiding in the shower, I decided.

I looked around the kitchen for a weapon. An electric mixer was the closest thing I could find.

Of course then I had to find an extension cord so it could reach the bathroom and still have power, because an electric mixer without power isn't much of a weapon, it's just silly really. So I found an extension cord in my junk drawer, and by the time I got the thing plugged in and ready I looked into the bathroom to find Mr. Pushcatela in the shower, peeking out from behind the curtain.

He was hiding.

This filled me with confidence, and I advanced, flicking the mixer on and off, holding it like a chainsaw. I planned on driving the spook back to the netherworld, or at least out of my apartment and into the hallway. Where he went from there was not my problem.

I paused in the doorway, with the mixer on medium and held like a gun. I made my demand, "Get out of my house!"

Mr. Pushcatela flung back the shower curtain and replied, "Your house? This is my house!"

"Ha!"

"Ha nothing!"

"Ha get out!"

He took off his belt, folded it in half, and stepped out of the shower.

"We'll see whose house this is," he snarled, "Let's dance!"

I don't handle aggression well. Sure, when the ghost was cowering in the shower I was plenty tough with the mixer, but things had changed. There he was with a weapon of his own—a much more traditional and battle-tested weapon at that—asking me to dance. My response was clear, simple, and direct. I dropped the mixer and ran.

I passed Mr. Puss hissing at a ghost cat as I bolted through the door, then I continued down the hallway with my knees and arms pumping, down the stairs, and finally out of the building and into the night, where I continued my retreat (bobbing and weaving through the crowds) for just over ten blocks, only stopping because I was out of breath. If my mind had its way, I would have continued running, out of the city, through all the other cities I came across, over mountains and through oceans, never stopping until I was dead, and could meet Mr. Pushcatela on his own playing field.

13
Strange A-Goings On

Now you know something about me. Something about the kind of man I am. There was a ghost in my apartment, an aggressive ghost at that, both on and off the toilet, and I left Mr. Puss, my cat, my friend, in there to deal with it on his own with no backup. What kind of a man does such a thing? A man like me.

I wonder if ghosts hang around and do their own thing even when no one is there to see them. It's like the tree falling in the woods question. Do ghosts float around being spooky for our sake, or for their own?

It's creepier to think that they would do it with or without us. At least while I was there I could see what Pushcatela was up to. But what if he took shits all over my apartment while I was out? How would I ever know? And a shit is a shit regardless of whether it came from flesh or from a flickering image of flesh. I decided to play it safe and that everything, *everything*, needed to be disinfected first thing in the morning.

What I needed to do first, was to answer the question that has plagued many human beings since 1000 A.D. when Kaldi, a sheepherder from Ethopia, fed his sheep the berries from an unknown shiny green plant and noticed that the sheep suddenly became hyperactive and jittery: will it be coffee or booze?

Pros and cons were weighed.

Coffee pros: the worldwide mean temperature increase of 1.5 degrees has caused more regions to be suitable to grow coffee beans, increasing the supply, and making it almost as cheap as water, so you can drink a whole pot of the stuff and still have money left over for silly things like breakfast.

It's tasty. It won't make you puke. You can't get sick off the stuff. It keeps you awake so you don't fall asleep and have nightmares about dump-taking ghosts. It doesn't kill brain cells. You won't pass out and wake up the next morning beside a car with something odd up your ass. If you drink enough of the sludge it takes the place of a meal nicely. Coffee shops are where smart people hang out so you can look smart too, especially when you add a pair of glasses and a book, increasing your chances of meeting a cat-eyed cutie reading a big thick novel.

Or you yourself could read a big thick novel that makes you look even smarter and you could hold the book so that everyone else sees the cover, and the title, while you sip java and think about having sex with the cat-eyed cutie while the big thick words in the big thick novel pass through your big thick head, like radiation. Or you could write some pretentious poetry of your own. Or you could smoke while staring out the coffee shop window and pretend you're film noir. Then you could eat a cheese danish to prove you're not. You could ask the guy behind the counter to put on some obscure Gregorian Chant/Electronica fusion band and feel as if you're among friends when he knows what you're talking about. You could write leftist proclamations on the bathroom walls. You could draw a vagina underneath those very proclamations for the sheer duality of it, then jerk off while staring at that very vagina. You could also smear your tiny baby juice all over that vagina drawing and tell yourself it's Art, and then walk out of the bathroom with the knowledge that you just did something sick, naughty, and dual-natured and no one, not even the guy who was waiting outside the bathroom door, will ever know it was you, except of course for your mother who knows because, you disgusting pervert, a mother always knows.

Coffee cons: see above.

Booze pros: hands down, the best thing about any form of alcohol, let's face it here, is that it gets you fucked up. It makes you forget about that ghost back home who is currently cleaning its nether worldly ass with your cat. It makes women in your league look like women out of your league. It makes women who you *thought* were in your league actually *be* in your league (as long as said women are also drunk).

It makes you laugh at things you should be crying about, cry about things you shouldn't even be thinking about, and, if you drink enough of it, you'll pass out and forget a lot of things that should be forgotten, it also kills off brain cells you don't need anyway. It kills germs that cause bad breath and gingivitis so you don't have to brush your teeth. It exercises the infrequently used reverse gear of your digestive system, it often comes with a free bartender to listen to your stupid stories, a free TV to watch sports on, free music to melt your eardrums, a free bathroom to piss in, a free stool to spread your cheeks on, and a free door to be thrown through after you scream at the faces on your free TV to go fuck themselves, throw a punch at your free bartender, puke in your free bathroom and fall off your free stool.

Booze cons: see coffee cons.

As I walked about considering these options, I suddenly realized that my ghost sighting kind of proved the existence of an afterlife. Maybe not a heaven and hell, but a something. This made me think about just what sins a person must commit in order to end up shitting away eternity on what was your, but is now clearly someone else's, toilet.

After I added up all of the sins I ever committed, and could remember, and estimated how many more I would commit over the course of a lifetime, I chose booze, as it seemed more appropriate.

Old timey guys (like truckers wearing faded blue T-shirts with long greasy gray hair pulled back into a pony tail) who see ghosts while on the road—often taking the form of a skinny old man riding a bicycle down the middle of the road at three a.m.—are the ones who go to coffee shops and all night diners to drink black coffee, eat soft boiled eggs, and mutter cryptic things about "strange a-goings on in the deeeeeeeeep, darrrrrrrrk night" and "I seen things no sane man should ever have to set his eyes upon."

Meanwhile, young men such as myself, on seeing things they can't explain, things that creep them out, typically go to all-night bars to get smashed and shout things like "Hey. HEY! WHO WANTS TO SEE MY PECKER?" hoping to spend the night sleeping in a urinal, a dumpster, a strange woman's bed, or anywhere but at home with said spook.

Unfortunately I'm not a big drinker, so I really didn't have any favorite bars to drop in on, but God knows there were quite a few to choose from. And they all appeared to do good business, so it was difficult to choose a place based on its popularity alone. The best thing to do, in my experience, is to just head right in to the first place where the lights aren't flashing outside or inside, where there are no cops mulling around by the door, and most importantly, a place where the people coming out of the bar aren't crying, screaming, or singing.

14
Shamash

After wandering around for close to an hour, a bar called Shamash, with a little gold bird design on its door, was the first acceptable place I came across. The amount of light and noise coming from it being so small that, from the street, I wasn't sure if it was even open. I usually don't frequent places with nonsense names, but I was tired and thirsty for some forgetting.

A searchlight swooped back and forth a few blocks away from the bar, and I considered following it to its source, but decided against it in case it was a trap. Just like the rainbow that holds nothing at its end but a psychotic cokehead leprechaun who'll skull fuck you for nothing but kicks, you should never trust mysterious beams of light.

I walked through the door of Shamash and found that the place was dead enough that the bartender was staring at me before the door even closed behind me. Everyone else either had their backs to me or their heads down looking into their drinks. At least I didn't have to worry about getting the bartender's attention, something which can make a grown man look like an awkward teenager. I suspect that many bartenders ignore male customers trying to get their attention on purpose, just so they look cooler than them in front of the ladies.

I don't know the bartender's name, and it's not that I can't remember but rather never got it. I'll call him Father Collins. Because from behind that bar he looked like a priest behind an altar.

Father Collins greeted me with a "What?" as I took a seat at the bar, his bar. People were saying less and less those days. And why not? When you walk into a bar and the bartender says, "What?" you know what he is asking you without the addition of "do you want" or "can I get you." Sure, he could mean "What...would you rather I do? Shoot you with double finger guns and wink, or smile at you for so long that it becomes uncomfortable." But the odds of that, thankfully, are slim to none.

It was a new form of speech, growing in popularity among the hip and young, but not a habit I myself ever picked up, but it was his bar, and I didn't want to make a scene, so I played along.

"Jack and root beer," I told him, keeping the "I'll have a" completely in my mind. I think *I'll have a* and then say "Jack and root beet." It's all wonderfully efficient.

Father Collins shook his head. "No."

There was also a lot less qualifying going on. People would say "no" without any explanation at all such as, "No, we just ran out of root beer." But who needs their "no's" explained really? Does it make a difference why the answer is no? No.

How about a "Scotch and soda."

And with that he began to make the drink for me without so much as a nod or a blink. It's like we evolved a form of telepathy between each other, but it was a telepathy that had no physiological grounding. It was psychological. Decades of saying the same set questions and answers to each other, as if there was a universal script, made it so we could super-abbreviate everything and still have everything make sense.

That'll be "Ten" *dollars.*

Can I start a "Tab?"

Sure, can I hold onto your "Card?"

I gave him the plastic disc which represented my available net worth in this world, thus ending our interaction for the time being and allowing me to get down to the grave business of getting utterly blitzed.

Sip.

It was a quiet bar. At one end of the counter, my end, there sat three guys and myself. At the other end sat a couple (not a Duo), and while it didn't look like they were in love, it did seem like they had sex quite regularly.

The girl was attractive in a primitive way, with the childbearing hips and large breasts that any man with any amount of man genes in him would have difficulty not at least glancing at, and the guy was large and in charge enough to warrant a serious effort on my part to NOT stare at the girl.

Sip, sip, sip.

There were four TVs hung high in the corners of the poorly lit room, all of them showing what I assumed to be a nature documentary from about thirty years ago. As I sat there I couldn't imagine being in such wide-open places like were shown. Most of the rainforest and savannah national parks that I saw on the news didn't look as natural and wild as what was on the TVs. I'd been staring at the screen for five minutes and hadn't seen a fence, armed guard, or tourist taking pictures once.

In the documentary there was a shot of a lioness laying by a tree licking herself, cut to a male lion yawning, cut to a bug doing the two-step on a branch, cut to the male lion giving it to the female from behind, cut to me glancing at the girl across the bar.

Siiiiiiiiiiiiiiiiiiiiiiiiiiiiiiiiip.

"Another?"

"Yes."

Glass, ice, hooch, squirt, boom!

Sippy sip.

The guy to my right was an interesting looking chap. A real bug of a guy. Small head, skinny arms, long neck, with huge eyeballs, bursting out of their sockets. Look out! They're gonna blow!

I wondered what would come out if they did? Goo? Pus? Is there a difference? Blood? Maybe if I stuck around long enough I'd find out. They were like time bombs.

Tick, tick, tick.

Sip.

With eyes like that it made me think that he'd seen some pretty fucked up stuff in his life, crazy stuff that made his once-normal eyes pop out—like ghosts.

He probably saw ghosts all the time, everywhere he went, even in that bar. It was a curse handed down from his mother's side of the family. A guy with eyes like that, he could tell me a thing or two about the paranormal, and I would have asked him about it, if I knew how to talk to people.

Gulp.

"Another?"

The couple across the bar was annoying. To me, they were Mr. and Mrs. Poke. It wasn't the girl so much as the guy, Mr. Poke, who ticked me off. Look at him. It's always the big fellas, the thick types, the guys who offer a sense of physical protection, who get the ladies. This is assuming that money and fame don't exist, and in my world they certainly don't.

I don't know why I was jealous of them, a couple of circus chimps in real people clothes, beating their chests, walking around with blank expressions on their faces, shoving their lips out, scratching their heads, chasing the smaller chimps around the pen, having their brains eaten for desert. Look at those cocksure monkeys trying to act like humans. Who did they think they were fooling?

"Nice try, you stupid apes!"

I had planned on only thinking that last sentence but ended up screaming it as loud as I could.

Father Collins and Mr. and Mrs. Poke were looking at me now, but they seemed more bored than angry. They must have heard people shout stranger things than that.

The bug man, Buggy, was still staring dead ahead, probably at the vision of some little girl spook in a pretty pink dress, riding a ghost tricycle, saying, "Why did I die? Why did I die?" over and over as she rode her bike in circles. At least that's what his eyes were telling me.

So far so good, I thought, judging from everybody's current state of affairs it looked like my stupid apes proclamation had passed into the cultural lexicon without incident. I just needed final confirmation from the gentleman to my left who—

"Who you callin' apes?"

I forgot to mention that the chap to my left looked like a primate and was probably called such many times by gentlemen far bigger and braver than I. I mean, we all look like primates, but he *really* looked like a damn ape. He had one of those edge-of-the-cliff brows, a slightly upturned snoz, deep set eyes—a lot like Lincoln except this guy looked like a gorilla. Lincoln at least looked like the missing link.

Gulp, gulp, gulp.

"I was talking to the TV," I explained. "There were some monkeys on the screen."

"Monkeys? Were they acting stupid or something?" he asked.

"You could say that."

"I mean, were they like shitting in their cages and stuff?"

"Not really, they were in the wild."

"The wild? They probably shit in there too though, huh? Those stupid apes shit all over the place. Even in their own homes. What kind of stupid motherfucker shits in his nest?"

Jesus. He was right. Shitting all over one's home is a clear sign of stupidity—insanity really. If I were to fill my hands with my own, or anyone else's, feces and then proceed to finger paint my walls with it, then one could safely assume I was insane, or as my new pal Koko Junior put it so well, a stupid motherfucker. A keen insight, I raised my glass to the beast.

Chug, chug, chug.

"Another?"

A ghost. A stupid motherfucking ghost was shitting in my apartment. I thought that Koko Junior might understand what I was going through. I needed to tell someone else about that ghost. About what he did. What he did to me.

"Someone is shitting in my home as we speak."

He raised his eyebrows. "No shit? Really?"

"Yes really. He's shitting alllllllllll over my place."

Koko Junior got real serious. "You can't let him do that. What, you gonna live in a place that's been shit in? Once a place has been shit in there ain't no getting it back to the way it was, all pristine. No way, it's done. Sure, you can clean up the mess but a toilet is still a toilet after you clean it, right? And who wants to live in a toilet?"

I found much truth in what he said. "You're right. My God, there is no going back. I should just burn the whole thing and start over. Hope for the best."

"That's right. I'll drink to that."

"To what?"

"To burning it all and starting over niiiiiiice and fresh."

"Here, here."

Clink! GULP.

That felt good. A little back and forth with my fellow man, my fellow barfly, my Koko Junior. I even got a little compassion out of the interaction. Not enough, but some and it felt good. I needed more.

Looking around I doubted I'd be able to interact with all of those people one at a time. Who has the energy for that? I needed to do it all at once. I decided to stand up and make a general announcement.

"THERE'S STRANGE A-GOINGS ON IN THE DEEEEEEEP, DARRRRRRRK NNNNNNNNNIGHT!"

It was out there. I just had to sit back and wait for the connections. Here they come...I could feel them...wait...wait...

Nothing.

I had informed these people that not only were there scary things going on outside this bar, but that they were going on in the night, in the dark, and I had some information about said scary things, and their reaction was to do nothing? Nothing but glance at me, smirk, and go back to totally faking-it human-like behavior? Is that what we've become? A species of do-nothing smirkers, a bunch of chimps trying to act like human beings, and failing miserably, even in the face of bone chilling spookiness? Does no one care?

Maybe the problem was with hoping to reach the masses. The multitudes. I needed to take this grassroots, back to the one-on-one approach,

"Did you hear what I just said, Buggy?" I asked of Buggy.

"Yes," said Buggy, putting down his big beer and turning those hardboiled-egg eyes on me.

I challenged him on this. "What? What did I say?"

"You said there were strange a-goings on in the deeeeeep, darrrrrrk nnnnnnnnight."

"That's right! I did. So what the hell do you think about it?"

He took a sip of his beer. "Nothing."

"Nothing? Nothing! Look at your eyes! Don't lie to me, Buggy, not you. I know that you know that I know that everybody in this bar knows that you have seen some bizarre shit in your days, so don't tell me that you think nothing of me saying there are strange a-goings on in the deep, dark night. Which, as you know, there are."

I began to hate Buggy. Hated him for not backing me up. An expert in the field sitting right next to me, and he wouldn't say a word. Everybody else looked at me like I was crazy, and all it would have taken for them to take me seriously was for him to stand up and say, "He's right. I've seen these strange a-goings on he speaks of with my own bugged-out eyes."

Father Collins, bless him, intervened with his first sentence of the evening, "It's time to sit down and shut up."

Sip.

Father Collins, any Father Collins, is an imposing figure. He has a certain authority when he's behind that bar. He's the priest at his pulpit, and we're the congregation, listening to the wisdom he chooses to dish out, confessing our sins to him, receiving bread and wine from his hand, sitting while he stands, singing along to the hymns he plays on the juke-box, kneeling by the toilet, looking to him for some salvation from the outside world, and trying to find a heaven inside a longneck. So when he tells me to sit down and shut up, I listen, unless I happen to be so full of the spirit that my actions are no longer my own but are the very hand of God. Who needs a bug to back you up when the spirit urges you forward? Not me.

"What do you know of time?" I asked Father Collins.

"Home," he commanded.

"That's not an answer! You have to answer my questions. You must respond! Forget your personal agenda and respond!"

"Go."

"It's like I'm not even here. I might as well be talking to myself. I can't go home, you prick. That's where the strange a-goings on are currently a-going on! If you don't believe me you can ask Buggy over here, because he knows, he knows ALL TO WELL. Don't you? Don't you, Buggy! BUGGY! MR. AND MRS. POKE! TELL HIM! TELL HIM I'M RIGHT! PLEASE! KOKO JUNIOR! DON'T LEAVE ME HANGING, YOU BASTARD MMMMMMMONKEY!"

Whoosh. Without a drop of effort on my part I was off the stool, through the door and spread eagle on the sidewalk. A horrible place to be but at least I could take comfort in knowing that I didn't waste any of my own energy getting there.

And even though everybody else (Father Collins, Buggy, Koko Junior, and Mr. and Mrs. Poke) were still inside and I was outside, I felt no more alone then than I did when I was with them. I closed my eyes and dreamt of a cat-eyed girl with thick glasses and a friendly face reading a thick novel aloud to me while firmly—yet lovingly—shoving hardboiled eggs up my ass. And no, I didn't mind. It was nice to have someone acknowledge my presence, both physically and mentally for once, even if only in my dreams, and even if it meant odd things had to go up my ass.

15
An Ancient Itch

I woke up in a church of sorts. I only knew it was a church because of the many stained-glass windows on the walls around me, each
illuminated by a small spotlight. I counted these windows—there were
twelve—each depicting what appeared, at a glance, to be your basic
holy tableaus from the Bible. On closer inspection however, it became
apparent that these scenes weren't quite right. The familiar characters
were all accounted for—the bearded old man God, the unshaven hippy
Jesus, the buck naked Adam and birthday suit Eve, the lipstick red
Satan—but the stuff they were doing was all wrong.

In one window God was getting his ass handed to him by Satan and
his gang of devil thugs in an epic war that I previously thought had a
much different outcome than the one depicted. Satan literally had God's
ass in his hands and was handing it back to God, who was missing a
large chunk of flesh from his ass. Now, I know, from years of forced
Catholic schooling, that Satan was a powerful guy and a real mean
bastard who could kick some butt, and from years of dressing up for
Halloween I know that he has a goatee drawn on his face with a black
magic marker and wears tight red pajamas with feet, but I don't think
that at any point in his infamous career that he ripped off God's rear
end and then actually had the balls to hand it back. Someone must have

taken a few liberties with the good book to come up with *that* interpretation.

After examining that first window I wondered if I was in a Satanic church. Is there such a thing? Don't Satanists just kill chickens and goats every full moon in Uncle Bob's tool shed, which they painted black to make the whole thing official and to please the Dark Lord who loves it when tool sheds are black like his soul? But even if Satanists did have actual churches, and not just Uncle Bob's tool shed, I don't think that they would bother with stained glass windows, which tend to scream, "Holy! Holy! Holy!" No matter what you put on them.

In another window, Satan was stealing God's stash of light—I never heard any stories about God stockpiling light, maybe prices were going up at the time—and stuffing it into Adam, who in the window directly before this one, was being molded out of clay along with Eve by Satan (wearing a beret), not by God as the story went.

Jesus, who had light shining out of his eyes like a friggin' poltergeist, was encouraging Adam to eat the apple in the next one, practically shoving the thing down his throat. While Satan, in the form of a snake—at least they got that part right—sat in the tree watching Jesus and Adam, with a horrified expression on his face as if what was about to happen with the apple was a terrible thing. Now that doesn't make sense no matter how you look at it.

They were all like this. The characters were right, the setting was right, but the plot was screwy. I wondered if maybe the church got some kind of deal on these windows since they were all misprints.

The only window that wasn't messed up was the one on the ceiling and it was the biggest of them all, by far. It was lit up by a spotlight on the floor directly beneath it. The window depicted the sun—or *a* sun— the typical yellow circle with rays of light sticking out of it. Behind this was a red triangle. I'm pretty sure it was a sun, either that or a yellow spider that had been stepped on. Floating in the middle of this sun were two open chubby hands that looked, despite being disembodied, rather welcoming.

Except for those concentrated beams of light on the windows, the room was dark.

The first thing I did after waking up and examining the windows was check to make sure I still had my wallet, and indeed I did. When you pass out in the street, doing this is as automatic as a knee reflex.

The second thing I did after waking up, examining the windows, and checking for my wallet, was to check if my belt was still fastened, and it was.

This too should be a knee jerk reaction, performed anytime one wakes from falling asleep, not just in the street, but anywhere not familiar. I once woke up in a strange bed, feeling as if I had been drugged, and not only was my belt not buckled, but I didn't even have any pants or underwear on. I screamed "I'VE BEEN RAVISHED!" five times before the gentleman across from me, and in a similar situation, informed me that I was in a hospital, and had just had my appendix removed. So the pantless situation was, therefore, OK. But under any other circumstances it would have been cause for serious concern.

The third thing I did after waking up in a church, examining the windows, checking for my wallet, and making sure my belt was locked, was scratch my neck.

My neck rarely itches. It's just something I do, and I think it's because my dad always did it when he woke up from a nap. I wonder if his neck really itched when he woke up or if it was just something he saw his father do. And if that's the case, then did my father's father's neck really itch? If not then was it my father's father's father's? Or must I go all the way back, through decades of motion to a much slower time, to my father's father's father's father's neck to find an actual itch? Or must I go back to a monkey? Did the itch have a beginning at all? Or has it just always been? Will it ever end? Am I the last generation of the itch? I feel like I am.

And finally, after waking up in a church, examining the windows, checking for my wallet, making sure my belt was locked, and scratching my neck, the fourth thing I did was get blinded by a spotlight.

"Are you OK?" said the light. From the deep bass tonal quality of the voice, I deduced it was a male light or, to make the leap of faith, a man standing behind the light.

I decided to speak to him, expressing myself freely. "I'll be OK when you get that light out of my face, you cocksucker!"

Whoa! Whoa! Whoa there, idiot. I needed to consider some things. Sure a bright light in the eyes is a horrible thing to happen to a hungover chappy, but I was in a church. That much had been established. There could, I told myself, feasibly be a man of the cloth behind that light. I didn't want to call a priest a cocksucker, now did I? You do know what it means to call someone a cocksucker, right? It means they like to suck on cocks, and not only that, but it's something they do often enough to be labeled as one who sucks cocks. Take a minute. Think about your own cock if you have one. That hairy, engorged vein with the goo inside, that tube of filth, is what I was saying the man at the other end of the light, in a church, a house of God, sucks on.

"Did you just call me a cocksucker?" inquired the man with the light. Who, at that point could have been a priest, or a man, or a nun with a deep voice. Whatever it was, the light made me feel like I was being interrogated.

"No." I lied and then quickly realized that this could be an agent of God and elaborated with, "Well, yes. I did. But I'm sorry for it and I'd like to repent."

"Good. If I were a priest I'd tell you to say fifteen billion Hail Mary's and two hundred ninety-nine million, seven hundred ninety-two thousand, four hundred fifty-eight Our Father's. But I'm not. So fuck you, you fucking fuck."

And with that the man (who at this point I can honestly say was NOT a priest, a nun, or a lady) walked off, taking his spotlight with him and leaving me alone again in the darkness.

At this point I thought maybe I really was in a Satanic Church.

"Cocksucker," I mumbled to myself, or maybe not to myself, as the light swung around and was back on me full force.

"The opening ceremony shall begin in four minutes time," he told me, "and I suggest you be gone from here in much less than that. Ba Hubba Tree Bob was kind enough to lift you out of the pool of your own blood and vomit in the street and carry you here over his shoulder. Now I suggest you be kind enough to lift yourself up off our floor and carry yourself back where you came from."

"Who brought me here? The hubble tree?"

"Leave!"

"If you tell me how to get out of here," I told him, "and maybe if you turn on a few overhead lights so I can see where I'm going, then I'd be glad to leave. I don't want to bump my shins."

"We can't turn on any lights yet."

"Why not? You already have a bunch of lights on."

"No, we don't."

"Yes, you do. For starters you have a light shining on those paddy-cake hands on the ceiling."

"That's the Father of Lights," he said, sounding quite offended, "His light doesn't count."

"Well, it should."

"Look, buddy, if I point my light at the exit do you think you'll be able to stumble toward it?"

"I could try."

"Good."

He swung his light off me and across the room, illuminating an open door.

"Thank you," I said as I made my way toward it, happy to be on my way out of that possibly Satanic chapel before their opening ceremonies began. Opening ceremonies? If the Satanic Olympics were about to begin I wanted no part of it.

But when I was only a few feet from the door, the spotlight on it went out.

"Hey! Could you at least wait until I get through the door!" This guy really was a cocksucker.

"My finger slipped! Sorry!" He said this, but he didn't sound sorry. He was more angry than sorry.

The light came back on quickly, but the door in front of me was no longer empty. May—my coworker, my girlfriend, well, at least when I'm whacking off she's my girlfriend—stood in it, staring out at me, wearing a yellow robe, and holding a small flashlight in her hands. The expression on her face told me at once that she and everybody else in that church were up to some rather goofy ass things and they didn't want outsiders to see them doing those things, since prancing around a room with a flashlight is only a goofy ass thing when someone who isn't prancing around the room with a flashlight sits in the corner of the room, shakes his head, and thinks, Lord Almighty these people sure look like a bunch of goofy asses prancing around the room with flash-lights. And though they weren't prancing around the room with flash-lights just then, May knew that they soon would be doing just that.

16
The Bright

May was squinting. "Is that you, Joe?"

"Yes."

"Oh Joe, you look like shit. Just like a shit. What are you doing here?"

I figured I'd try saying something better than "I got drunk, passed out in the street, and was carried here by something called the hubble tree." I didn't want May's pity, I wanted her sympathy, in the hopes that it would lead to her touching me, somewhere, for more than just a few seconds. So I lied.

"That guy over there, with the light, beat me up and took my wallet."

"Oh my God!" cried May as she clutched her shoulders, "Phillip, how could you?"

"I didn't touch him!" said Phillip as he scurried over to us. He too wore a robe, but his was a darker shade of yellow than May's.

Damn you Phillip, you were supposed to be over there, not over here. I didn't like the mingling of over there and over here that Phillip engaged in.

"Don't lie to me, Phillip. Did you beat up Joe?" demanded May, giving me the feeling that she liked me more than Phillip, which, I'll admit, gave me a little smirk. I felt May liked me more than anybody else in the entire room at the time, even if there was only one other person in there besides me. The room was a closed system and for a moment I wished that the doors would be sealed off forever so I could live with those odds until my dying day.

But that dream was broken by Phillip, who had the nerve to defend himself with, "I didn't touch him, May. No one did. Ba Hubba Tree Bob picked him up drunk on the street last night."

"That's where you're wrong, Phil," I said, pointing my finger into his light, "Ba Hubba Bubba beat me up, took my wallet, and then, THEN, he carried me back here."

"Ba Hubba Tree Bob beat you up? Please."

Phillip wasn't buying it, but maybe, just maybe, May was.

"I don't know if I believe that, Joe."

She wasn't.

"Well, believe it. Because it happened."

"But Joe, you do smell like alcohol." May pointed out, and she was right. I needed to explain that.

"That's not drinking alcohol you smell. It's gasoline. Ba Hubba Three Rob was just about to set me on fire when I plea bargained with him to beat me and take my wallet in lieu of setting me ablaze."

"Ba Hubba Tree Bob?" asked Phillip.

"That's the one."

"Doused you in gasoline and tried to set you ablaze?"

"That's right."

"Why?"

"How should I know? Probably because I wouldn't drink goat blood out of a chicken's skull, pledge allegiance to the Dark Lord, and fondle his penis all at the same time."

May covered her ears.

Phillip turned red.

"Fondle his penis! First you refer to the Father of Lights as 'paddy-cake hands' and now you insult our prophet?"

"Oh please Phillip, I'm not that naïve. I saw those satanic stained-glass windows over there. I know what's going on here."

"This is a Church of The Bright, Joe. We're Bogumils," said May, whose sympathy was now replaced with the pity I feared earlier, and instead of the doors being sealed off forever, I now wished that the whole room would take off like a rocket ship, taking May, Phillip, and the whole structure somewhere deep into space and leave me on Earth. I had no idea what she was talking about with the Bogumil or the Ba Hubba Tree Bob stuff. Not a clue. Maybe the alcohol from last night cast a haze over the speech centers of my brain, or maybe they were talking gibberish. Regardless, I didn't want to look dumb so I just said, "Bogumils eh? I see. Well, I'm off."

I slid past May through the doorway and made my way to the exit, which I couldn't see, but hoped was close. I didn't make it though, because behind me I heard:

"Wait, Joe. Aren't you going to join us for the Opening Ceremony?"

I suppose it was her use of the word 'join' that got me. She didn't say watch, observe, investigate, probe, check out, consider, see, survey, study, or assist with. May asked if I would join them, and that sounded like something I might be interested in doing.

17
Opening Ceremonies

Twelve people—five men, five women, one Phillip, and one May—all wore long robes of various shades of yellow and they all stood in a circle, or ellipse if you want to get technical, in the center of the room with all those kooky windows. Each of them held a flashlight, turned on and pointed at the center of the circle, creating a single point of light that fluttered with the natural movements of people's hands.

They also wore huge, thick, dark sunglasses, like the kind you would wear if you wanted to stare at a solar eclipse without burning your eyeballs off. May gave me a pair of the glasses and told me, warned me really, to use them to watch the ceremony.

I sat outside the circle in a folding chair that Phillip the Cocksucker was nice enough to bring out for me, and sipped the second—after downing the first in one gulp—cup of coffee the vending machine in the hallway was nice enough to dispense for me. I took the glasses off shortly after May gave them to me since they made me look stupid and I was afraid that May would sneak a peek at me and see me looking like a bug. Besides, it was so dark in the room, I couldn't see anything with them on.

It started out as a pretty lame opening ceremony. A bunch of people standing around in a hokey pokey circle so early in the morning the sun hadn't even come up yet, not saying a word, in the dark, with no music playing, no torch, no releasing of doves, and hell, they weren't even holding hands.

My sips were the loudest sound in the room by about six decibels, but no one gave me a dirty look nor shushed me. They were meditating, I thought, waiting for enlightenment or something else that would never come from standing around playing with flashlights. I was so bored that anything in the way of movement or speech would have been welcomed, but nothing happened.

I had been sitting there for a good ten minutes when, out of boredom, my thoughts drifted away from the scene in front of me, making an initial stop into my innards, where the coffee was beginning to shake things up, continuing from there to the bedroom with May, where she was naked on the bed and I sat in a chair across from her wearing a big, puffy snowsuit of some kind and playing a fife. This scene could have unfolded in a number of beautiful ways if only the image of Martini doing a jig a playing a fife hadn't popped into my head, ruining everything.

Damn that Martini. What had become of him? I knew the Duo had him at some time and in some place, if not at what time and in what place, but not what they could have wanted from him. His company? Doubtful. So why didn't they take me instead? Were they observing me on the train those two times? Sizing me up and coming to the conclusion that I was unsuitable for their needs. Needs which Martini could have been fulfilling, perhaps, right then. It had been so long since I had filled someone's needs that by not being abducted by the Duo I actually felt rejected. I felt like a runner up, kind of like how the monkeys must feel when they look at us.

In an attempt to ease the pain of rejection, I was just beginning to ponder an image of a naked Martini getting a stoic midget stuffed up his ass by a determined skeleton man, when all of the spotlights on the windows and all the flashlights in the room went out simultaneously. If there was a signal for this to happen I had missed it completely. The place was dark and quiet enough for me to get spooked, so much so that after a moment of sitting in my chair, worrying that a disturbingly small, old woman with red lipstick smeared over her lips might be scurrying around me in ever decreasing concentric circles, I stuttered, "Hello? Phillip?"

That's when the sun came up, the first sliver of its light peaking through the windows. I figured the robed folks were going to stand there in silence and watch the sunrise, that it was their peaceful little way of welcoming the new day.

I thought it was pretty nice, to come together every morning, stand together with other people, people who you may even be friends with, or at least familiar faces, and watch the sunrise. I sure as hell would never have the patience to do it, but I thought that they were almost noble in that simple daily communal act free from the bells and whistles and mucking up that is almost a part of everything else in people's lives today.

My thinking on this matter was way off.

A column—no, a shaft—a shaft of light poured down from the giant sun window on the ceiling, so bright that I swore I felt the thin surface layer of my eyeball flesh sizzle off like flash paper.

Maybe I should have kept the glasses on.

The light was accompanied by a sound similar to those sound effects you hear in movies when a space ship turns on its tractor beam. That low humming.

When the light from the window hit them, the robed folks, their backs now to the center of the circle, spun around and tilted their heads back, as if they were soaking up some rays at the beach. They held that position for a moment and then lowered their heads in unison, clicking on their spotlights and pointing the beams out the stained glass windows around them. It looked as if they were a type of filter, with the shaft of light going into them and out into twelve smaller beams.

A section of the floor in the center of the circle slid open, much like a manhole, releasing a soft blue shaft of light. It penetrated the center of the white shaft of light, a blue straw in a glass of lemonade. From the hole rose a man, not tall and not short, thick like a walrus, wearing a white robe and sunglasses and sporting a huge pearly white smile. He was bald on top but from the sides and back had long albino white hair going down to his shoulders, and his skin was white as glue. When the platform lifting him was even with the floor, he began to speak in a voice so high it sounded as if he had been sucking on helium.

"We are all of the Bright—the perception, conception, and presumption of which is essential to true love bliss—and we must return to the Bright, where The Father of Lights waits for us all—no matter what we look like or what we've done—with open hands. This is my divine revelation to you: I am all that which has already happened. I am the Wholeness, the Oneness, the Great Yes, the Bright, the Complete, the One, who is everything and Everything, and that too. Know me, pay attention to me, and all can be yours, for all of the complexity of the Bright maze can be simply realized in the relationship with Me: Da Adi Sumra, Ba Hubba Tree Bob, La Love-Jamuti Te-ta, The Ba, The Bee, The Ba Bo Bee.

"Now, that said, take yourself back, way back, to, oh I don't know, let's say age sixteen. A good age. Or, if not that, any age you can comfortably remember. But get as close to sixteen as you can, follow your light path. The twists and turns. The bends. The dips. The loop-da-loops. What are you doing? What were you doing before that? And after? What then, hmmmmm? Fill in the blanks. Ah ha! You can't! That's what you say. And I, Ba Hubba Tree Bob, say you can, with me."

He went on like this for what was in my mind way too long. Putting me to sleep with his silly yapping about light paths and beams and the Bright. When he finally wrapped it up they all sang "This Little Light of Mine, I'm Gonna Let It Shine." That, at least, I could identify with and I even found myself singing along and doing a few of the hand motions, but I don't think they were talking about the artificial light coming out of their flashlights or about the little smiling candle flame I imagined as I sang. The light they thought of was clearly more of a, how can I put this, New Agey bullshity type of light—the kind that doesn't exist or, if it did, won't for very much longer.

As the group sang, Ba Hubba Tree Bob made his way around the circle, giving everybody a long hug.

I watched each embrace like a dog watches his master eat a bucket of chicken wings, amazed that a creature could have an actual bucket full of food, contemplating every drop of sauce, every finger lick, every crunch, with mouth hanging open and eyes wide, holding out the hope that there will be at least one bone with a speck of flesh left for him to nibble.

For me, there was. After hugging the last person in the circle, Ba Hubba returned to the center and walked toward me. As he moved, the circle moved with him, always keeping him dead center. The outer rim of people soon passed by me, enclosing me in their group. Ba Hubba walked right up to me, looked me in the eyes and smiled. He opened his arms wide and, with a sigh, gave me a hug.

I didn't mind this at all.

It felt like I was being held by a big, warm, white walrus, and I even wouldn't have minded slow dancing with the man for a song or two. But it didn't stop there. Ba Hubba took my head into his hands as the singing of the group quickly swelled and the robed folks began to dance around in circles, their flashlights now on and twirling along with them, while the other lights in the room, including the white and blue shafts, rotated like at a rock show.

I tried to turn my head to get a better look at this light-show but couldn't as Ba Hubba's hold wouldn't allow it. Assuming he wanted me to look only at him and that he would explain everything to me, I turned my eyes on him hoping for a shrug, a wink, or a laugh but instead getting Ba Hubba Tree Bob's tongue shoved down my throat.

I tasted vanilla.

18
Bogumils

May rode the subway back with me. She was on her way to work and I was on my way home to clean up before doing the same.

It was early enough that the train wasn't packed. The seats were full but the aisles weren't, and we managed to sit next to each other. In the narrow seats, designed for what must have been a race of people far narrower than us, our hips were actually touching, no, pressing against each other from knee to butt and, traveling up the torso, we also found our shoulders touching as well. Not a bad ratio of touching to not touching, especially for me. I wanted to close my eyes and focus on the contact, but first, I understandably had some questions about the opening ceremonies.

"What the hell was that?"

I figured I throw in the word 'hell' to come across as slightly edgy. I considered using 'fuck' but decided that it was too early in the morning for 'fuck.' I also crossed my arms and raised one eyebrow as I said it in an attempt to project that fatherly aura, the wise old man who is actually slightly edgy and young, a combination I believe that women, try as they may, cannot resist. I only needed a pipe and maybe a small tattoo on my neck to complete the multi-layered effect.

"Church," she said, while applying lipstick to her big thick lips, and missing the multi-layered effect I was so subtly crafting. If someone is talented enough to create a multi-layered effect solely for your benefit, then the least you can do is have the common courtesy to notice it. You don't have to stand up and shout "bravo!" but for the love of god, have yourself a look-see.

"I've been to Church, May." Pause for effect. "That was no Church."

"It's the Church of The Bright. It's *new*."

When she said "It's *new*" her eyes lit up as if she was talking about the new hot copy guy at the office. Who's that? Oh, that's Edward. He's *new*. And just as I would be jealous of Edward for making May light up like that, I was jealous of this new Church. What did it have that I didn't? What more could it offer to a lost soul than I could? I could offer my soul to a lost soul. Beat that.

"So that warm fellow who frenched me was a priest?"

"Ba Hubba Tree Bob? He's not a priest, he's the Bright."

"The bright what?"

"Just The Bright."

"Capital T, capital B?"

"Yes."

"I see."

She pulled a small book out of her bag and handed it to me. The cover had that sun with the hands and triangle thing on it. I flipped open to the first page where there was a big yellow dot with lines coming out of it. The lines were each obviously drawn on with different pens, markers, and pencils, and not printed like on. At the bottom of the page it read, in small black letters: "Howdy Bogumil!"

"This book has been defaced," I pointed out, "It's ruined. Worthless."

I told her this to make sure she didn't blame me for the graffiti when I returned the book.

"It's meant to be defaced, Joe."

"You did this? You drew all these lines?" I could have added 'young lady' at the end there, but chose not to as that would have been going too far with the father thing.

"Only one," she replied.

"Which one?"

"I can't remember. It really doesn't matter, they're all the same."

"Can I draw some?"

"You can draw one."

"Why only one?"

"Because each line represents a person and you're only one person."

"But how will you know which line is mine?"

"It doesn't matter whose is whose."

"Can I label my line?"

"Label it what?"

"Label it 'Joe.'"

"No."

May did however say that I could keep the book for a few days to read over it and draw my line, so I tucked it into my pants pocket. As I did, I performed a quick scan of the train, looking for the Duo. It would be just like them to pop up then, while I was connecting with a female on so many levels, and ruin everything with their staring and snatching.

The train was, however, void of Duos. In fact, May and I were the closet thing to a Duo on that train at that moment, a wonderful fact that didn't escape me.

I decided to find out more about this Church.

"What's with the robes?"

"The lighter the yellow, the closer you are to the Bright."

"Does having his tongue in your mouth get you any closer?"

"There are different ways. Just read the book, it explains everything."

"Everything?"

"It did for me."

"Good, because there are a few things in my life that could use some explaining."

"Like the Duo?"

"*Exactly* like the Duo."

It took a moment for my brain to realize that I never told her about the Duo. I never told anyone besides Mr. Burk, which meant something was afoot.

"I've been assigned," she said.

"Assigned to what?"

"Your top secret project."

This also made her eyes light up. And I was now jealous of my own top secret project. I was also shocked, and showed it with a sudden and dramatic change in the position of my eyebrows.

"Oh Joe, don't look so surprised. Did you think you were the only one?"

"No, Martini was my assistant, but he's been captured."

"By the Duo?"

"That's right. It's a dangerous mission May."

"Mr. Burk told us that you were just being silly about all that."

"Silly? I've seen them May, seen them on the subway, in the past, and I saw them nab Martini. Did you say *us*?"

"Yeah, he briefed four of us."

"Four!"

"It's a big project, Joe. You're going to need help."

"What about the tours?"

"They've been cut back until this is completed. We're only giving a few private ones. Don't get mad at me but I think you're leading one today at noon."

"Leading a tour?" I was crushed by this betrayal. "Mr. Burk has lost faith in my abilities."

"No he hasn't, he just wants this taken care of as quickly as possible. Oh, I need to transfer here. Maybe I'll see you in the caf."

"The caf?"

"Cafeteria."

"What cafeteria?"

"The one on the eighth floor."

"There's a cafeteria in our building?"

"Yeah. Everybody eats there."

"I never knew."

"Well now you do."

And before I could call out, "Thanks for the scoop!" she was gone, and the doors closed.

And before I could draw a line in my mind from lunch in the caf with May to May and I waking up together after a nap, I looked up and saw the Duo sitting across from me.

19
Reunions

The doors shut, the train started to pull away from the platform, made it about twenty feet, stopped, backed up into the station, stopped, the doors opened, the Duo stood up, the Duo sat down, the doors closed, the train pulled out of the station again, and this time continued on out of the station.

The Duo exchanged a worried look while I thought about how the behavior of the train made me think of the behavior of Mr. Puss with his back and forth trick.

Thinking of Mr. Puss made me think of the ghost in my apartment, wondering if he was making himself a cat and eggs breakfast.

And thinking of a cat and eggs breakfast made me, I admit, a bit hungry, but it also made me think of death and how my poor cat was far too young to die and be eaten by a ghost and how I myself wasn't ready to die.

And thinking about how I wasn't ready to die made me return my thoughts to the matter at hand—the Duo.

I gathered all the strength I could muster after a night of drinking followed by a few hours sleep on the floor of a new church.

I sat up straight, planted my feet on the floor, put my hands on my hips, stuck out my chest, stared right into all four of their eyes, took a deep breath, and said, "I demand to know the whereabouts of one Tullio Martini!" In the most grave, full of rage, don't-fuck-with-me voice I could fake.

Martini wasn't my friend, and really, I loathed his presence, but he was a co-worker, and I did know his full name, so I felt a certain amount of loyalty to him. And he was in the union.

The Duo didn't answer my demand but only returned it with confused stares. They sat there looking at me, being themselves really, and doing what I was beginning to learn they did best. Clearly words weren't enough to get through to their kind so I grabbed May's flashlight and pointed it at them, my index finger on the switch and my brow furrowed.

"Last chance, fellas. Where's Martini?"

Simultaneously they both raised their right arms and pointed to their right at what I feared was either a naked bloody Martini hanging from the ceiling by his penis or nothing at all, a diversion to get me to look away so that they could grab me, take off all my clothes, bloody me, and hang me from the ceiling by my penis.

I wasn't going to take any chances and I also wasn't going to miss what they pointed at, so as I swiveled to see what was there I switched on the light. That way, I figured, if it was a trick on their part to divert my attention, I could swivel back and hit them with the light full force, causing some minor eye damage, or, at the very least, causing them to blink a bunch of times. And in matters of life and death, it's those who blink who end up road kill. If, however, it was Martini hanging by his little wiener, I would merely illuminate the horrifying scene and nothing more.

I swiveled, and the flashlight did end up illuminating one Tullio Martini, but instead of hanging from the ceiling he was standing in the aisle, shoulders hunched, still wearing the "I fucked your girlfriend" t-shirt, and writing in a notebook.

"Hey Joe," he said, shrugging his shoulders.

"Martini. You're alive."

I was stating the obvious, I know, but what else do you say to a guy who you don't care much for but thought was turned into a naked bloody piñata? If I did care for him I would have said something more elaborate such as, "Martini! Thank Jesus you're alive! Oh this truly is a gay day!" But I didn't, so I didn't.

"That light is making me blink, Joe. It hurts."

The spotlight was in his eyes and his talk of blinking made me remember the Duo, sitting there, unmonitored, free to do as they pleased. Not on my watch!

I swung the light back around to light up the two seats in front of me. The two empty seats.

"They're gone," said Martini.

"I can see that."

But I couldn't figure out how since the train hadn't made any stops. I swung the light back to Martini. "Where did they go? And how?"

"Oh sure, no 'Hey Martini, are you OK?'"

If I wanted any information out of the man, I knew I would have to humor him, turn off the interrogation light, and pretend like I cared for his well being.

"Well are you?" I asked.

"Am I what?"

He knew what, he just wanted to hear me say it.

"Are you OK?"

"Physically?" He asked.

"Sure."

"No."

"No?"

I had visions of the poor bastard opening his long coat to reveal a long metal pole protruding from his stomach, blood soaking his gray pants, rolling up his sleeves to show me hundreds of deep bite marks up and down his pale white arms, lifting up his pant leg to display the colony of cockroaches that had taken up residence underneath his skin.

"Physically," said Martini, "I'm extremely hungry."

"Hungry? That's it? Oh please."

He was offended. "You know, hundreds of thousands of people die of starvation every year, you assface! They get hungry, they forget they're hungry, they're unknowingly hungry, they never eat, and then they die. Eating is vital, Joe. It's the foundation on which civilization was built!"

Not knowing how to reply to that I decided to instead turn the conversation away from his physical condition. "What about emotionally?" I asked, "How are you feeling?"

"Oh, *emotionally*, I'm fine."

"Well that's good to hear."

"For the most part they were very nice."

"Great." I wasn't interested. "So who are they and where'd they go?"

"In fact, since you asked, I'm going to miss their company quite a bit."

"I didn't ask."

He had crossed his legs and was twirling his pen in his hair. "You know how it is when you meet someone you really like, but they live far away and you only get to spend a little bit of time with them? But you really wish you could spend a lot of time with them, because you think that, even though there'd be some ups and downs, maybe in time you'd be great friends with them? You know what that's like?"

"No."

"Well this is like that."

"Are you going to tell me what happened? Or are you going to go tell me about some of the lost loves in your life?"

He pondered this.

"Can I tell you about both?"

"No."

"Fine. I'm not saying anything until I eat something."

And then he slapped his hand across his mouth to show that he meant business.

"What do you want to eat?"

"I want to eat breakfast," he mumbled through his hand,

"Don't you eat breakfast?"

"Sort of."

"Pancakes. I need steaming hot pancakes."

"If I buy you pancakes, will you talk?"

He grimly nodded once. I took that for a yes.

"Then let's go get some pancakes. Any place in particular?"

His eyes got wide and he quickly nodded ten times.

"OK. Where?"

20
Battered Bart's Breakfast Barn

My daily breakfast beverages consisted of either two cups of coffee or tea, with two sugars and three creams in each, or two glasses of purified cold water.

Regardless of which liquid it happened to be each morning, the first cup or glass would always be chugged to quickly reintroduce hydration, and the second savored and accompanied by either one cigarette, one stick of processed meat jerky, or one Kerpluey brand snack cake.

My breakfast therefore, on any given day, was limited to one of the following menu choices:

Two cups of coffee and one cigarette
Two cups of coffee and one meat stick
Two cups of coffee and one Kerpluey cake
Two cups of tea and one cigarette
Two cups of tea and one meat stick
Two cups of tea and one Kerpluey cake
Two glasses of water and one cigarette
Two glasses of water and one meat stick
Two glasses of water and one Kerpluey cake

I found each of these nine combinations to be just the right balance of nourishment and pollutant, enough to both wake me up and get me through until lunch, which normally consisted of one of the nine combinations available to me in the mornings, although rarely would my breakfast and lunch be identical.

Oh sure, there were days when I would wake up to two glasses of water and one meat stick only to find myself at lunch having two cups of tea and one meat stick, but rarely, almost rarely enough to be never, did I repeat an exact combination twice in one day.

On days when I began my day with a caffeine drink I did, I'll admit, feel pressured to have a caffeine drink again at lunch to take some of the pressure off of the morning caffeine, which may have felt pressured to keep me going all day long. No one and no thing deserves to be asked to do that much.

And on days when I began my day caffeine free, and then caffeinated myself at lunch, I did feel the nudge to have a caffeine drink that following morning to take the pressure off the previous day's midday caffeine, which may have felt as if it had been asked to do the Herculean task of both allowing me to get to sleep at night and getting me going in the morning. A preposterous request, and one I try to never make of my beverages or my friends, of which I have none.

The sugar, only completely absent in one of the nine meals available to me, gave me the physical energy to do things like move my body parts about.

The caffeine, absent in three meals, gave my brain the alertness to do things like fire neurons at itself.

The creams, also absent in three, gave my stomach the coating it needed not to eat itself, and the smoke and/or preservatives, always present, tended to keep my entire system occupied and distracted by the disturbing presence of chemicals, lethal in large doses, necessary in small ones, until such time as my nightly dinner of soup could be consumed.

I don't consider myself a smoker. I never smoke more than two cigarettes in the course of a day, and they are an essential part of my diet. And that goes the same for the shot of whiskey I tend to splash into my nightly dinner of soup. It's all part of a delicate balance.

Which is why the sight of two large pancakes sitting in front of me, dripping with raging rivers of melted butter and stagnate pools of syrup, threatened that balance and caused some nausea without a single morsel breaking those guardians of the inner temple known as the lips.

The pancakes seemed like a good idea when I saw them on the menu—I thought that since a pancake was, at its root, a cake, and that a Kerpluey cake was, at its root, a cake, that one could easily be substituted for the other—and so much so that when the waitress asked me what I wanted, I heard myself saying, "Pancakes." The words sounded so strange coming out of my mouth, mainly because I never eat out, and when I'm at home I never say the name of the food I'm going to eat before I eat it. I don't sit down to a nice bowl of soup, pause, and say "Soup" to myself before I eat it. That would be crazy. Not that I don't have the urge to, because, honestly, I almost always do. But once you start actually *doing* the abnormal things your brain suggests, and not merely thinking them, it's only a short slide to shuffling aimlessly through the streets, wearing empty tissue boxes as slippers.

This is why at the diner I thought it was Martini who said "Pancakes" and not I, but that thought was quickly corrected when Martini said:

"French toast and breakfast sausage links, if you don't mind. And some milk."

"I thought you wanted pancakes?" I asked him.

"I was swayed. The menu swayed me."

"How? It's just a list of items. There aren't any pictures or descriptions to do the swaying."

"There *are* descriptions. See what it says by the sausage links?"

"It says nothing by the sausage links but 'sausage links.'"

"It says *breakfast*, Joe. It says they're *breakfast* sausage links."

"How is a breakfast sausage link different from a regular sausage link other than the fact that it's served in the morning and has a tendency to get syrup all over it?"

"Have you ever had a breakfast sausage?" He asked.

"I've had sausages before."

"But a breakfast sausage?"

"Sausage is sausage."

"Sausage is *not* sausage."

"If you eat a sausage at 8 p.m. can it be a breakfast sausage?" I asked.

"What time did you wake up that day?"

"You woke up at 7 a.m."

"Well then it depends."

"On what?"

"On the sausage."

"No."

"Yes."

"Sausage."

The conversation was starting to get away from me.

"Look," I said, "I don't want to say 'sausage' anymore. It's starting to sound weird."

"What is? Sausage? How can sausage sound weird? It's a perfectly normal word. Listen: sausage. *Saus*age. Saus*age*. *Sausage*. Sssssssssss—"

"Enough!"

He put his head down like a scolded child. In the ensuing awkward silence I stared at my fork and thought "fork, fork, fork, fork, fork" over and over in my head to see if doing so would make 'fork' sound as weird as 'sausage.'

It did.

Martini lifted his head, looking hopeful. "Couldn't you just say 'links' instead?"

"No."

"Patties?"

"Leave me alone."

"Why? So you can go back to thinking about your precious fork!"

"Leave the fork out of this!"

Shortly after that we were eating. Me with the oozing pancakes and he with the egg-soaked pieces of fried bread sopping alongside two meat logs, all the while sitting in a two-person booth (which may have had two places to sit but only really had enough table space to accommodate one plate) at Battered Bart's Breakfast Barn. Which wasn't a barn at all but a small, rather greasy and cramped diner, which was bursting with dinerees. Not an uncommon thing according to Martini.

"It's always like this," he said, while under the table we engaged in a passive aggressive battle for legroom.

There were only two booths in the place, the rest of the seating either at the counter or at small, two-person tables. A smart move by the owner, seeing as how very few people went out anywhere with more than one other person those days. There were families to think of, but this place was hardly of the sort where mom and pop would bring the kids for Mother's Day brunch.

I wondered if Bart was an actual person, and if so, if he was battered, as in physically deformed from years of abuse, possibly self-mutilation, or was it just a clever pun for a breakfast diner? I asked Martini and he told me that he always thought both sides were true, the title Bart's Battered Breakfast Barn was both clever, because of its catchiness, and ironic, due to the beaten-down nature of Bart. I considered asking a waitress to confirm this but decided against it for two reasons. One, because if Bart was a battered man I didn't want her to bring him out and put him on display to prove it to me, and two, I had more important questions that needed answers.

I waited until Martini had finished the bulk of his meal before starting. He was staring down at his plate, alternately shoveling in huge chunks of food and taking long, slow pulls of milk. Somehow he made it look as if even eating was a burden, with his slow chewing and frequent sighs.

I tried my best to ignore my food, but it was difficult to do this while the sloppy pancakes were uncomfortably close to me, because half my plate hung off the table and jabbed me in the chest. It was also hard to ignore my pancakes because while he ate, Martini wouldn't stop rocking his body side to side and softly singing,

Mixin' pancakes
Stirrin' pancakes
Pop 'em in the pan!
Fryin' pancakes,
Flippin' pancakes,
Catch 'em if you can!
Lickin' pancakes,
Sniffin' pancakes,
What you doin' man?

I tried pushing my plate more onto the table, which pushed Martini's plate more towards him and jabbed him in the chest, which stopped him from singing, but it also had the unpleasant side effect of making him sob gently, so I pulled my plate back. He dried his tears and began the song again, just as softly as before,

Pooin' pancakes,
Pukin' pancakes,
Right back in the pan!

The song didn't finish until his plate was clean and glass was empty.
"Talk," I said.
"Wait," he replied.
"Wait for what?"
"I want to see the magic show."
"What magic show?"
He pointed to the scruffy man standing in front of our table. The

guy could have been standing there for quite some time for all I knew.

The man wore a faded, old orange tuxedo with a matching top hat. He had a mustache that curled up at the ends. In his right hand he held a wand. In his eyes there was a twinkle. From the smell of his breath and the color of the vomit stains on his shirt I suspected the twinkle was alcohol induced.

He bowed, tipped his hat to us, and burped. The burp smelt so bad I could taste it. It tasted like a rotting corpse's armpit.

"Molloy is the name, and magic is the game," he said. "A little here, a little there. There's magic everywhere!" With some difficulty he pulled out a bouquet of dirty, torn fake flowers from his sleeve.

Martini gasped and grabbed my hand. "We're in for quite a show!"

I quickly pulled my hand away. "Shut up, Martini."

The magician bowed again, almost falling over this time. When he rose, a grubby open hand was thrust in my face. "For my next trick," he said, "I will need a member of the audience to place a dollar in my hand."

"I don't have any cash," I lied, "And neither does my friend."

He thought this over. "I see. But you do have pancakes, yes?"

I looked down at my uneaten stack of flapjacks. "Yes."

"They'll do."

"The whole stack?"

"Yes, it is most necessary for the trick to work that it be an entire stack."

I gladly stacked the pancakes on his hand.

"And now, gentlemen, you are about to witness the most—um, could you put some more syrup on them. Just a bit more. That's it. And a pad of butter. Don't overdo it. Perfect!"

He cleared his throat. "And now! Feast your eyes on the most amazing illusion ever performed in the history of the Earth! First performed by The Great Manicotti, this trick has baffled billions of people all over the world! And yet, there are only three living who can execute it! I, Molloy, am one of those three!"

Martini was practically bouncing out of his seat with excitement by this point.

Molloy continued, "Keep your eye on the pancakes, keep your eye on the pancakes..." He waved the wand over the pancakes as he moved the stack back and forth. "Do not be alarmed, gentlemen. I am a trained professional and you are all completely safe. Get ready! Here it comes! The great! The amazing! The spectacular!"

And then he shoved the entire stack of pancakes into his mouth. With that much food in his mouth he really couldn't run away, and as he frantically chewed, syrup dripping down his chin and melted butter oozing out of his nostrils, one of the cooks came out, grabbed him by the arm, and dragged him out of the restaurant.

As we watched him go it sounded like he was trying to say something through the pancake mush in his mouth. It was hard to make out, but what it sounded like was, "Poof," over and over again.

Martini looked confused. "Did he say 'Poof'?"

"I think so."

"Poof? Just, Poof, and that's it? After all that build up? Poof and he devours the pancakes?"

"Yep."

Martini huffed. "Rather anticlimactic, don't you think?"

"It could have been worse. He could have magically spit them back up all over us. Now, can we talk about something more serious?"

"Like what?"

"The Duo. I want to know everything. Who are they? What do they want? What did they do with you?"

"In any order?"

"Who first."

"OK. They're spacemen."

That's how he began.

"Astronauts?" I asked.

I could see that. A couple of retired NASA guys still chafed that the Agency was able to send a chimp named Adam safely to Mars and back while the only manned flight there ended with the entire crew of three tumbling uncontrollably into deep space, cyanide tablets their only way out.

Maybe the thought of their friends rotting in a tin can as it gently rolled its way out of our solar system was too much for them to bear and they lost it.

"No. They're aliens, Joe."

"Oh please." That was too much, "They're weird, I'll give you that, but that doesn't make them aliens."

"They took me to their home planets."

"Really, Martini," I figured he had been duped, "Did these home planets happen to look like deserts?"

"A little."

"They probably took you to Arizona, porkface."

It took me a good fifteen minutes of apologizing to make up for the porkface comment and get him talking again. I also had to buy him a piece of pecan pie, a la mode at that, and promise to eat all of the actual pecans on top of it since he only liked eating the goo.

"Is Arizona populated by a race of little people?" He asked as he wiped away tears and ate his pecan goo with a knife and fork.

"No."

Not that I knew of anyway.

"I see. Well, is it populated by a race of tall, skinny old men?" He asked next.

"No."

I don't even think dwarfs and old men are considered their own separate races.

"Then they didn't take me to Arizona."

"How's that?"

"Because the first place they took me was populated by midgets and the second by tall old men and both places had two suns."

"Two suns?"

"They have names for them. Names I can't pronounce. Sometimes, when they talked, I could see their lips moving but couldn't hear any sounds coming out. Kind of like when a girl whispers across the room 'I love you' except you can't tell whether she's saying 'I love you' or 'Olive juice' but you don't really care because it's so sexy when girls whisper, regardless of what they're saying."

Anger boiled up within me. "I think you need to back up. You're not making any sense. So why don't you, uh, STOP LYING AND TELL ME WHAT REALLY HAPPENED, YOU LYING SAD SACK OF SHIT!"

Martini spit out a mouthful of pie, making sure to get every last bit out with repeated spits. He looked up at me with food mush on his chin and tears forming in his eyes, "Why don't you believe me?"

"Because what you're saying is unbelievable."

"No, that's not it. If May told you the same things you'd believe her," he blubbered.

"I wouldn't."

"You would."

He was turning red, the tears welling up again as he blubbered, "You hate me. I can see it in your eyes."

"Calm down, I don't hate you."

"I knew this would happen!"

I could see why the Duo chose to take him. They knew that people would get fed up trying to get the story out of him and their secrets would be safe.

"That's why I took notes."

He slammed a small black book down on the table.

"You made a report?"

He was angry, but proud of himself. "Yes."

"How long did they have you?"

"It's impossible to say. I was light-headed and disoriented the whole time. And a certain *someone* didn't give me a watch for my birthday, even though I hinted at my desire for one on numerous occasions."

I had gotten him a can of soup instead—split pea.

"And you took notes the whole time?" I asked, hoping to avoid another heated watch/soup argument.

"What else did I have to do? It's not like I could talk to anybody."

"Could I borrow it?"

"What?"

"The book."

He looked suspicious. Like he had something to hide. "I don't know."

I forced a smile. "Please."

"No," he said.

I don't know why I even bothered asking. This was Martini I was dealing with here. Tapioca puts up more resistance than he does.

"I'm taking the book, Martini."

He sighed. "It's just as well, I don't see how I could stop you. The energy just isn't there."

"I know."

I picked up the book.

"Even breathing can be such a burden sometimes," he said.

To illustrate this he began breathing in and out, slowly, and loudly, as if it was as taxing as carrying a stack of logs up and down eight flights of stairs.

I edged towards the end of my seat. "I'll see you at the office."

"Not to mention moving about."

"Goodbye, Martini."

I was standing now, looking down at him as he showed me how hard it was to bring a piece of pie from the plate to his mouth.

"And then there are combinations of the two. I don't know how one is expected to breath and move about at the same time. It's a bit much, a bit much to ask really. Watch."

He began doing the heavy breathing while struggling to eat the thing as I slowly backed away from the table and out the door. I continued backing down the street until I came to a corner where I stopped, pivoted, and then took off in a full sprint toward my apartment, eager to both read Martini's report and get far away from him.

Some people are much easier to deal with in written rather than living form.

21
Words, words, words

Martini's notebook didn't have any dates in it, his entries (or 'items' as he called them) were only numbered. It also had very few paragraph separations. There were a few spaces here and there, but it was mostly page after page of straight text, running down each page like a column—similar to Burk's account of the pterodactyl in his lab. On the subway ride home I flipped through some earlier entries out of curiosity, and I didn't get to the section on the Duo until I was home on the toilet. There were many pages before that on topics such as why Martini hates Saturdays, Tuesdays, Thursdays, and even-numbered years. How his pet fish, Martini Junior, could be a total asshole sometimes. How he was tormented by an unidentifiable ticking sound in his bedroom for two years, twenty-one days, four hours, and thirty-three seconds. How he suspected Martini Junior of generating said ticking, how he got his revenge on Martini Junior, how he dreamt of flying one night, how he attempted to fly the next morning, and how, during one rainy afternoon, he used multivariable calculus and miniature marshmallows to determine the exact volume (to 3 decimal places) of his nostrils.

But before I could get on the toilet to look over the notebook, I had to gather the strength to actually walk into my apartment. Getting into the building and up the elevator wasn't a problem. It was my front door that I had to stand in front of for a moment, preparing myself for a possible nasty scene involving my kitty and a ghost.

As I stood there, listening carefully for any signs of a struggle coming from within, Mrs. Vercelli came scooting up to me. She lived down the hall and always carried a small white mutt with her whenever she did her daily scoots through the building. And this mutt invariably had what appeared to be tomato sauce stains around its mouth, but which could have been blood.

I could hear Mrs. Vercelli coming because she always wore a pair of slippers, the kind with plastic on the bottom, which scraped against the carpet as she shuffled around the building. I often wondered if I would be able to use her slippers to create fire if ever the apocalypse came down upon us and left me alive.

When the scraping stopped I knew that the hard of hearing and always shouting Mrs. Vercelli had arrived next to me. Both her and her dog were panting.

"LOST YOUR KEYS?" she asked.

I tired not to make eye contact. "No."

"WELL THEN WHY DON'T YOU GO ON IN, JOE?"

"Because I'm afraid."

"AFRAID? WHAT EVER IS THERE TO BE AFRAID OF?"

"Well..."

She sounded concerned, like she actually cared, so I decided to tell her the truth. She's old, I figured, she could give me some advice, use her many years on this planet to tell me that everything would be OK, that I wasn't crazy, that she's seen much worse than a ghost on a toilet or a cat inside a ghost on a toilet or a cat coming out of a ghost on the toilet, and that all I needed to do was put some clean sheets on my bed, have her tuck me in, and I'd be fine, fine, fine.

"It's Mr. Pushcatela," I told her, "He might be in there. On my toilet."

"HE'S DEAD!" She shouted, turning from sweet old lady into

ticked off old bitch in one sentence flat. Her lips pursed, her brow furrowed, her eyes raged, and her dog barked at me, yipped really, and continued to do so punctuating everything Mrs. Vercelli said.

"I know he's dead," I tried to tell her, "But he was in there last night taking a poo."

"HE'S DEAD!"

"Yip!"

"I heard you."

"HE'S DEAD!"

"Yip!"

"I heard you!"

I didn't know what to say to her, outside of lying, to make her understand. She held her dog away from me, as if at any moment I might have tried to grab the pooch and shove the whole thing in my mouth at once, while she watched in horror as I labored to chew. And believe me, I would have, had I the stomach for such a thing.

I decided there was no use trying to make her understand, so I turned away and went back to staring at my door which returned a neutral stare at me, containing no more understanding than Mrs. Vercelli, but no less either.

During the ensuing forty-two second silence, Mrs. Vercelli had some time to think things over. Apparently, time didn't heal all wounds.

"HE'S DEAD!"

"Yip!"

"Dead!"

"Yip!"

"Yip!"

"HE'S DEAD!"

"Yip!"

"Dead!"

"Yip!"

"Yip!"

"Yip!"

"Dead!'

"YIP!"

"Dead!"

"Dead!"

"Yip!"

When I could no longer determine whether the dog was saying "He's dead!" and Mrs. Vercelli yipping or the other way around, or even perhaps back and forth, I decided, screw this, I'm going in.

I charged into my apartment and slammed the door shut behind me. With my back to the door, and the faint sounds of yipping behind me, I scanned the room for any oddities.

The living room and kitchen looked normal. No piles of glowing ghost shit anywhere to be seen. Mr. Puss was sitting on the table looking at me, giving me the guilt trip for leaving him alone with the ghost man and ghost cat last night. I gave him the, 'I'm in no mood, cat' look.

I tiptoed into the bedroom and then down the hallway into the bathroom. It appeared the ghost of Mr. Pushcatela had vacated the premises. So after disinfecting the toilet seat with bleach I myself took a seat on the throne, something I had wanted to do since shortly after my first cup of coffee in the church.

I opened Martini's book and found the page where his time with the Duo began—once again, I've done my best to recreate this account here for you as it truly is, or was, or will be, but without access to the hard copy, I had to rely on my memory and therefore, had to improvise here and there:

Item #8,726

They have me. For the first time in my young life I have become an object: nothing more than a souvenir, picked up by two older men. The homoeroticism is apparent, it's even obvious, perhaps cheap, but before I go into that, or anything, I shall play the age-old game of favorites. The tall one, he is my favorite. He smiles at me, sometimes, and even

138   CHRIS GENOA

has been so bold as to lightly touch my shoulder with one finger, giving me an instant outbreak of goosebumps. His smiles are sad things, but they are smiles nonetheless. It is true that his smiles are always preceded and followed immediately by a frown that starts small and gradually is made deeper, pulled down by the gravitational force created by the immense weight on his soul, and it is also true that his ratio of smiles to frowns is depressingly lopsided in favor of the frowns, but a smile is a smile and exists in a vacuum. So he smiles. The short one, my co-possessor, despises me for what reasons I do not, and fear will never, know. I call the tall one The Tall One and the short one The Short One. Now, onto descriptions. No. It is enough to say that I call one The Tall One and the other The Short One. That will do. Neither of them speaks a word of English. They speak. Just not English. Nor Spanish, Russian, German, French, Japanese, Chinese, Greek, Latin, Pig Latin, Dutch, Arabic, Italian, Navajo, Swahili, and so forth. Oftentimes they move their lips and yet say nothing, nor does any sound come out. As if some prick is pushing a mute button on and off as they speak. If I find that this prick exists I shall kill him for his cruel mind games. Then perhaps someone someday will sit themselves down and write a tragi-comedy about Martini and how he killed the prick who tormented his tormentors. Perhaps. Or maybe when they move their lips and no sound comes out they are saying something that I cannot hear because my ears are only human. Perhaps a dog could hear them, or a bat, or an infant. Either way I'm confused. Dear Lord I'm bored. Maybe I should sing something to pass the time. But what to sing? I know! Coo-roo, Coo-roo! Well...that didn't go very well. I barely got to the "Then my dada for his lunch/Wolfed me down in one big munch" line before The Short One threw a rock at me. Oh well! I must press on! The Tall One tried to talk to me, he's at least made an effort to communicate something, which is much more than I can say for The Short One who does little more than laugh, grunt, bark, shake his head, spit, frown, pace, smell the air, smell me, smell The Tall One, and fart. He doesn't mind the smell of his farts, which is strange seeing as how into smelling he is, and neither does The Tall One, but I however, most certainly do mind them. They make me feel faint. The only thing I can gleam from The Tall One's attempts to communicate with me is that he and The Short One are extremely concerned about _____and that they must stop _____ soon or else _____ will happen and ruin everything. What _____ is I do not know. I think they want me to know _____. At least The Tall One does. The Short One looks more like he's here because someone forced him to tag along with The Tall One. Perhaps The Short One's father made him go with The Tall One just like my savage father made me get the tender tip of my prick hacked off. The two want something from or of me, of this much I am certain. In this way they remind me of my relationship with my mother. How is mother today? Tied herself to her rocking chair again? Mother, I understand how you are able to tie both your ankles and one of your wrists to the rocking chair, but the second wrist as well? How now? Something is amiss, mother. I'm on to you. No, on second thought, I'm not on to you. You're safe...for now. Happy? I suppose I should start from the beginning. Yes, that would make sense, to start where it started, get to where we are now, and then go on from there. Like a nice straight line, or an arrow of time, we shall go forward. It started in the hospital while I was with Joe. That's when they took me. Took. Stole. I'm a prisoner. A victim! I'm not sure how, but my possessors must have taken me through a wormhole that transported us from the hospital to this field. It didn't feel as if I had been through a wormhole, sensation wise, but there is no other explanation for it, and what's the point of keeping a journal if not to explain the momentous happenings in one's life. So one moment I was talking to Joe and the next I was standing in a big wide-open place with lots of tall green grass, what one could call a meadow, and a big blue sky. I figured we had gone back very far in time indeed. It was there that The Tall One first tried to talk to me in a language I could not understand nor place nor hear completely. There have also been times when he would grab me by my shoulders, thrust his face up close to mine, and stare deep into my eyes, his face muscles straining, as if he is trying to send a message directly from his brain to mine. It didn't work, either he's not sending or I'm not receiving. This has however allowed me to have a few wonderful staring contests with The Tall One, which pass the time better than being sniffed, laughed at, and farted on by The Short One. The Tall One even tried using charades to communicate with me, twisting his long spindly frame into various odd contortions. At first I thought that he was doing some modern dancing to amuse me, and then I thought he was doing yoga to relax after the strenuous modern dancing, and then I swore he was just being silly, but finally I understood that he was trying to tell me something using his body. Unfortunately, I didn't get anything out of that either, except for a few laughs and a unwelcome stiffy. The Short One sat on a rock while all this went on, chuckling to himself, shaking his head, and occasionally yelling at The Tall One. After a series of sixty-eight contortions, The Tall One, exhausted and frustrated, went over and sat with The Short One on the rock. They are there now, moving their mouths towards each other as I sit a few feet away in the grass and write all this. I suppose they are arguing, or at least it appears that way. The Short One was pointing off into the distance behind him a moment ago, smelling the air, and then he was pounding his fist into the ground, and now he's pointing behind him again, wagging his tongue around. It looks like he is describing to The Tall One something he wants done, but The Tall One doesn't seem to agree and is showing so by flapping his arms up and down as if he's trying to fly away. The Short One just farted AGAIN. The Tall One is doing a soft shoe dance. I must say that I

am now someplace completely different. How'd that happen? The Short One and The Tall One came over and stood next to me as I sat in the grass writing, someone flicked the lights off and then right back on again, and now here I am in a desert. Since I was outside and since I am still outside I suppose I can't say that someone turned the lights off and on, rather, someone turned the sun off and then on, or rather, turned the sun off and then the suns on. An explanation is in order. I'll explain my trip from there to here by saying that I went through another wormhole, although again it didn't feel like I did. There wasn't any fooping, for one. I believe that I am on a different planet. I know this not from the ground I'm sitting on, nor from the plants around me, but from the two suns burning in the sky above me and also from the large group of tall old men and what I assume are tall old women gathered around me in a wide circle. They all look similar to, but not the spitting image of, The Tall One, but similar enough so that I can't tell if The Tall One is here among them. I suspect he is, for why would he abandon me to these maniacs? The Short One is here too, but he is still very much of the aloof nature, standing outside the circle of tall ones around me. I can see him between their legs. The Tall Ones, plural, are talking to each other and pointing at me, every now and then one of them comes forward and tries to communicate with me. Some try talking. Others try the staring thing. And still others have a go at The Tall One's version of charades. Despite their efforts nothing came of this besides the aforementioned disturbing reaction that such charades have on the distribution of blood in my body. The Short One came forward to the center of the circle as the tall ones continued to converse amongst themselves. He's standing above me now as I write, looking down (down! The Short One!) at me with such contempt.

❖ ♑ ♒ ♎ ♐ ◆   ♦ ☻ ⌘ ☒ ❖ ♌ &

He took my book! He wrote that gibberish in it! Now he's pointing at the gibberish. Yes, I see it, The Short One, very nice. Now he's tapping the gibberish. Stop touching my journal, The Short One. Stop it. I'm going to hold my breath until he stops touching my stuff. I'm doing it. I'm not taking in any air, my friend. I can't believe him. I'm going to pass out and he's still tapping? I feel lightheaded. Death is upon me! Be gentle, Grim Reaper, for I shall not resist your touch. I will take your hand willingly, as my nude, hairless body melancholically skips alongside you into the technicolor abyss.

He slapped the journal out of my hand! Oh, how DARE you! I hate you, The Short One! I HATE YOU! At least I can breathe in good conscience again. But look at him stomp away. I'm the one who should be angry here, The Short One, not you. I need to get my mind off him. Our relationship is nothing but destructive. What else can I think about? That scuffle has taken all the energy from my frail body and tender soul. I suppose I could describe the planet, but why bother. I'll say this. It is very hot. It is slightly windy.

It is not hot at all. It is extremely windy. The change in the weather has come about due to another change in my location, which has come about from another lights-out/lights-up experience. A new planet now and I'm in a clearing in a thick forest. Good thing I didn't bother describing that last one in too much detail, as that would force me to describe this one as well, for reasons of symmetry, and I really don't have the energy for symmetry at the moment. I will however say this: there are still two suns. And they look like the same two suns from before, only from a different distance and angle. The planets must subsist in the same solar system. Neighbors! How quaint! This must be The Short One's home for I am now surrounded by a whole group of Vegas style The Short One impersonators, female ones too, and once again I cannot tell if The Short One is among them. The Tall One, now no longer a needle in a tall stack, is standing outside the circle of The Short Ones. I can see him over the heads of The Short Ones. He looks worried. I wonder if it really is The Tall One. Could he have been replaced by one of the others? Unlikely. I wish I could ask him if he is The Tall One. And I have other questions besides that one for him. I should list them.

Why am I here?
Where is here?
Who are you?

Do you think I need to lose a couple pounds?

Do you have a girlfriend?

Don't you just hate The Short One?

I wonder if they find it odd that I'm writing while all this is going on. But what else is there for me to do? The Short Ones don't seem to be nearly as interested in communicating with me as The Tall Ones did. They just stand around bickering with each other. Every now and again one comes forward to inspect my body. To caress my skin, poke my belly, smell my hair, or peer into my eyes. And the farting continues. But mostly they just bicker with each other or with The Tall One who continues to stand behind them with his head bowed. The Short Ones seem so determined, strong in their convictions, and cocksure. I wonder if they'll arrange a wrestling exhibition to impress me. And if so, will I have the honor and pleasure of supping with the winner? Will he order for me? And if so, will he order the oysters, or the snails? Or, dare I dream, both?

The answer, sadly, is no. I'm back on earth. I'm home. I'm on the subway, feeling a tad ticked that The Short One didn't see to it that I was returned to the time and place of my departure and a tad hurt that The Tall One didn't see to the same. More importantly, I'm very hungry. Haven't eaten for hours. HOURS. To make matters worse I'm also standing, hanging onto a pole while The Tall One and The Short One are sitting together farther down the car, all buddy-buddy. I feel chewed and spit out. Like a toenail clipping. But are they the same The Short One and The Tall One from the start? Of course they are. I can see it in their eyes. And I don't even care as long as I'm not alone. Joe is sitting across from them, doing something odd with a flashlight. At least they saw to it to see that I was returned to a familiar face. My journey must be coming to an end. It's not there yet. But it's coming. Joe's journey may just be beginning. Lucky Joe! I wonder what that end will be for me? Has it already happened and did I miss it? Or will it be death? Too much to hope for. It'll be breakfast most likely.

Strange. Breakfast is usually a beginning. Speaking of breakfast, I realize now that I have forgotten to record quite a few things that happened during my trip. Vital information I suppose, but what's the point getting into it, using all that energy to get it out and down on paper when no one will believe me anyway. And it's not like I'll ever forget those things! Ha! I should stop writing now because Joe may see me and want to know what I'm writing, and he may try to snatch my book, and if that happens what can I be expected to do on a stomach so utterly devoid of pancakes? Nothing.

After reading Martini's journal entry for the first of many times, I could only think one thing: Mr. Burk needs to be made aware of this, and he needs to be nicer to me, and buying me a cup of coffee would be a good start. Just so you know, thinking that Mr. Burk needed to be nicer to me, and that buying me a cup of coffee would be a good start, was something that I thought many times before that, ever since I began my career as a tour guide in fact. So it really had nothing to do with reading Martini's account and everything to do with the childish name calling and lack of coffee buying I had to endure for months. Even so, perhaps strangely so, I was nearly bursting with delight knowing I had something of import to tell him, that my suspicions about the Duo were true and that Martini was loopier than loop dee loop soup. I figured a pat on the back or at least a head nod of approval was headed my way.

Things were looking up.

22
Meet the Mrs.

"You're off the case."

Mr. Burk didn't react as well as I had anticipated, even daydreamed, to the news that either two aliens were mixed up in the beating of his younger self or that one of his tour guides had in fact lost his mind.

"But without me there is no case," I pointed out, "We're one and the same."

"I beg to differ. I'm a differ beggar. You've lost focus, Joe. I'm putting you back on tour duty."

I was deeply hurt by this. The promotion to Chief of Probes was the only promotion I had ever received, and I fully expected it would be my last, so I treasured it like an old stray dog treasures its first and last pat on the head before being shot. And to take that away from a man or dog, that little act of kindness that means little to the giver and everything to the receiver, no matter how you look at it, is a disgusting crime against humanity.

Luckily, I found the words to perfectly express my feelings on this to Mr. Burk.

"This sucks."

"You suck."

I didn't bother debating him on his decision as I was in no mood for the childlike back-and-forth banter that the discussion was bound to degrade into, especially seeing as it had already done so.

I was assigned, re-assigned, to lead a tour group composed of, as Mr. Burk put it, "a bunch of bible ya yas and my wife." They were going to see The Great Supernova of 2015, which to me wasn't all that great, just a bright flash of light in the Eastern sky that stuck around as a patch of light for a few months and enabled people to parade around at night as if the world had become one giant football stadium with the exploded star as the artificial lights. Neat-o, but not great.

The Neat-O Supernova of 2015.

But to each his own. I'm not here to judge other people's ideas on greatness. I just lead the way and explain all that can be seen in an impartial way, letting them decide what's great, what's neat, and what's stinky, and also letting them point me in the direction they want to go. These folks were pointing to a supernova.

I met the tour group in the briefing room, that's where we, well, I'm sure you can guess what we do there. I knew what to expect. A bunch of couples giggling at how funny they looked in their retro clothes, some of them nervous about going through a wormhole for their first time, discussing with each other whether they thought it would hurt at all or if it was dangerous or if it was possible to get stuck midway between holes in a type of limbo, or something else just as absurd as that. I wasn't looking forward to it, especially while May and the other guides took over my mission. They were getting to do something that had a purpose, a goal, an ending to shoot for, a mystery to solve, a mission to complete, while I led a Church group and my boss's wife to see the sky get brighter. I hated them.

True, we were all looking for illumination, just in different forms, but the illumination I was heading for had already been illuminated for me and many others many times over, while their illumination would be a first and would come about due to their actions, not the random actions of stars.

Increasing my hatred was the fact that astronomical happenings were always such a bore to me. Kind of like an earthquake on the other side of the world. Put it on the news, yes, but don't expect me to have a spiritual awakening because of it, or to be able to even grasp the loss of thousands, because it's just too far away from my little apartment for me to think much of it. The same goes for a bunch of planets being in alignment, or for a comet passing by, or even for a supernova. Thousands, or millions, or billions of miles away, it doesn't matter. If it doesn't happen too close to home, there's something in me that won't let me do much more than oooo and ahhhh, and then go on with my life, no matter how pathetic it may be.

My expectations of what I would find in the briefing room were way off. What I walked into was a room full of yellow-robed men and women. I felt as if I had made a wrong turn into the Church of The Bright from this morning, and I wasn't far off.

"What do you people think you're doing?" I asked. I was familiar enough with 2015 to know that long yellow robes were not all the rage then and that a group of twelve individuals dressed as such would draw much attention to themselves, something absolutely against company policy.

"We're going to see the light," piped up a short little man in the corner. He was sweating and his hands were folded in his lap, a man I could take, as in slap around, if it ever came to blows between us.

"Not dressed like that you're not." I pointed at the small man as I said this. He blinked twice and then folded his arms across his chest—this from a man I could take?

"Yes we are," he said.

I decided to advance on him—just two steps. Enough to physically manifest the terrifying reality that I meant business while leaving room for the possibility of more steps, if needed, to reinforce that reality while staying well outside striking distance.

"There are certain rules," I told him, "Rules that I didn't make up, and that I may not understand. But somebody made them up, and somebody understands them. And I think that we owe it to those who bother to make things up and understand them, to follow."

The little man fluttered a few blinks, stuck his neck out, and said, "He said we could."

After deciding to name him Mr. Tuttle, after a turtle, I said, "He? He who? He where? Te hee hee? Show me he!"

Mr. Tuttle, blinking far more than necessary to maintain proper eye wetness, pointed to something in back of me. I turned to follow his outstretched finger, briefly catching a glimpse of a red-skinned, buck-toothed fellow to my left who was looking rather nervous about something, before making it all the way around to see Mr. Burk standing in the doorway with a woman wearing one of those robes.

A note on this woman: But why bother? She was rather plain, a shade from unsightly, but not quite there. Her hair was nice enough, but the nose was all wrong, the cheeks were too tight, the chin too narrow, the forehead too wide, the lips too thin, the neck too long, the ears too small. It was hard to make out the body underneath that robe, but I would later find it almost completely without curves, nothing but straight lines all the way down. This was Mrs. Burk, and on the outside I must say that she was a slice of American cheese—plain and tasteless, but comfortingly inoffensive and unstinky. Inside, there must have been something more than American cheese, something perhaps even beautiful, maybe Manchego, but damned if I ever had a chance to find it.

At the moment though, I wasn't concerned with her. The robes weighed on my mind, and their presence was a direct insult to my authority.

"Mr. Burk, look at these people. Look at what's going on here."

"I don't have time for this, Joe. I have some grim knitting I need to get done before the end of the day or all hell is gonna break loose."

Under different circumstances I would ask Burk to clarify what kind of knitting is grim (although for the sake of my own peace of mind I suppose that's something better left unknown), but I had other things on my mind. "Look at what they're wearing!"

"Yellow is a year round color, and might I add very flattering. They'll be fine."

"It's not the color. It's the robes."

"If anyone asks, tell them that you're a bunch of Buddhist monks."

"But what am I to do? I don't look like a monk."

"Well, it sounds like *you* are the problem here, Joe. Not them."

"I have to wear a robe?"

"Yes."

"Have to, have to?"

"Yes."

"I see."

Since it was a matter of have to have to, I merely shot Mr. Burk a nasty look to show my disapproval before turning to go find a suitable robe that didn't make me look too fat, but I didn't get far. Mr. Burk grabbed my arm, pulled me out the door with him, pinned me against the wall, and said, as if asking if it's bad when there's blood in your poo, "Let me ask you something. Do your ears hang low?"

"What?"

"You know...do they wobble to and fro?"

"Not really."

"I see." He thought about this. "Well, can you tie them in a knot? Can you tie them in a bow, Joe?"

"Why do you want to know this?"

"Just answer me. Can you throw them over your shoulder?"

"What do you mean? Like a Continental Soldier?"

"Yeah."

"No."

"Then it's hopeless."

I have to be honest with everybody here. Mr. Burk didn't really ask me all that stuff about my ears wobbling to and fro. He did pull me out of the room, he did pin me against the wall, and he did say something that lacked any semblance of meaning, at least to me, but it wasn't that exactly. In truth, I've forgotten what he said. But since it was meaningless I figure it won't matter much if I substitute something with an equal amount of meaninglessness to whatever he said. The important thing here is that after he said the jibber jabber, he spun me around and pushed me back into the room where I saw Mr. Tuttle standing in front of me, within striking distance, holding up a robe, a dark yellow robe about my size, and smiling a smile that held much meaning indeed.

23
Star light, star bright, first star I see die tonight

This I'll admit: In an effort to live vicariously through my robe I was naked underneath it.

If they were going to make me wear the silly thing, I figured I might as well get something out of it. Furthermore, yet another rationalization, we were going to be in the painted desert of Arizona in mid-August and I wanted to stay as cool as possible. That's a lie. We were there late at night, well after midnight, when the air was cool and the stars, while hot and many, were much too far away to cause a person to leave his underwear at home. The truth is that I liked the way the robe felt against my nudieshow flesh, and how it allowed the air to run all over and in my body. Also, I felt that none of the women in the group posed the threat of an arousal, certainly not American Cheese, so the concern for my bishop poking up and out was not a major one.

Light pollution being an issue when it comes to viewing celestial events, The Great Supernova of 2015 tour always took place in the desert, far from any large cities or even towns, the nearest development being a small Native American reservation that, in an effort to both save electricity and make a run at the world record for stubbed toes, never left a single bulb burning after bedtime.

Before the tour began, two associates from the company's Quality Control department went through the wormhole to de-futurize the area for our arrival. We call these impeccably well-dressed, menacing, and predominately slightly deformed individuals the Qualcons.

They are well dressed to come across as official looking, menacing to discourage any sass, and predominately slightly deformed to predominately slightly scare people—three qualities which make the act of de-futurizing much less of a hassle.

De-futurizing a tour site is simply clearing it of the previous tour group. If it wasn't for this procedure, new tours would constantly be bumping into old ones, and with tours occurring daily, events would quickly become so crowded that they'd look more like a theme park than a real event.

The Qualcons round up the past group and order them to turn around and march right back through the wormhole they just came in on. They only encounter one previous group because they de-futurize before every tour, so they're on top of things. And while my present-self has never seen them in action, my past-selves certainly have. But as the Shaved Cat tells us, the present-me doesn't remember ever seeing them because all of my past-selves that did see the Qualcons are now living out their lives on separate timelines.

The same goes for the turned-back tourists, who are only turned back on a separate timeline, and as long as they leave through the wormhole they came in on, and not through the one the Qualcons came through, then Dactyl—at least the Dactyl on this particular timeline— will never receive any complaints along the lines of "Why the hell did two well-dressed, menacing, and slightly deformed people prevent me from seeing The Great Supernova of 2015?"

For people unfamiliar with the peculiar laws of quantum mechanics I developed the following eight-step method for one to fully understand the delicate science behind de-futurizing:

1. Cower in a corner. Any corner will do.

2. Close your eyes.

3. Imagine the entire known universe as a wagon overflowing with potatoes. Now imagine the wagon being pulled up a steep, endless hill by a donkey with one pointy ear and one floppy ear.

4. Imagine Time as a hobo sitting in the wagon on top of the taters.

5. The hobo picks up one of the taters, looks at it, slaps his knee, and begins to laugh hysterically.

6. The donkey heehaws along with him.

7. The hobo laughs so hard he eventually falls off the tater wagon and rolls down the hill, still laughing as he tumbles.

8. The donkey falls silent. His floppy ear becomes pointy and his pointy ear becomes floppy. He continues pulling the tater wagon up the hill. While you no longer see the hobo, you will always hear him faintly in the distance, laughing at that potato.

The lesson here is this: Time is too busy laughing at a potato to sorry about what's happening to the universe as a whole, which is being pulled by an ass. And that is why asinine things like de-futurizing can take place.

The Qualcons came back through the supernova wormhole, gave me a slightly deformed thumbs-up, and we were off. As soon as the tour group came through on the other side, the Bogumils—I found out that they were members of May's church from Mrs. Burk—gathered into their little circle again with the flashlights they brought along and illuminated their faces, waiting for a star to die.

When I first saw them forming this circle I assumed, from habit, that it was so they could all be at an equal distance from me as I spoke on the science of supernovas and their effects on the earth. So I walked into the center, and directed my flashlight at my face, not to fit in, but just so they could see some of the facial expressions I had planned to highlight key points—my favorite being an expression, used to convey the explosive nature of a supernova, I like to call Skinny O, where the lips are drawn tight into a skinny O shape, the eyebrows are extended as high as they can go, the eyes are opened wide, and both arms are straight down (flush against the body), with fingers at full extension.

I began by giving the speech I had given dozens of times before:

"All stars, like everything else in the Universe, eventually die. Take our own sun for instance. It's a star. It too will die. Just like my dad died. Some will die like the star known as Betelgeuse, which we'll see die tonight, in a quick and violent explosion of light! Kablooie! Others, like our own sun and my dad, will die slowly, over the course of many years, running out of fuel and (this is where the comparison involving my father ends) collapsing into a red dwarf, or perhaps even a black hole, which is something so black, so big, and so insane that none of us could ever hope to comprehend it. So don't try. But don't be sad, neither for the narrowness of your minds, nor the fate of star, nor the fate of my dad, because, as Carl Sagan said, so long ago, on his classic TV series *Cosmos*, 'Billions and billions and billions and billions and billions and billions and billions and billions and billions and billions and billions and billions and billions and billions and billions and bill—"

"Shhhhhhhhh! Shhhhhhhhh! Will you please just shhhhhhh!"

I wanted to put this man over my knee and spank him but instead I fired back with mild fury, "Don't shush me during the enrichment, sir. You are *way* out of line."

"We don't want the enrichment," he said, with his face quite the opposite of the Skinny O, in fact, it was the antithesis of the O, all scrunched together into an expression I'll call Pruney Magoony. "We didn't come here to listen to your babble."

"You mean *you* didn't come here to listen to it. You! You shush for no one but yourself!"

"SHHHHHHHHHHHHHHHHHH!!!" The group, en mass, shushed for itself. They even went as far as to put their index fingers to their lips, every one of them, as if I needed both the shush and the finger. One would have done, people.

Thus rejected by the entire group, I bowed my head and excused myself over to a small rock, well away from them.

"I'll just be over there if anyone needs me."

Far less than a guide, I was nothing more than a babysitter at that point. I considered curling up in the corner of the couch, ordering a pizza, and calling up my best girlfriend Sue on the phone to talk about how cute Seth was and about how much of a bitch his girlfriend Julie was, how I hated her, how we hated her, how I wished she would just throw up and die. Not having any girlfriends named Sue, not knowing anyone named Seth or Julie, not having a couch to curl up on, and not knowing any pizza places in the desert I decided to instead have a look around.

I stood at the top of a small plateau near Monument Valley. For those of you who've never been to Monument Valley it's an area of a desert, half in Arizona and half in Utah, where there are various massive, odd rock formations scattered about, and which draws tourists like women are drawn to me (in my dreams).

As I said, we were near Monument Valley, not in it. There was only the small Indian reservation nearby, but as none of them had any idea that a star was about to blow up, and as it was 3 a.m. on a Tuesday, they were all asleep in their teepees.

Ok, they didn't live in teepees but they were all asleep. Except for the Chief, who was doing a rain dance around a large bonfire, eating smoking hunks of buffalo meat, and shooting flaming arrows into the night.

Ok, the Chief wasn't even there, he lived in Flagstaff, in a little brown house with a pool out back and a Kokopelli on his mailbox, and he too was asleep. But he could have been having a dream about a bonfire, flaming arrows, and buffalo meat.

Despite the lack of historically stereotypical Indian behavior, they were honest-to-god Native Americans, I swear, even if they ate flatbread instead of buffalo chunks and slept in trailers instead of teepees.

Like I said, it was dark. The moon was nothing more than a finger-nail clipping. A perfect night for viewing the stars and watching one of them die, and perfect for finding comfort in the sucking of one's thumb and not being noticed doing so.

So I sucked away and watched the group as they stood muttering to each other. I couldn't hear exactly what they were saying, but I could tell they were all confused about something. The shuffling-about noises, the rise in inflection at the end of their sentences, there was some definite confusion. Too bad for them, I thought. Serves them right for not letting me finish the enrichment.

A few of them had their flashlights off their faces and searched around, actually using the flashlights for their God-given purpose. I continued sucking my thumb while I watched all this activity, the light beams falling on various rocks, shrubs, and people, bringing these objects in and out of my field of vision, and thus in and out of existence. I reasoned that they could have been playing flashlight tag but refused to confirm this for fear of feeling left out and thus crying.

And then the illuminated face—which looked as if it was floating—of Mrs. Burk came towards me from the circle. Why she chose to shine her flashlight on her face, as if she were about to tell a ghost story around a campfire, and not on the ground in front of her, so she could see where she was going, escaped me. I suppose she did it for either dramatic effect or out of sheer stupidity. Regardless, it allowed me to keep my thumb in suck until I had to speak, as there was no way she could see me.

The floating face stopped a few feet in front of me—I coughed to stop her from running into me—and spoke.

"We can't find Joe," she said.

It took me a minute to figure this one out. Maybe since she had the light on her face and not on me, she couldn't see who I was, that I was in fact Joe, and that she had indeed found me.

"I'm Joe," I told her.

"Not you. The other Joe."

"There's more than one?"

"Is your name Joe?"

"Yes."

"Then yes, there are two Joes—minimum."

Her logic was airtight.

"Did anybody see where this other Joe went?" I asked.

"No, but Joe is an Indian."

Again, confused, I asked, "What?"

"Isn't that an Indian village down there?" she asked.

"It's a Native American reservation."

"Well, maybe Joe went to check it out?"

"Oh I see. To see how his ancestors lived eh? Get in touch with his roots."

"I suppose. Do you think he'll come back?"

I could see that she was faking concern, trying to get me to go after him to make her fake concern go away and allow her to continue playing flashlight tag with the rest of the group. I wasn't having any of it.

"Maybe you should go check on him," I suggested.

"Maybe you should come with me," she modified.

"Maybe I will," I concluded.

I did. For two reasons: One, because I was getting bored sitting there in the dark with nothing to look forward to but the supernova (again). Two, because I suddenly got the urge to strike up some sort of friendship with American Cheese, mainly because when you have a sandwich with no cheese and there's nothing but a slice of American cheese in your fridge, you make do.

I had an idea that friendships were often formed that way, by walking somewhere and then back with a person. It seemed like a good way to make friends. Granted, I walked next to people almost every time I went out in the city, but there were too many of them around to ever single one out.

I would like to make it clear though that at this time I had no intentions of wooing Mrs. Burk into any kind of illicit affair involving total or even partial nudity. None. Things *did* happen, I'll grant you that, but I never planned any of it. It was friendship I was after, pure and innocent.

As we made our way down the plateau I tried to think of things to say to her. Things that would get rid of the awkwardness between us and get a little of the old back-and-forth going. All I could think to say, however, was, "It's dark."

"Yes," she said.

"Dark," I repeated.

"Very dark," she added.

"Yes," I said, "Very, very dark."

"Very," she re-enforced.

We walked a bit further in silence while I searched for something, anything, to say that wouldn't seem like a non sequitur. There are few things I fear more in this world than not having relevance to what preceded me.

"There's nothing like darkness," I furthered.

"Not that I know of."

"It's pretty much its own thing."

"Yes, it's very unique," she said.

"Very."

"*Very.*"

"Kind of like...me, " I said with an aw-shucks look on my face.

She was amazed. It was almost as if I had told her that I knew where the Holy Grail was. Her eyes lit up and her jaw dropped as she asked, "You are? *Really*? How so?" She grabbed my robe and shook me. "How!"

"Well... "

The life of the conversation, our relationship, our future together, our unborn children, depended on me thinking of at least one way in which I was unique, in which I was my own special thing, like darkness.

I had nothing.

We walked on in silence as I desperately tried to think of something to say. I looked over my body but there are no special features there—just the usual bumps, lumps, and clumps of flesh. Then I thought about my habits: some of them are perhaps rare, but unique?

Mrs. Burk's initial hope that I would come up with something soon faded and she looked at her feet while she walked, clearly disappointed. All hopes of me connecting with this woman were dying with a whimper.

Soon we were down on level ground with the reservation in sight. Time was running out, so in an act of foolish desperation I opened my mouth and, like Jesus, let God take care of what happened next.

"I'm naked underneath this robe."

That stopped us both.

I would like to point out that I was not looking to turn her on by putting the image of my naked body in her mind. I was just looking for a conversation. It was clearly God who was looking to turn her on because those were His words, not mine.

Nevertheless, I still hoped that a conversation would ensue, with her saying something like, "Naked eh?" To which I would have replied, "Yes, isn't nudity the bees knees?" And from there the conversational sky was the limit! We could have talked about various times we've been naked, amusing naked antidotes, what our earliest memories of being aware of our own nakedness were, how partial nudity can be much more awkward than full nudity depending on which items of clothing are still intact, especially if the only intact item is a single sock or a t-shirt and socks with no pants, or nothing but a belt.

Unfortunately what she said instead of "Naked eh?" was, "So am I."

"So are you what?"

She looked down at her feet. "Naked underneath my robe."

"Oh."

"Yes."

I looked down at my feet as well. "Yes."

This changed everything. We now had something in common. We shared a quirk. A quirk that could be easily exploited. Who needs conversation when you have that!

We both looked up and stared at each other. There we were, two adults with nothing more than two thin yellow robes between us and full frontal nudity. Think of the simplification. There wouldn't have to be any fumbling around with zippers, belts, bras, socks, locks, and latches. The awkwardness between that first button unbuttoning and that last sock coming off would be minimal, nonexistent even as the first and last maneuver would be one in the same. All partial nudity issues were null and void. It was like having a buy-one-get-one-free coupon for Sippin' Sticks, and even though you rarely have a hankering for Sippin' Sticks, you feel compelled to take advantage of the offer, seeing it as a deal too good to pass up. It's why coupons are such great advertising, because they make people feel like they should buy things they don't really need or want, just for the sake of a bargain. That night I was given a coupon for American Cheese.

Before I could think about silly things like the fact that her husband was my boss, or the fact that she wasn't very attractive, or the fact that I was technically at work, or the fact that a member of my tour group was missing, or the fact that this was a church outing, I was rolling around the ground with Mrs. Burk, both our robes hiked up and bunched around our necks.

I won't lie. The contact was wonderful. Two naked bodies, skin cool to the touch from the night air, legs a tangle, chests pressed together, with a warm sky full of stars overhead and the cool ground underneath. I didn't even want to have sex, even though we most certainly did. You get two naked people together and rolling around and it just kind of happens.

What I really wanted was to simply lie on top of her, or, better yet, have her lie on top of me as if we were a sandwich with her as the thick slice of warm cheese and me as the hunk of meat. But it appeared that she preferred the spooning position, because anytime I would get on top of her she would roll us over a quarter turn to our sides, and then I would counter with a another quarter turn in the same direction, clockwise, so that she was then on top of me in the prime position, but then she would immediately roll us into the spoon again, and so on, until it wasn't so much sex as it was stop, drop, and roll.

It was all this rolling back and forth that led to the actual sex. As we tumbled, my blind pet snake, if you will, just popped in there, and out of there, and in there. I must say that I didn't even realize he was doing such things as I was far too focused on getting and staying in the sandwich position to be aware of anything going on down there where he lives, in his cage. I'm not saying that my snake has a mind of his own, but rather that he has no mind at all and relies on pure chance to get anything done. Once I realized that he was doing what he was doing, well, there was no sense in just pulling the poor thing right out. If you accidentally walk into a toy store with a child, you can't just grab his arm and yank him right out. No, you have to let him run around a bit, check out the merchandise, and after he's had his fill, then you can leave. If he isn't finished doing his thing when you want to leave, well then you must forcefully yank him out of there yourself, and later on, when you're both away from prying eyes, you slap him around for being so stubborn.

My child had his fill rather quickly. Her little brat took forever.

And when it was over I looked forward to the chat I expected would follow. The minutes (dare I dream hours!) of holding her with maybe a discussion scattered in on what just happened, our plans for the future, or even an exchange of observations on how lovely an evening it was. All the while I could keep my pet in his vacation home, letting him rest a bit before taking him home again, to stare at the blank walls of his cell.

None of that happened. No sooner had we come to the end of the act itself when she, in a reversal, pulled the vacation home out from the vacationer, leaving my pet snake feeling cold, confused, and cheated—like a newborn baby.

"What time is it?" she asked.

I checked my watch. "3:43."

"I have to get back. It's soon," she said, hopping up from me and throwing her robe over her head in one grand sweeping motion.

I had forgotten about the supernova, and I must say was a little ticked that she hadn't.

"Will you go get Joe?" she asked.

"But I'm Joe." I said, suddenly bringing us back to square one. It was as if nothing had happened. We went through some of the two Joes issue again before I remembered that a tour member was missing. I agreed to go find him only because I was naked and she wasn't, and it's hard to say no to a person who has that kind of leverage on you.

As soon as I said I'd go, she hurried off with the flashlight shining on her face again, walking backwards like I did earlier with Martini.

The illuminated face of Mrs. Burk, no longer just American Cheese to me (because after you have sex with cheese, let's face it, it's no longer cheese), left just as it came to me: disembodied.

I laid on my back, looking up at all the stars I missed out on every night at home since the light from my city drowns out the lights from all of the stars. Did the monkeys ever think that one day they would drown out the stars? At first I tried to find the few planets I could see every night in the city, curious to see if they looked any different when they were amongst others. But they all looked the same to me. They looked lonely.

Then I turned to look at Betelgeuse, the star that was about to die. Just like people who are about to die suddenly, the star didn't look any different from its neighbors. It was twinkling away as it quickly approached its explosion just like a man who whistles a happy tune as he walks into the path of an unseen oncoming car.

Shaking these thoughts off, I stood up and quickly pulled my robe down. To be honest, I was feeling cheated and used and didn't want to be reminded of the sex any longer. A hand or a hotdog could have brought about the conclusion to what happened between Mrs. Burk and I, and that's what I felt like. Like a hotdog used for something other than its true purpose, cast aside, and left to die without ever achieving its destiny—to be absorbed by another living thing.

With the flashlight dance at the top of the plateau building to a frenzy, I headed further down into the dark reservation, which I might as well call a trailer park from here on out, because that's what it was. There was a light on in only one of the trailers, so I figured I'd start my search there. We had researched the location in detail many times before and there had never been a light on in the trailer park during the supernova. Something had changed.

As I entered the reservation, looking around at the dry, dead land, I wondered why they called it a reservation. Reserving land like that makes about as much sense as reserving a table at Battered Bart's Breakfast Barn.

I had a feeling that I would find Indian Joe staring into a window, seeing how horribly his relatives lived on the reservation. I envisioned coming upon him with a single tear falling from his eye, as he gazed through the window at a mother not unlike his own, sleeping with her arm around a baby not unlike himself as a baby. I prepared myself to put my arm on his shoulder for comfort and say, "There, there, Indian Joe. It's gonna be alright, fella. What do you say you and I grab a couple beers and go watch that kooky star go boom boom while your friends play flashlight tag?"

As I got closer, I saw that Indian Joe was indeed by a window of the lighted trailer. It was the side window and he was doing more than just looking in, he was trying to squirm in. At the same time, at the front of the trailer, a young Indian woman came out the front door looking suspiciously for something, probably Indian Joe, whose legs were the only thing hanging out the window at that point. The woman was wearing pajamas with a floral print.

I had my flashlight on to see where I was going but as soon as I saw her I flicked it off and hit the ground to avoid detection. It didn't work.

"Hey! Did you just tap on my window?" she asked.

"No."

"Why are you sneaking around my yard?"

"I'm not sneaking."

"Then what are you doing on the ground?"

"Looking for my dog."

"Does he walk that low to the ground?"

"Yes. He's a wiener dog."

"I don't believe you."

I decided to turn the tables. "Well, what are *you* doing sneaking around?"

"I'm not sneaking."

"Yes you are."

"It's my house."

"Prove it."

"I'm going to get my gun."

"Wait. I'm a monk."

I told her that I was leading a stargazing tour for a small group of my Buddhist monk brothers, and that one of the brothers had wandered off. I was trying to find him before some non-monk stole his wallet and raped him, as we monks know nothing of the modern world and its ravages and are easily taken advantage of. When she asked why I didn't tell her that at first I told her that I feared that she, on finding out that I was a monk, would take my wallet and rape me.

She bought it. It must have been the robe. The woman asked me in to her trailer for a cup of coffee and I gladly accepted, eager to get inside to see what the hell Indian Joe was doing.

As I walked through the front door, which led directly into the little home's kitchen, the woman introduced herself as Susan. Not truly expecting but hoping that her name was something more along the lines of "Threatens With Gun" or "Sees through Some Lies But Not Others," I was disappointed with her real name. When I told her that my name was Brother Joe she smiled and said, "That's my son's name."

"Your son's name is Brother Joe?"

"Joe."

"What?"

"That's his name."

"Brother Joe?"

"No. Joe."

"What?"

"Joe!"

"WHAT!"

And then she made us coffee.

"Lovely place you have here," I said as I walked around, pretending to admire her home and having trouble finding things to even pretend to admire, while really looking for Indian Joe. From what I could see, the home had two main rooms, a kitchen and living room, with two doors at opposite ends of the trailer. The window Indian Joe crawled through was beyond the door next to the living room.

"It's small, but we manage," she said to the coffee pot.

"Where is your son anyway?"

"He's asleep in his room," she said as she nodded toward the room where I assumed Indian Joe was, the room where Little Joe laid asleep, the room where Indian Joe had seen something that made him want to go in, to either get a better look at or perhaps take back with him as a souvenir—oh, how I hoped it was only a souvenir arrowhead and not the boy's virginity.

Before storming in, I needed to figure out what could be in there that Indian Joe would want, and I decided on the direct approach.

"So...Susan, by the way I love what you've done with your kitchen. Is this wall plastic or wood? Because it looks like wood, it really does. Would you say that Little Joe's room had anything in it that would be of interest to an older Indian man?"

"What?"

"What is that wonderful smell? Is it the coffee? Potpourri? A wet dog? Let's say there was an adult Indian male looking into Little Joe's

166   CHRIS GENOA

bedroom—in the middle of the night. He's standing outside with his face pressed against the window, breathing heavy, eyes wide open. Would there be anything that would make him climb through that window? Anything of interest?"

"What are you talking about, Brother Joe?"

"Well..."

A crashing sound, glass shattering, came from Little Joe's bedroom. Susan put down the two coffee cups she had been carrying over and walked quickly to the door to her son's room.

"JOE?" She shouted.

"Yes?" I replied as she stormed past me.

"Joe?" She said again, knocking on the door, "Joe, are you alright? Joe!"

As Susan jiggled the locked door handle, the name Joe danced around in my head. I marveled at the chain of events that had brought three Joes to this one trailer, from the discovery of time travel to the founding of the Church of the Bright, to Susan getting knocked up by some guy, possibly named Joe, who no longer appeared to be around.

As Susan opened the door I pictured how neat it would be when Little Joe met Indian Joe met Brother Joe. Susan would say to her son, "Joe, I'd like you to meet Joe. Joe, I'd like you to meet Joe." And then to Indian Joe and I, "Joe and Joe, I'd like you to meet Joe." And then the three Joes would all simultaneously wave to each other and say, "Hello Joe," which would throw the entire room into hysterics for days. It would be one for the history books.

But the greatest introduction of the century didn't get a chance to take place, because Susan turned on the light in the room to illuminate Indian Joe standing over Little Joe's bed with his hands around the boy's neck and the boy's head decidedly blue.

Susan jumped from the doorway to the bed in a desperate attempt to save her son, and I should have done the same, even though he wasn't my son, even though I don't think I could have jumped that far, and even though he was just a person in the past, nothing more than a shadow really, but I couldn't seem to move. I was too busy standing in the doorway saying, "Hello Joe."

Just as Susan put her own hands around Indian Joe's neck, with the clear intention of making his face turn more blue and her son's face turn less blue, there came out of Indian Joe, from within Indian Joe really, a blinding beam of light, like a mini supernova, starting in the region of his chest and quickly growing to cover his entire body. It was so blindingly bright and grew so big so fast that even though I threw my arms in front of my face for protection, I thought the light had incinerated everything in the room, including me.

When I lowered my arm and opened my eyes I saw nothing but endless whiteness, which I took to be heaven. That's how I always envisioned heaven anyway, as a bed of clouds with people in soft focus sitting at white tables on white chairs playing chess and drinking white tea, people riding white bicycles, eating white steaks, wearing white suits, flying white kites, napping in white hammocks, playing white guitars, picking white apples from the white apple trees, and so on. I made it, I thought, I'm in heaven. Bring on the white shit.

But as I walked around heaven I began to get worried. Where were my parents? Where were my old pets? Sparky? Where's Sparky? Where was anybody? Was I the first person in the history of mankind to gain entrance to heaven? Who would keep me company? Hello? God? Jesus? Holy Ghost? What the fuck!

"Hello?" I called out, "Anybody there!"

Finally, someone called my name.

"JOE! JOE!"

It was a woman and she sounded scared.

"I'M OVER HERE!" I shouted back.

"ARE YOU OK? JOE!"

She sounded desperate, and she only wanted to know if I was OK. I truly was in heaven.

"I'M FINE! WHERE'S ALL THE WHITE SHIT?"

"SHUT UP!" She shouted.

"HEY! YOU CAN'T SAY SHUT UP IN HEAVEN!"

"JOE? ARE YOU OK, HONEY?"

"I SAID I'M FINE!"

"SHUT UP, BROTHER JOE!"

"YOU SHUT UP, LADY!"

Wait. *Brother* Joe?

That's when I realized that it was Susan's voice I heard. She was calling out her son's name, not mine. I hadn't died, and I certainly wasn't in heaven.

I took a moment to be thankful that the afterlife wasn't an eternal white abyss with lots of yelling and no pets, and then I joined Susan in the search for little Joe. My vision began to come back before Susan's did. I guess the arm protection did something after all. My blurred vision saw Susan feel her way along the wall and Little Joe slumped in his bed, quite blue, and quite dead.

There was no trace of Indian Joe.

I went over to the bed and looked at little dead Joe. He looked a little like the older Joe. Not me Joe, Indian Joe. Then I looked up at his mother stumbling her way towards me. She too looked a little like Indian Joe.

I decided to leave.

As I power walked up the plateau, my arms pumping and my butt shimmying, the burst of light from the supernova had already reached Earth. In the distance I could hear the Bogumils cheering and pictured them holding hands, dancing around, and flashing each other.

In 2015 many people thought that the world was coming to an end when they saw the supernova. Even though the star was much too far away to cause much damage, few knew that at first. So there was much freaking out had by all, and anything that the Bogumils were doing would have fit in just fine had others been around to see them.

What neither the Bogumils nor the rest of the planet knew was that real harm had indeed been done that night, maybe not the first time that night came and went, and maybe not the next eighty or so times, but it did eventually happen. Not deep in the cosmos, but in a trailer park in the middle of nowhere Arizona, by what I later pieced together was a suicidal Native American man named Joe who wanted to spare his younger selves the pain and disappointment of the future life they were destined to lead, by killing himself as a child.

By doing this he wiped his existence off the record of time from that point on in a burst of light.

Poof.

As I shuffled the Bogumils through the wormhole, ignoring their protests that their allotted time wasn't up yet, and left that time behind, I had a feeling that Mr. Burk's Shaved Cat Principal was seriously flawed. And what we know about the nature of time, and the effects of traveling through it, is about as much as a mite living in my eyelashes knows about all of the horrific things I see with those very eyes.

Part 2

Wow

1
Howdy Particle!

I never gave May her little yellow book back. I suppose some would call me a thief. Well I'm not. I didn't give it back because I just got around to reading it recently. And I wasn't about to return an unused borrowed object, because the whole point of lending and borrowing objects is to share a part of your life or learn about a part of someone else's life, and neither of those things can happen if you just let the borrowed item gather dust.

If, for example, you let your neighbor borrow your husband, and she does nothing but paint his genitals blue for the duration of the lending period, then she will have learned absolutely nothing about you. That is unless you regularly paint your husband's genitals blue, in which case by doing the same your neighbor will understand what it is to be you somewhat more. She will have walked a mile in your shoes so to speak.

And if you are lucky enough to then borrow your neighbor's dog, and you put the beast to good use guarding your supply of blue paint, then you too will have learned something about your neighbor, but only if she too uses the dog to guard her blue paint. The end result being that you will understand where your neighbor is coming from when she looks at you with glazed eyes and says, "Dogs are *great*, aren't they?" and she in turn will understand you when you grab her shoulders and declare, "You can never have enough blue paint. NEVER."

So the book was my golden chance to get to know May and to understand where she was coming from, but back then I didn't have the time. But looking back, I don't understand where all my time, during that time, went. Especially since I had many days with little to do but stare at the walls in my apartment after Dactyl was shut down for a federal investigation.

During that time I often found myself standing by my apartment window, looking through binoculars down at the street where I would regularly find at least one person carrying that yellow book with them. Some would be reading it as they walked, others would have it tucked under their arm, others would have it peeking out of their briefcases or pocketbooks, and still others would have it in both hands, raised above their heads, parading it down the street.

It was everywhere, and if the people who were walking about the city, on their way to and from places, had the time to read, even parade, the book, then why didn't I, who didn't have anywhere to go but occasionally to the bathroom, have the time?

And it wasn't as if I just forgot about the book's existence, not at all, for I was constantly reminded of it on the morning, afternoon, and evening news which all frequently ran human interest stories on the followers of the book, both new and old. From these I learned what Ba Hubba's odd name meant. His mother told him that the first sound he ever made, other than crying, was "Ba." In early adolescence, his Uncle Jimmy used to say "Hubba, hubba" whenever a young Ba Hubba walked past him. A "Tree" is one of Ba Hubba's favorite symbols because a tree's roots firmly connect it to the Earth. And "Bob" because Ba Hubba's real name is Robert.

My favorite TV spot was one on a lady waiting at the end of a line that coiled around several blocks and led to a bookstore. The people waiting to buy a new pamphlet Ba Hubba had written called "The Itsy

Bitsy, Teeny Weenie Booklet of Ultimate Delight." The booklet was the size of a matchbook and came with a little magnifying glass that you had to use to actually read the tiny text.

Since he now had far too many followers to personally speak to all of them, Ba Hubba had taken to releasing one of these best-selling booklets every month or so to spread the word. A reporter asked the woman in line what drew her to Bogumilism. Her response went something like this:

> "Well, I was feeling pretty spiritually starved. You know, something was missing. I had tons of money, a nice husband, two beautiful kids, I had it all. But life felt so...meaningless. I felt like this separate little capsule floating through life. So I planned to kill myself, just end it all. Either that or have an affair. One or the other. I gave myself four days top find someone to have an affair with, and if I couldn't, I'd kill myself on the fifth day.
>
> While I was paging through the personal ads, looking for someone to have an affair with, I got a call from an old friend who was living out in Los Angeles. She said she had just met some guy who called himself La Love Bob who was a teacher and had changed her life. I thought, 'Cuckoo, cuckoo.' She met him in some book-store/meditation center she stumbled into one after-noon, and she wanted me to fly out there the next day and meet him. I figured that my friend was nuts, but I had nothing better to do so I went. At the very least, I thought, I could have an affair with her or maybe this La Love Bob guy.
>
> So I packed a bunch of pills to kill myself with if things

didn't work out, and headed out there. As soon as I walked into the bookstore I felt something. There was a warm Energy filling the place. But La Love Bob wasn't there, so my friend and I laid down in the meditation hall and took a nap. When I woke up, my friend was gone, my shoes were missing, someone had brushed my teeth, and, most importantly, I didn't want to kill myself anymore, *or* have an affair. All of that mess had been lifted from my soul. There was also a pamphlet lying on my chest. It was called 'The Elbow of Understanding.' The first paragraph in it changed my life:

'Misery is disconnection, being unconnected, partial, a self-fatiguing tablet of life-force. Misery is disconnection and disconnectiveness. And misery is the prime truth of personal life. The questers' quest in life, for all miserable tablets, is to re-connect to the Love-Vigor.'

I didn't meet Ba Hubba that day—he was out getting a manicure or something—but the experience of being so close to his presence changed my life forever. I had begun the long journey to re-connectedness.

From this interview I got the impression that even people who actually had things to do outside their homes, even people with families to tend, were managing to find the time to read that yellow book and the pamphlets. How—I wondered while I was in one of my daily staring-at-my-feet stupors—did those family folks (between waking up the kids, feeding the kids, dropping the kids off, picking up the kids, feeding the kids again, scolding the kids, putting the kids to bed, sobbing quietly in the bathroom, screwing quietly in the bedroom, sobbing quietly in the bathroom again, sleeping, packing lunches, cleaning the muck, creating the muck, ingesting the muck (albeit unknowingly), spanking the kids, spanking the husband, spanking the wife, spanking the self, walking the dog, feeding the dog, encouraging the dog to run away, going to work, being at work, wanting to go home, coming home from work, wanting to go back to work, hiding in the closet, soiling the bed, burning the sheets, and so on) have the time to read *anything*, let alone a silly book about a silly religion?

I concluded that even though it felt like I didn't have the time, I must have had it—I just didn't have the inclination.

The Dactyl work stoppage had unsettled me, knocking me out of the life I had gotten used to and into a broken-down elevator of sorts, where I could do nothing but stare at the floor indicator stuck on 6, with my mouth hanging open, my eyes unfocused, and my ears more aware of the beating of my heart than of the mutterings coming from the people trapped there with me. If you will.

Mr. Burk attempted to continue the tours and avoid an investigation by keeping what he called POIJO, "The Poofing of Indian Joe Occurrence," an internal affair. This failed rather quickly when news of what happened slipped out through one of the Bogumil group members who witnessed the event (I suspect Mr. Tuttle was the culprit, just to spite me). It was reported on local news one night and the whole thing was world news less than an hour after that.

All Dactyl tours were immediately halted, all employees sent home and told to stay there until further notice. I took this literally and stayed in my apartment, as if I had been sent to my room, for the duration of the hiatus. Not that I was physically confined to my building by means of a lock or a guard monkey patrolling the halls—not at all. I was, in fact, free to go outside, walk about, eat in fancy restaurants, see the sights, but I couldn't come up with a compelling enough reason to do so. Oh I'm sure I would have enjoyed a nice stroll through the park, or a good bite to eat, once I was actually doing it, but it was the getting started that mystified me.

The investigation quickly concluded that Indian Joe had gone back in time not because he was a Bogumil interested in seeing a grand celestial event involving light, but to kill his younger self, and that by doing so he had somehow—Shaved Cat Principle be damned—caused his entire presence in time to disappear from that point on in a burst of light, leaving only the boy's lifeless body behind as the sad period on a simple life sentence that had at one time been quite complex and painful.

The fact that Indian Joe disappeared in a burst of light when he killed his younger self was quickly latched onto by the Bogumils as proof of their faith. They claimed we were all made of light beams, and that those beams all shot out from one source, known as The Bright, but could just as easily be called God.

The idea that everyone had a soul connection to God, that He was a ball of warm light and we billions of rays of that same light, shooting out from Him through time, was very new to people who had been told for centuries that a bit of funny business with a reptile and some fruit had caused a huge rift between us and Him. They were told that the only way back was by following a strict set of rules, etched in stone, that forbade a number of awful, as well as a few incredibly enjoyable, acts. That they were written in stone strongly implied that these rules weren't open to revision or amendments.

Thousands of years later the people, apparently, had had enough of these static stone rules because Ba Hubba Tree Bob and his religion of always moving light beams spread like a virus, going from localized infection to epidemic in less than a month.

According to Ba Hubba, in order to find happiness on Earth and in the afterlife the trick is to be able to mentally trace yourself through the past along your light path back to The Bright. To connect the dots—all of them.

And it was Ba Hubba, and Ba Hubba alone, who claimed to be the only man able to guide people through this process, and that he was able to do this only because he spent a decade meditating his way back to The Bright while living in a warehouse apartment in Red Hook, Brooklyn. The warehouse grew to be considered a shrine, and many Bogumils took a pilgrimage to see it. But that all stopped when the current resident of the warehouse apartment in question, a Mr. Nabokett, unable to sleep for many nights on end due to all of the flashlights and singing constantly outside his window, went a bit nutty and torched the place. The heartbroken Bogumils on the scene reported that Mr. Nabokett ran outside and laughed and danced as the entire warehouse became engulfed in flames. I believe I would have done the same.

To get a feel for what Ba Hubba's book was like, I offer you a little taste:

> Let me now introduce myself! For I have been known by many names, such as: The Life Vigor, The Shebang, La Love Bob, La Love, The Bob, The Ba, The Dee, The Da Doe Dee, That Guy, Hey You, Puttana, and Robert S. Noonan, III—among others. But you may address me as I am now, at The End of my Metamorphosis (and at your beginning), as Ba Hubba Tree Bob. And you? Who are you? You are a particle. A particle of light. Howdy, particle! YES. And every second of every day you are creating a twisty and turny path of light through space and time. You (like a Comet! Whooooosh!) leave a trail of Light wherever you go. Good for you! And it is I, Me (Ba), in my infinite Ba Bo Bee Wisdom, who has come to show you (Little Speck, Little Dot) and all (Little Specks, Little Dots) the way back home to The Bright (The Source, The Whole Shebang, ALL. Follow me, and you too will know The Bright.

> But you ask, "What is The Bright?" And I answer, "What, you do not know? You have no idea? Ha!" Do you see? Do you now see why you need me? If you don't know what you're looking for, then how can you expect to ever find it, hmmmm? Impossible! You are lost and I will show you the way!

Everything that ever was: is Whole. Everything that ever
will be: isn't Whole...yet! Weeeeeeeeeeeee!

Similar nonsense with exclamation points abound throughout the
book, and the whole thing gets really fucking annoying by about page
three. But that didn't stop Bogumilism from sweeping the goddamn
world, now did it?

On the day after Indian Joe went poof I was on my way back to the
apartment and everywhere I looked I saw one of those yellow books in
someone's hands. Commuters were reading it in the subway stations
(nodding along with all of the !s) and on the trains (contemplating each
! as they bobbed to and fro), they carried it as they walked to and from
work (flipping it open to reread a favorite section of !s whenever foot
traffic backed up), they smacked it shut when they came to the end
(the smack acting as an ! to the act of them finishing such a !-filled
work). They often looked up from their reading to see me staring at
them, only to smile at me, tap tap the open book, and give me thumbs
up. I hated them. Hated them because no matter how many times I
began to read it I couldn't get past the Howdy on page one, and I hated
anyone who could.

To capitalize on POIJO, Ba Hubba Tree Bob (in several highly
publicized interviews) explained to the world that what happened was
that since we are all nothing but beams of light extending through time,
if you cut off the light beam at a certain point, you thereby cut off the
person from that point on. So when Indian Joe went back and killed his
younger self he cut off his light beam right then and there and extin-
guishing the beam of him that had extended up to the present.

Imagine a flashlight beam shining against a wall. The front of the
beam is you, the path it takes to get to the wall is your life, and the wall
is your death. Now put your hand in front of the beam. What happens?
The light stops at your hand and the part of the beam that was between
your hand and the wall disappears without a trace.

If you had told me this foolishness about our lives being like light before POIJO, I would have nodded my head in agreement while thinking, "Now here's a crazy son-of-a-bitch." But after, I didn't know what to think.

The POIJO investigation, with Burk's full cooperation, sent a team back in time to preempt Indian Joe's suicide by stopping him from ever going on the tour in the first place. They ran into a slight problem: there no longer was an Indian Joe who went on the tour because there no longer were *any* Indian Joes past the POIJO point. From that moment on his existence was erased.

The team also went back to the reservation on the night of the supernova and watched in awe as the young, sleeping Indian Joe disappeared in a burst of light on his own this time, even without the now-erased older Indian Joe present to choke him. The act couldn't be undone.

Time, that supple old fool, somehow adjusted to make up for Indian Joe's absence. So even though the present me clearly remembers doing it, the past me no longer went to look for the missing Indian Joe, because Indian Joe never left the bed in that reservation trailer.

One member of the team found this paradox so ridiculously fruity she decided that any sort of reality that allows such a thing to be true was no reality for her. She promptly became unhinged and spent the rest of her days in the booby hatch, walking up and down the center of a hallway as if she was on a tightrope.

The question of just how someone knows if he or she is living in the past, present, or future is one that most people avoided except for a small number of philosophers and scientists who seemed to enjoy writing countless pages on the subject, none of which came even close to making sense. Most just figured that the fact that forward time travel seemed impossible, proved that we were living in the present, or in Bogumilistic terms, at the front of the beam.

I did manage to attend one Bogumil mass, at the invitation of Mrs. Burk. I walked into the church with her at my side but walked out alone. The opening singsong, which adopted the first person voice of Ba Hubba, drove me out. It went something like this:

(To the tune of Lord of The Dance)

I shined in the morning when the world was begun
I shined like the stars & the Moon & the Sun
I came from The Bright & I shined through Earth
At Brook-a-lyn I had my birth:

Shine then, wherever you may be
I am your guide to The Bright, said He!
And I'll lead you all, wherever you may be
And I'll lead you all to The Bright, said He!
(...lead you all to The Bright, said He!)

I shined for my dog & my fam-i-ly
They would not shine & they wouldn't follow me
I shined for the bums & for the hipp-a-ies
They followed me & The Bright went on:

Shine then, wherever you may be
I am your guide to The Bright, said He!
And I'll lead you all, wherever you may be
And I'll lead you all to The Bright, said He!
(...lead you all to The Bright, said He!)

A group of robe wearing adults waving flashlights and belting out lines like, "I shined for my dog & my fam-i-ly" just didn't do it for me. So as more and more people got into the religion, I spent less and less time outdoors.

Luckily, none of the folks in my apartment building got into Bogumilism. They had way too many years invested in their chosen religions to start switching at that point in their lives.

With all that free time on my hands I found myself wandering around the apartment building most of the time, discovering the joys of mindless activities that pass the time.

2
Was His Name O?

The Bingo hall in my apartment building was on the first floor and was nothing more than a large open room with a tiled floor, fluorescent lights, a small stage at one end, five rows of twelve folding tables, and each table surrounded by ten folding chairs.

When all of the chairs were full, and they frequently were, the room held an army of sorts. One that would fight only with fist-shaking and general orneriness, yes, but an army nonetheless.

On the evening I left my room—fed up with Mr. Puss's refusal to wear a hat I made him out of a sock, opting rather to do some form of intricate soft shoe dance across the kitchen counter—and wandered down to the Bingo hall, all of the tables save one were filled.

At that table, in the far right corner of the room, only one woman sat, but she had so many cards spread out across the table that there was barely room for any one else to set up camp.

The woman—a short, hunchback type, with long wet gray hair, wearing an old thin (too thin, too transparent) white dress—had three perfect rows of cards lined up across the table top—thirty-six cards in all—with one eight by twelve empty square of space in a corner of the table. It is on this corner that I squeezed in my card.

"I won't be in your way here, will I?" I asked the many-carded lady as I sat down.

She stood near the center of the table, with her arms down by her sides, and her body leaning forward as if she was in midair of a ski jump. She had a worried look on her face as her eyes darted from card to card. I had a feeling that this was the first time she attempted so many cards at once.

Her voice was soft and low and she trembled as she replied with, "Don't mess me up. Oh please don't mess me up. Please oh please oh please." She was unable to take her eyes off her cards for even a second to look at me.

"I won't. I'm just going to sit here and play my card if that's OK, Miss..."

Her eyes widened. "Betty."

I smiled. "Miss Betty."

She shot me a look that made me want to scamper back into the womb (any womb) and then whispered, "Don't mess, don't mess, and don't mess me up."

The tap tap on the microphone and quick clearing of a man's throat amplified throughout the room was, I fear, the only thing that broke her stare. At the first tap Betty's entire body clenched and her focus jerked to the stage, where a man wearing a bowler hat and an old tweed suit stood on one side of the Bingo machine—which looked much like one of those plastic balls a hamster scoots around in, only much bigger. On the other side of this man stood a woman wearing an outfit I thought only acrobats were allowed to wear. She appeared to be his assistant.

The woman held a crank connected to the plastic ball while the man held the microphone with one hand and his hat onto his head with the other.

Betty, shaking, raised her left arm, palm up and opened, and whispered in awe, "Behold the tumbler."

The caller finished clearing his throat and announced, "Pardon me, pardon. Par-r-r-r-don. Thank you. We're going to get going now, ladies and gentlemen. Hope everyone is, uh, ready."

He smiled nervously before belting out, "Because the beginning is upon us!"

I looked around the room and noticed that only Betty and I were paying any attention to him. I think he noticed this too because he began to shout.

"FOLKS! THE TIME HAS COME. LET THERE BE BINGO!"

He nodded to his assistant who, with a nervous smile of her own, began to crank the crank, turning the tumbler, and thereby mixing up the little balls inside.

"It begins," said Betty, shooting me a look that was a disturbing mix of awe, joy, anger, and sheer terror. The look gave me chills and I found myself frozen in her eyes, as if I was staring into a cave of unfathomable size and darkness, wanting to look away, knowing that it would be best to look away, but unable to do so. If I ever get the chance, I thought, I should introduce Betty to Boogedy and Nibbles. I imagine they'd get along famously.

"N! 14!" The caller belted out. "N! 14!"

In one movement Betty turned away from me and slammed two little blue chips, one in each hand, down on two of her cards on opposite sides of the table. She held that position, arms stretched out across the table, as if she was playing the timeless game of Twister, until the caller announced the next ball.

"I! 2! I! 2!"

This time Betty had three matches. She slammed down the three chips, jumped up on one of the chairs, and did jazz hands while the rest of the people in the hall scratched their heads, stared at the caller in disbelief while thinking such things as, "who the hell does this guy think he is?" while others murmured things such as, "did he say G or D?" "I don't understand...this game. Or anything really." and "Defeat comes to the wicked."

After looking up at Betty on the chair, towering over everybody else in the room, and then looking around the room, confused as to how nobody else found her actions to be of any interest, I looked down and noticed that I too had G2 on my card. I also had N14. Not bad for a beginner. Not that any of aspect of Bingo had something to do with anything besides dumb luck, or probability (whichever you prefer to call it), it's just that sometimes it's nice to do well at something—even if that something is dumb luck.

But after only two rounds, something went wrong with the tumbler that Betty held in such high regard.

"Just a minute! Just a minute! Just a minute!" The caller announced into the mic before turning his attention to the tumbler. One of the little balls was jammed in the ball exit hole. The caller, still holding his hat down, squatted down to get a good look at the problem. The assistant widened her nervous smile and waved to the crowd which, seeming more bewildered than angry, waved back. Somebody in the crowd turned to his neighbor and asked if they were at a parade.

Betty, still doing jazz hands, slowly began to sing the following ditty, picking up the tempo as she went:

> *There was a corner who had a bum and Bingo was his name*
> *O*
> *See the bum N-G-O.*
> *And Bingo was his name O.*
> *There was a corner who had a mum and Bingo was her name*
> *O*
> *See the mum N-G-O.*
> *See the bum N-G-O.*
> *And Bingo was their name O.*
> *There was a corner who had a Hun and Bingo was his name*
> *O*
> *See the Hun N-G-O*
> *See the mum N-G-O*
> *See the bum N-G-O*
> *And Bingo was their name O.*

She went on like that until there was a bum, a mum, a Hun, a nun, a rat, a cat, a dog, a frog, a lad, a dad, a doc, a croc, a sucker, and a fucker all standing on this corner and all named Bingo. This was some corner.

The ball was still jammed when Betty got to the fucker named Bingo standing on the corner, so she started the song over from the top, this time singing it a bit faster with sped-up jazz hands to match. I figured that I could either sit there and watch Betty take her little song and dance to a level of insanity hitherto unseen in a Bingo hall, or I could go up and see if I could help get the little ball out of the hole. I got up.

As I stepped up onto the stage the caller had his front teeth clamped on the ball and was grunting.

"What's the problem?" I asked.

He released the ball. "It's jammed. And, well, we may have to cancel Bingo." He paused to let this sink in before adding,

"Forever."

I looked back toward my table and saw that Betty had added an alternating kick dance step to her routine and had gone from stir to puree.

"I'm afraid I can't let that happen," I said.

The caller had a crazy look in his eye. "Sometimes things happen that we have no control over. And when they happen, it isn't our fault. It isn't anybody's *fault*. It just *is*. This is one of those things."

"Stand aside."

He held up his hand as a warning. "Don't meddle with things you don't understand. Things you can't possibly even comprehend!"

"Stand aside, I say!"

I brushed his hand away and crouched down to look at the stuck ball. I immediately noticed that the ball in question was bigger than the other balls in the tumbler and was too big to fit through the hole.

"Who put this ball in here?" I asked the caller. "It's far too big."

"Oh no you don't. It's nobody's fault. I told you that. It's just one...one of those...things that...well..." He shot an accusatory finger at his assistant. "IT WAS SHE! SHE DID IT!"

The assistant took a few steps back. "I...I didn't know," she pleaded, "How could I have known? No one told me. You, you can't blame *me* for this. You just can't. I can't be blamed. Do you hear me? I CAN'T BE BLAMED!"

"Do you see? Do you see the guilt?" the caller whispered in my ear, "It's her you're after. She is the one who can answer your questions. Take her! Spare me, you fool!"

I shoved this lunatic to the ground. "Stop it! I'm not going to take anyone."

A crowd was gathering around the stage. They weren't interested in the assistant sobbing to herself and clawing at the curtain, and they didn't care too much for the caller who was frantically throwing his belongings into a suitcase. They were there only to give me some pointers.

"Son, you gotta poke it."

"Don't listen to him! You gotta tap it. Nice and easy like."

"Poke it. Poke it, son. A good stiff poke."

"Oh he doesn't know what he's doing, someone go up there and do it for him."

"Any idiot can tap."

"Well that's true, but he ain't gonna tap now is he. He's a-gonna poke."

"Like hell he is."

"What about my shoe?"

"Oh Lord, here we go again."

"Does anybody require the services of my shoe?"

"What the hell good is a shoe going to do?"

"Lots of good. It's pointy. Good for pokin' or tappin'."

"Like hell it is."

"Lord, guide that boy's hand to do the right thing."

"I think he heard you."

"Who? The Lord?"

"No. The boy."

"My God, he probably has this whole place bugged."

Behind the onlookers, who quickly came to consist of everyone in the hall sans Betty, I could see Betty on blend and quickly approaching liquefy. I was desperate. I turned to the crowd for assistance.

"You. Give me your shoe," I asked the man who had offered the services of his shoe.

"My shoe?" He was suddenly horrified at the suggestion.

"Yes."

"Well, I don't know. Everything's happening so fast."

"Give me the shoe, dammit!"

He perked up. "I have the shoe!"

"I know you do. Give it."

Another man stepped in front of him. "No. The shoe won't do!"

"He's right!" said a third man.

The chances of me getting the shoe were looking bleak (and I would have used my own if I hadn't happened to have been wearing slippers at the time) until another man came through the hall doors and proclaimed:

"I have returned with a stick!" holding it high above his head.

While the crowd murmured about whether it was a stick or a rod, I (having no time or patience for semantics) took the stick and put it to use.

I opened the hatch on top of the tumbler, reached in with the stick, and as the crowd held its breath, gave the ball a firm but gentle tap. With a pop the ball was born and cast out from the womb into the cruel world where it would find few people who welcomed it, many who were indifferent, and some who regretted the day it was born.

The caller threw his suitcase aside and scrambled to grab the bouncing ball. He slowly walked over to the microphone. Looked at the ball. Looked out past the crowd and declared, "B! 5! B! 5!"

There was a pause when time didn't so much stand still as fart. Looking from face to face I could sense synapses looking out with their mouths hanging open, neurons squinting with lips pursed, and cerebral cortexes scratching their asses with both hands, yawning. A stimulus had been delivered and the response was coming, but it was in no hurry.

When it finally came, understanding swept over the crowd like a wave of ah ha, causing everybody to disperse almost at once.

I returned to my table to find that Betty, sweating, had already covered her B5s (an impressive five in all) and was poised—hands by her sides, head down, and panting—for the next call.

I too had B5 and attempted to place a chip down on it slyly, without Betty noticing. I didn't want her to see how close I was to my victory and her defeat. While I was confident she didn't see or hear me do the deed, I have a strong feeling that she knew anyway. Somehow, she was in touch with every aspect of Bingo in the room.

I wonder if anything went on in the Bingo players' heads? Since the game itself requires so little of the human brain—hell a chimp could hold his own at Bingo—what, if anything, did those people do with that extra computing power? Did they think about the past? The future? Or were they just staring at their cards, waiting for someone to call out the next move, hoping that they would have the ability to make it.

"G! 71! G! 71!"

I had it.

As I was focused on discreetly covering G71 I barely noticed a man sit down next to me, until he spoke.

"Hey, hey, hey! Look who almost has Bingo!"

It was Mr. Burk, and he was sloppily rearranging Betty's cards to make room for his own.

All was not right with the world.

Especially since through Betty's eyes I saw her mind toss around the idea of setting itself and the entire room on fire because of Burk's disturbance to her cards, resolve itself to do just that, and then shift from "should I?" to "I should, but how should I?"

"Mr. Burk?"

"O! 42! O! 42!"

I had O42. I had Bingo. But I chose not to put a chip down, fearing that doing so would push Betty over the edge, forcing her to quickly answer the question of how to set the entire room and everyone and everything inside it on fire. I thought that I was in the clear until I looked over at Mr. Burk who had his mouth wide open and had a ridiculous grin on his face. He was anxiously waiting for me to yell out, "Bingo!"

Betty gave me a sideways look. There was loathing in her eyes.

I tired to change the subject. "What are you doing here, Mr. Burk?"

"I'm here to play Bingo."

"I don't believe you."

"Joe, you have Bingo. You get to yell it out."

"I'd rather not."

"Do it, Joe. Quick!"

"I don't want too."

"N! 20! N! 20!" The caller shouted.

Betty had two N20s, but still no Bingo.

"You're going to miss your chance, Joe. This lady with a shitload of cards is about to win."

"I don't care. Why are you here?"

"Put down a chip and I'll tell you."

"Tell me and I'll put down a chip."

"N! 20! N! 20!"

"Didn't he just call that ball?" I asked.

"Maybe he was reiterating," said Burk.

"N! 20! N! 20!"

"There, he said it again."

"No he didn't."

"Of course he did."

"You're hearing things, Joe."

"N! 20! N! 20!"

"See!"

"See what?"

"What he said."

"How can I see words?"

"Hear!"

"Where?"

Something was up and Mr. Burk was trying to confuse me. The caller was indeed calling out N 20 over and over. At first, the crowd seemed happy with the extra time to find any N20's that they might have had, but after the sixth time folks started to ask one another, "How many N20 balls are in that thing anyway?" While they discussed whether or not it was legal to have multiple N 20s in a Bingo game, I—ignoring Mr. Burk's attempts to get me to watch how far back he could bend his thumb—went up to the stage to see just what the hell was going on.

I jumped up on stage and stood a few feet from the caller, watching as he continued to call out the same ball again and again. There was something odd about the way his body moved—there was an exact pattern to it. He would call out N20, take a step back, hold the ball up to the exit hole on the tumbler, step back up to the mic, and call out N20 again. Each time exactly the same as the last, forward and reverse, down to the movements of his facial muscles.

Looking over at his assistant I saw that she was stuck in a pattern of her own. Her head turned to watch the caller hold the ball up to the hole and then followed him back to the mic, and then back to the hole again. Her facial muscles, straining to keep that fake smile up, also appeared to be somehow locked in a subtly repeated pattern.

I took a step closer to get a better view and was about to take another step when I was stopped by Mr. Burk shouting out, "BINGO! BINGO! WE GOT BINGO OVER HERE!"

This threw the crowd into an uproar since how the hell could someone just be realizing, after twenty-seven calls of N 20, that he had Bingo.

I decided not to get involved and took another step closer to the caller, putting my hand on his shoulder with the intention of giving him a good shake. But instead of shaking, I immediately took my hand off the caller's shoulder and took a step back. The strange thing is that while I did physically take my hand off his shoulder and take a step back, mentally I did nothing. I had every intention of shaking the caller, but my body decided against it. I was overruled.

"N! 20! N! 20!"

I tried again, stepping up to the caller, placing my hand on his shoulder but once again, against my will, I immediately reversed the process. Determined to let my body know who was in charge I tried again, and again, and again, failing each time, unable to will myself past the first step. It's as if the moment I placed my hand on the caller's shoulder I became a puppet, my movements controlled by an unseen puppeteer, my mind a blank. I was aware of what was happening as I took the step backwards, but I couldn't think about anything as I did so.

"N! 20! N! 20!"

"Problem, Joe?" asked Burk, who had come up to the foot of the stage and had Betty piggyback on his shoulders, like a sleepy child. The crowd behind him had fallen into two camps of about equal size: one group, the skeptics, was closely examining my card to see if there were any irregularities and to figure out how the twenty-seventh called N 20 won the game for me, while the other group, accepting defeat, had fanned out across the room and were going about the business of collecting all of the cards and chips, ready to move on to the next distraction.

"Something's going on here, Mr. Burk. Something fishy."

"It's Betty, she smells like trout."

"N! 20! N! 20!"

"I know, but that's not what I'm talking about. These people are stuck in some kind of force field. It's making them repeat the same action over and over again."

"N! 20! N! 20!"

"Maybe there's just a ton of N20s in there," suggested Burk, even though he knew damn well that was not the case.

"Maybe you'd better shut up," I told him.

"Maybe you'd better make me."

"Maybe I will."

That's when the assistant screamed.

3
A Mild Blip

"A mild blip within a localized loop-dee-loop."

Back in my apartment, that's how Mr. Burk explained the Bingo incident to me, with a good deal of nobigwhoopedness in the tone of his voice. He sat at my kitchen table with Betty—who he insisted on carrying from the Bingo Hall to my apartment on his shoulders, just to prove to me that he could do it. Not that I ever said he couldn't, and I even reminded him that I never said so, twice, but he swore that the thought must have at least crossed my mind and at most caused me to have an inner smirk. This is why an understandably sleepy Betty was sitting next to Mr. Burk, leaning on his shoulder and looking at me as I stood a reasonable distance from them both.

"Just a small, brief fluctuation in the space time continuum, Joe. Happens all the time."

"Well I've never seen it happen before."

He sighed heavily. "It happens all the time with protons. I've seen them do it with my own eyes. First, they start shaking violently." He shook his whole body violently to illustrate, rattling my table.

"Then they hop around all over the place, like this." He hopped around my room like a bunny rabbit having an epileptic fit.

"Eventually they'll hop through walls, dimensions, and even back and forth through time." He threw himself at my kitchen wall, bounced off it, and fell to the floor, in what must have been an attempt to pass through it like a particle. I swore he knocked himself out, but he hopped right back up, unfazed, and took a seat.

"This kind of stuff happens all around you, billions of times every second."

"These were people sir, not protons."

"What's the difference?"

"Protons don't play Bingo."

"True."

And then Betty began to softly, and surprisingly beautifully, sing.

(To the gradually increasing rhythm of a metronome ticking in an insane woman's head)

I like to eat eat eat apples and bananas
I like to eat eat eat apples and bananas
I like to ate ate ate ay-pples and banay-nays
I like to ate ate ate ay-pples and banay-nays
I like to eat eat eat ee-pples and banee-nee-s
I like to eat eat eat ee-pples and banee-nee-s
I like to ite ite ite i-pples and bani-ni-s
I like to ite ite ite i-pples and bani-ni-s
I like to oat oat oat o-pples and bano-no-s
I like to oat oat oat o-pples and bano-no-s
I like to oot oot oot oo-pples and banoo-noo-s
I like to oot oot oot oo-pples and banoo-noo-s

"I think she's hungry, Joe," said Burk. "Get her a banoonoo."

"Banoonoo," whispered Betty.

"I don't have any banoonoos."

"Then get her an ipple."

"Stop humoring her! I demand to know why you are here!"

Betty stood up and shouted, "Banee-nee!"

"Scratch that ipple, Joe. The lady wants a baneenee."

"Both of you, stop it! Nobody's getting anything to eat until I know why you're here."

The smile left Burk's face as he looked me in the eyes. "I need you, Joe. The mission is back on."

I turned away and looked at the floor. "Why don't you get the other guides to help you. Like you did before."

"Because. They're all dead."

"What!"

"To me. They're dead to me. They don't have the it-factor, Joe."

"Oh, and I do?"

"Yep."

"Really?" I would have twirled my hair and batted my eyelashes if either were long enough. "You think so?"

"I know so."

Even though I don't really know what the it-factor is, I felt special that Burk thought I had it. Like a hopelessly ugly child who is told by her aunt that she's beautiful, I felt like staring in the mirror at myself for hours on end, admiring my newfound itness.

Burk pulled a picture out of his pocket and flicked it at me. There was a brief scuffle as Betty dove across the table for it and tried to wrestle the picture out of my hand. Her tenacity though was no match for my brute strength as I was able to drag her out of the apartment and throw her into the hallway, locking the door behind me.

The picture was a photo of Mr. Burk in his 20s, naked in a closet, bent over a chair, with his hands tied, a gag in his mouth, and a broom handle shoved partly, but thankfully not entirely, up his ass. The expression on his face was not a happy one.

"There's a broom in your ass, sir."

"I know. This disturbs me, Joe."

"I can imagine."

"This must stop."
"How?"
"You."
"Me?"
"You."
"Me what?"
"You go."
"Me go where?"
"You go back."

4

Slouching Towards WOW

On our way out of the city—smoothly riding along in Mr. Burk's super slick, orange-cream colored, egg-shaped car—I saw several more incidents of mild blips within localized loops.

In one such scene a man in a suit walked up and down the stairs into an office building while a small, baffled crowd gathered around to watch.

In others, a car pulled out and then into a parking space, a group of school children led by a teacher crossed an intersection halfway then retreated back to the curb and then halfway out again over and over (the motorists waiting for them to cross shook their fists and honked their horns), a teenage girl sat down and stood up at a bus stop, and a cop drew his pistol and holstered it (whoever he had originally drawn it on had apparently long since gone).

Each time I pointed out one of these occurrences to Mr. Burk he insisted that stuff like that had been happening all the time since the beginning of time and there was nothing to worry about. I didn't believe him.

The two of us were heading to Mr. Burk's house, which would be used as the staging area for the mission. Since the house was over 22 minutes outside the city, and since we were one-on-one in the car, we had to make two stops along the way so Mr. Burk could get out of the car and either be in a crowd or be alone for a few minutes, until the hives subsided.

Burk's house was in an affluent neighborhood where the residents still had their own yards and didn't have to wait in line to do things like get to their front door. For this luxury they paid dearly.

While Burk was explaining my assignment—which was to once again attempt to locate the person or persons responsible for creating the disturbing photos of multiple young Mr. Burks, hog-tie the fiends, and return them to the present—I saw something move out of the corner of my eye, turned to see what it was, and discovered we were not alone in the car.

"I have some bad news, sir," I said.

"What is it?"

"There's a ghost in the back seat."

Mr. Burk glanced into the rearview mirror, shrugged, and said, "So?"

"So?" I whispered, "Sir, I think it's Martini."

Mr. Burk glanced into the mirror again, shrugged, and said, "Yeah, that's him."

"I didn't know he died."

"Who said he died?"

"I'm sure his ghost would say so."

"Maybe. Maybe not."

I turned around to get a better look and confirmed that it really was Martini and, just like Mr. Pushcatela, really was a ghost. Thankfully he wasn't going to the bathroom like his comrade. The Martini ghost was just sitting back there, with his hands folded, and looking contentedly out the side window. Turning back to Mr. Burk, I asked him when he last heard from Martini.

"Last I heard from him was when he was in this car. He rode in the back then too. At first he said that he wanted to ride back there because he liked to pretend that I was his chauffer and that he was a famous explorer. But later he admitted that the real reason was because the back of my head is more aesthetically pleasing than the front. So be it."

"When was that?"

"This morning."

"And you don't find it in the least bit unsettling that his ghost is back there now?"

"No. People see ghosts all the time. Don't you?"

"Well, yes. Have you?"

"Sure. I saw your ghost last Wednesday."

"That's impossible. Where?"

"Eating pancakes at Battered Bart's Breakfast Barn with Martini."

"Ha! Impossible! I was alive and well last Wednesday!"

"And I saw my own ghost taking a shower a few weeks ago."

"No, no, no. Don't you understand, only dead people have ghosts. That's what ghosts are, they're dead people."

"Well my observations certainly don't support that absurd theory of yours, so I'm afraid we're going to have to discount it as pure hogwash and from now on call you Malarkey in honor of the stream of hogwash you spew forth."

I didn't believe him. Not that he wouldn't call me Malarkey, because he most certainly did, but that he wasn't concerned about the ghosts. He was playing the whole situation way too cool and I had the feeling he knew exactly why dead people's and living people's ghosts were appearing and that he was somehow responsible.

The fact the he quickly changed the subject back to the mission, with Martini's ghost still twiddling his thumbs in the back, made me suspect him even more.

Since the Dactyl offices and the two particle accelerators within were still closed down by the government for the POIJO investigation, we had to use a new type of particle accelerator that Burk had been secretly working on at home. He referred to it as "The Where or

Whencesoever Device", or WOW for short.

"That's in the process of being trademarked, Malarkey. So don't even think about taking it. Because I'll sue you," he warned me.

"I wasn't going to."

"I know, I know, I know. You're a good man, Malarkey, the only man I really trust. I love you like a son. But if you try to steal my trademark I will hang you from a tree by your intestines, bat you around like a tetherball, and then set the tree on fire."

"I wasn't going to steal it."

"Thanks...son. Wait until you see it. Your eyes will open wide, your mouth will hang open, you'll drop to your knees, throw your head back, and scream 'I have seen the future and it is grand!' And then—spent—you'll weep."

"Why?"

"You'll see."

"I want to know now."

"Words can't do it justice."

"I want to know what I'm getting into here, sir."

"Relax. You'll love it."

"Is it safe?"

"Yes."

"Have you tested it?"

"Yes."

"On humans?"

"No."

"Then on what?"

"Monkeys, Malarkey. Chimps."

"Where did you get chimps?"

"Where *didn't* I get chimps?"

"I can think of six hundred and eighty three places where you didn't get chimps. And that's just off the top of my head."

"I'm not going to lie to you. I had some made."

"OK that's it. Let me out. Let me out!" I tried to open the door but it was locked.

"Relax. A friend of mine is a geneticist. He owed me a favor."

"So you had him make you some monkeys?"

"Not some—a barrel full."

5
To Each His Own

Martini's ghost disappeared somewhere along the way to Burk's house and my second encounter with a spirit was, on the whole, much more pleasant, and puzzling, than the first.

As we pulled into Burk's driveway I could see that he wasn't joking about the monkeys. There were fourteen windows on the front of his house, and in each one of those fourteen windows was a monkey.

What follows is a description of what those monkeys did as we pulled into the driveway. I refer to each monkey as a he only because I lack the training and sense of smell to distinguish male from female:

Number one had his eyes closed tight and his finger up his nose. He appeared to be tunneling deeper than he had ever dared or dreamed before.

Number two had his lips puckered and was scratching his chin.

Number three was smiling and his eyes were shut. He was possibly stoned.

Number four tentatively sipped a steaming hot cup of something. Maybe coffee, maybe blood.

Number five licked his lips and as much of his face as possible.

Number six rocked back and forth.

Number seven was swaying side to side.

Number eight wore spectacles and made notes in a journal.

Number nine was smoking a pipe and blowing smoke rings.

Number ten was French kissing the window.

Number eleven was knitting a scarf while shaking his head in a disapproving manner.

Number twelve ate a banoonoo while holding a second banoonoo to his head, as if it were a telephone.

Number thirteen was sucking his thumb and falling asleep.

Number fourteen was pressing his cheek and the entire front surface area of his body against the glass.

When the monkeys saw the car pull up—and they all noticed it at the same instant—they all stopped what they were doing, pondered the car, and then became rather excited, all of them jumping up and down and pounding on the glass, engaging in more normal monkey behavior and putting me at ease by doing so. Then Mr. Burk double honked a hello at them and they all disappeared away from the windows and into the house.

"Where'd they go?" I asked, admittedly a little unsettled to see fourteen monkeys act in unison, regardless of what they did.

"You'll see," he said.

The smirk on his face and the wink of his right eye made me think that Mr. Burk had been doing more with those monkeys than sending them back in time. In fact I had a hunch he was training those monkeys to obey his every command, ruling over them with discipline, fear, and rewards. I imagined that as prisoners of their own minds the monkeys didn't realize that monkeys aren't supposed to do things like knit, press their bodies against windows, or act in unison. They had been brainwashed, and Mr. Burk had set himself up as their great leader.

In short, I didn't want to get out of the car.

The walkway from the driveway to the door looked like a one-way trip toward a mad social experiment from which I'd be lucky to escape with my sanity.

"GET OUT OF THE CAR, JOE," yelled Mr. Burk, now outside the car and by the door to his house.

"NO," I yelled back, still in the car and with no intentions of moving.

"IT'S THE MONKEYS, ISN'T IT?" he yelled back.

"YES."

"THEY'RE HARMLESS."

Then the monkey who had been smoking the pipe sauntered out of the house, still smoking, stopped a few feet past Burk on the walkway, did a 360 spin on one leg, did a full split, took the pipe out of his mouth, curtsied, put the pipe back in, and then sauntered back into the house.

"SEE WHAT I MEAN?" shouted Burk, "*HARMLESS.*"

I could have brought up all sorts of arguments that highlighted how, on seeing such things, one should definitely not get out of a car and should in fact lock the doors and curl up into the fetal position. The problem was that all those arguments would have fallen on deaf ears, as Mr. Burk, it was becoming clear to me, was the sort of man who sees monkeys evolving into mutants before his eyes and thinks to himself: harmless.

It was becoming clear to me that Mr. Burk and I were very different kinds of people.

Realizing there was no use arguing with such a man, I decided to get out of the car and go into the house. I was also afraid that if I didn't do so, I would have to watch all fourteen monkeys come out one by one and do their favorite dance moves in an attempt to make me see how *harmless* they were.

So in I went, and what I saw as soon as I stepped through the door was, in a word, horrific.

6
Watt?

That monkeys shouldn't independently form two columns of parallel lines facing each other, all the while standing upright and saluting, goes without saying. That, as two men walk between these columns, the monkeys shouldn't salute the men and then, after the men have passed through, do the Virginia Reel with no musical accompaniment, goes *with* saying AHHHHHHHH!

I'm not sure whether Mr. Burk taught the monkeys to do these strange things, whether they learned them on their own during their forced travels through time, or whether their strange behavior was a side effect of the always muddled cloning process. But what I do know is that what I saw unsettled me. As if the prospect of being the first human to use the WOW device wasn't enough to worry about, the fact that a certain barrel of monkeys who had recently used WOW now acted less like monkeys and more like a confederate military dance troupe on leave from Fort Lalalaloopeepee took that strain to new heights.

Because what if it really was WOW that did that to them? What could I expect it to do to me? Would I end up walking on all fours and flinging feces while the waltzing monkeys looked on disapprovingly? Was that my fate?

No, it wasn't. But all things considered I kind of wish it was.

WOW turned out to be a device that looked a lot like a steering wheel, only smaller, and light enough to make it portable. This enabled a person, any person really, to bop through time almost as easily as one could bop through television stations. You just punch in the date you desire to travel to on the keypad, select an exact location on the GPS screen, put both hands on the wheel, hold it at arms length, press the yellow button, and…foop.

WOW was demonstrated to me by Burk, who opened and closed a couple dozen wormholes of various size in his sitting room, while the monkeys—who must have thought it was time for more trial runs—ran around the room in circles, confused as to which holes they were supposed to go through. One chimp finally gave up, came up to me, stuck out his lower lip, shrugged, and did the Charleston out of the room.

"I'll corner the market with this baby—a WOW in every home. Think of it," said Burk, starry-eyed as he continued to haphazardly pop open wormholes.

"Don't you think that's dangerous?" I asked, ducking under a hole and knowing damn well that it was and worrying what the world would be like if everybody had access to the past.

The thought obviously never crossed Burk's mind, as his response was, "Whaaaaa?"

"In light of POIJO and all," I explained, "people might use their WOWs to do mischief."

He stood up with a shot. "Good God! You're right." He closed all of the remaining wormholes in the room. "Good thinking, Joe. I owe you one."

I was relieved.

Mr. Burk paced. "I got it! We'll put a warning on the box that reads: WARNING: BE NICE WITH WOW."

"Wait, that's it? You're just going to include a warning that says 'Be Nice?'"

"It's all inclusive, Joe. And it relieves us of any liability whatsoever.

Anybody who uses WOW to be anything but nice will be using the product in an inappropriate, unsanctioned manner."

"Oh that's a bunch of bull."

"Is it? Look, see this pen? If I were to take this pen and shove it through your heart, would you be able to sue the pen makers?"

"Well no, but I think this is different."

"It is one and the same! And now, if you'll excuse me for a moment, I need to prepare things for your expedition."

Burk left me alone in his sitting room, and I call it that only because there were about twenty different chairs in there, certainly enough to label the room as a place for sitting, and certainly enough to gather a group of people—or monkeys—together for a meeting, briefing, storytime, or good talking to.

There were also three large bay windows in the room, which looked out onto Mr. Burk's porch and the yard beyond. The porch was enclosed in a glass dome, which allowed it to be air conditioned, which allowed people to actually sit out there and not melt from the constant heat.

It was through the bay windows that I saw Mrs. Burk, Ba Hubba Tree Bob, and one of the monkeys having tea and cake together at a small table. They all wore white bathrobes and slippers and nothing else underneath, which made me wonder what activity they were doing beforehand that put them all into robes, and whether or not they had been doing that activity together, and whether or not that activity broke any laws—of nature. I feared it had.

There was a pot of tea and a small plate of petits fours between the three of them. Ba Hubba had his sleeve rolled up and was admiring his arm which had six watches on it. Mrs. Burk absent mindedly tapped each petit four with a spoon, and the monkey was resting his head on one of his hands and drumming the table with his fingers.

I decided to go out and say hi, hoping that Mrs. Burk would smile at me and then I could smile back, and then she could blush and turn away, and I could look down and bite my lip, and so on and so forth until I too was wearing a white bathrobe.

I found the entrance to the porch, walked up to the table and announced my intentions with a "Hi."

In response to that, the monkey saluted me, Mrs. Burk did a double take, and Ba Hubba put down his tea, got up with his arms outstretched, said, "Ah ha! There you are!" And before I could scream he once again had me in his arms and again I felt wrapped in glowing warmth.

"Together, our beams are twice as bright," he whispered into my ear, my head in his chest hair, before letting me go and returning to his tea.

"Would you like some?" He asked, offering me a cup.

"Sure." A cup of tea sounded pretty good right then. The hot, fragrant liquid, infused with tea leaves from an exotic foreign land. There is a flood of history, from Emperor Shen Nung to the East India Company, in every sip. Unfortunately, the cup I was given wasn't filled with tea. It was unmistakably filled with urine.

"What's wrong?" Asked Ba Hubba when he saw me make the kind of face one makes after he almost drinks someone else's bodily fluids.

"This, sir, is pee pee."

"Of course it is!" he said, "And what of it? Drinking urine is an ancient tradition that has been around for *centuries*. Even today, it's a common practice in many cultures to drink and gargle with urine shortly after intercourse, which is what we're doing now. The flow contains vital chemistry from the sexual organs that your body, dear boy, would do well to retain."

"It's very rejuvenating," said Mrs. Burk before taking a sip.

The monkey raised his cup to me, winked with one of his green eyes, downed the rest of his beverage, and then wiped his lips with the back of his hand.

My mind raced as it tried to figure out which one of them just had sex and supplied the supposed invigorating brew. Was it Mrs. Burk after having sex with Mr. Burk? Ba Hubba and Mrs. Burk? Dear

Lord, was it the monkey!

I put the cup down. "I just came out to say hi."

"Ah simplicity!" said Ba Hubba, "Good, good. What do you call your beam?"

"My *beam*? Well, nothing really. A girl I dated in college called it Chester McThunderstick once."

"No, no, no. You! What is *your* name?"

"Oh. Joe, but some people call me Malarkey."

"Hello, Joe," said Ba Hubba.

"Hello, Malarkey," said Mrs. Burk.

The warmth from Ba Hubba's hug made me forget about Mrs. Burk and the white robes. I wanted to know more about him and why he was always so warm.

"Can I ask you something, Ba Hubba?"

"Of course."

"What's with the watches?"

"Oh these? They're part of my collection."

"Ba Hubba has a sacred collection of wristwatches. It's the largest in the world," said Mrs. Burk with a proud, and possibly turned-on, smirk.

"Guilty!" said Ba Hubba, "To gaze at a watch, one might penetrate the very nature of light and perception. They are instruments of such precision and beauty they transcend themselves. The time they tick off is more real than the time we feel in our bones passing each day. Tell me Joe, and be honest, which one is your favorite?"

He shoved his watch-filled arm in my face.

"Um, I don't know. That one is kind of nice, I guess."

"Ah! He picked the 1940 Panerai!"

Mrs. Burk and Ba Hubba both stomped their feet, wiggled their fingers at each other, and squealed over my pick. It was a neat watch, but I didn't get all the excitement over it. Nor did I really care. The thing didn't even have a second-hand. To avoid a lengthy discussion on watches I quickly changed the subject.

"I also wanted to ask you about The Bright. Is it the sun?"

"The sun?" His eyes lit up. "You mean that thing in the sky that gives us heat and light? The thing that's responsible for all life on earth?"

"Yes. Is that The Bright?"

Ba Hubba gave me a dirty look. "No. Don't be silly. Have you even read my book?"

"No."

"Well then, maybe you should."

"I tried. It didn't work out. Couldn't you just tell me?"

"No. But I could have Watt show you."

"What?"

"Watt."

Watt was the monkey and I suddenly found myself being led out of the porch bubble and into the yard, hand in hand with Watt.

As soon as we left the air conditioning of the porch I started to sweat. It was so hot out that I wanted to let go of Watt's hand and head back inside, but the monkey wouldn't have it. He had a vice grip and instead of allowing me to go back, offered me a handkerchief to wipe the sweat from my forehead. I accepted but only because I was feeling uneasy and slightly fearful for my life, and rightly so. For all I knew, Watt could have been leading me into an ambush by his thirteen friends. Maybe they wanted to grind me up and make me into petits fours for their future teatimes. Maybe they wanted to cut my thumbs off. Or maybe Watt just wanted to lie down and hug a small, grassy mound of earth about the size of Ba Hubba's belly, which he did.

Watt let go of my sweaty hand when we reached the mound, got down on his knees, laid over it and wrapped his arms and legs around the sides. It looked like he was cuddling the ground.

This made me even more uncomfortable. It felt like I was intruding on a private monkey moment and the thought entered my mind that the mound was where Watt's dead mommy was buried. A vision of a small coffin containing a monkey skeleton, its bone hands folded, wearing bifocals and a decayed white dress, and of a picture on that skeleton's chest of a smiling baby Watt sitting in a stroller and sucking his toe, flashed through my mind.

Not knowing what my next move would be—whether to pat Watt on the shoulder or run away and hide behind a bush—I looked back to the porch for some guidance and saw Ba Hubba and Mrs. Burk's robes draped over the chairs, but they themselves were gone. This caused another unpleasant vision to enter my head so I quickly turned back to Watt to erase it, and that's when I noticed there was not one but two mounds in front of me. One was occupied by Watt and the other up for grabs.

All things considered—from going back into the house and possibly seeing a naked Mrs. Burk and a naked Ba Hubba playing musical chairs in the sitting room, to having run-ins with the thirteen other cloned monkeys, to becoming the first human WOW user—I decided to go ahead and join Watt in hugging a mound. He had a peaceful look on his face, as if he was drawing something from the mound that made him feel good, and if that was true I wanted me some of that.

At first I felt nothing. At second I felt nothing. At third I felt a bug on my leg. At fourth I felt nothing. At fifth I felt drool spill out of my mouth. At sixth I felt nothing. At seventh I opened my eyes and saw that Watt was still at peace. At eighth I closed my eyes again and felt nothing. At ninth I began to feel warm. Not the sweating warmth that I had been feeling ever since stepping outside, but a glowing sort of warmth. A warmth that wrapped around me, holding me tight, making me forget where and even who I was. It was as if I was ceasing to be Joe, as if everything that had made me a detached entity—my Joe-ness—was being burned off by the warmth as it flooded in, drawing me out of my body and into something else. Just as I felt I would leave the Joe in me behind forever and go into the something else completely, the warmth was sucked out in a snap and the Joe-ness rocketed back in by a shout from one of the second floor windows. It was Mr. Burk.

"HEY! MALARKEY! WATT! QUIT HUMPING MY LAWN! HUMP EACH OTHER IF YOU WANT TO HUMP SOMETHING!"

7
Malone

After the intrusion, Watt and I laid there for a moment, looking into each other's eyes. Nothing needed to be said for there was an understanding between us. An understanding that Mr. Burk was a cocksucker.

I tried bringing the warmth back in, but it wouldn't work. Every time I closed my eyes all I saw was Watt humping various people and things from the mound to me. Looking at Watt, it appeared he was having similar difficulties with assorted images of me.

So I got up, brushed myself off, and headed back into the house, leaving Watt lying there with his eyes open and his mind possibly contemplating what was the best way to kill Mr. Burk, who sat in the sitting room as I walked in.

"Let's do this," he said, shooting me the double finger guns.

Burk pulled out the picture of him with the broom up his ass and pointed out several clues that led him to calculate the exact date the picture was taken. The first clue was the broom in question, a neon green stick with white bristles that Burk had in his possession for only one year: when he was at Oxford living in the basement of a home owned by a dysfunctional British family. That gave him the year.

Next came the scarf around his neck, that gave him the season (winter), and more precisely post-Christmas winter since the scarf was a holiday present from his lab partner (a short young lady from London who Burk aptly referred to as Lily Oh Lily (but I wouldn't find out how apt it was until later)), and even more precisely the date was January 1st, which was the day after he received the scarf from Lily Oh Lily, just before they counted down to the New Year together over champagne and sausage rolls in the basement. That New Year's morn, as he walked Lily Oh Lily home, was the only time he ever wore the scarf. Not that it was an ugly scarf, mind you, it's just that Mr. Burk thought that scarves made people look, as he put it, "like gift-wrapped blobs of human flesh" and it also had a lot to do with Lily Oh Lily dying a tragic death a few days after giving it to him, and him witnessing it. When I asked him exactly how she died, Burk answered by looking at the ground for a moment before saying, "I forget. The only thing I remember is the blood."

"What about it?"

"It was slippery."

As alarm bells began to blare in my head, he shoved WOW into my hand and began to give me my final instructions.

"The broom incident must have occurred sometime after I got home from dropping Lily Oh Lily off. I'm going to send you to Lily Oh Lily's house. There, you'll locate and follow me home. Don't try to stop the incident from occurring, we want to catch these bastards in the act. When you find those responsible, press this green button. I preprogrammed it to set off an alarm on my watch and also open a wormhole in my bathroom that will connect directly with your location. If you need to use the bathroom at that time you may go through the hole and do so, but be quick about it. Number one is fine. Number two is out of the question. Understood? I'll be sending Malone through to help you at that point as he has extensive training in hog tying."

"Who's Malone?" I asked.

"He's a chimp."

"I don't want to do this."

"Don't be silly."

"Why can't Malone handle it by himself? It sounds like he's a lot more experienced than I am."

"Well, he is. But he's blind."

"Blind! And he can hog-tie?"

"Just be sure to point him in the right direction."

"I don't like this."

"It's sort of like Pin the Tail on the Donkey. Only don't spin him around, because he'll puke."

"No!"

"There's no time for no, Malarkey."

"I don't wanna go. You go!"

"Impossible. I don't want the younger me seeing the now me. Can you imagine what that would do to his morale? And I'd send one of the other chimps back to point Malone in the right direction, but none of the other chimps seem to like Malone very much. He's a loner. And I believe the others, with their primitive minds, fear that his blindness is contagious. Either that or they're sick of being hog-tied by him for no reason. So it's you or no one, and these outrages mustn't continue. They just mustn't." By this point Burk had tears in his eyes and his lower lip was quivering slightly.

"I see," I said, afraid to go against the wishes of a man who knows how slippery his dead girlfriend's blood was, and thus accepting my fate.

8
The Sliding Doors

As I hid behind the bushes of Lily Oh Lily's house, waiting for the two lovers to walk up, I seriously considered smashing WOW into a wide assortment of chunks and fragments and staying in that time indefinitely. Not that that, or any time, is the perfect time to be in. It was just that, all things considered, I'd rather be sitting behind the bushes there forever than have to confront whoever was doing odd things to young Mr. Burk, and no, having Malone on my side didn't change that feeling one bit.

Old Mr. Burk wasn't sure what time he dropped Lily Oh Lily off at her house, just that it was sometime after 8 a.m. To be sure that I didn't miss their arrival, I was sent back to 7 a.m., giving me an hour to set up. Having nothing to set up, and after the desire to smash WOW passed, I decided to have myself a walk around the house to kill some time.

It was a cute little home, very modest in size and veneer, with a small unkempt backyard featuring an overgrown garden, a dirty birdbath with two small birds cautiously dipping their feet into the brown water, and a concrete porch with a sliding glass door leading from it into the house. It was through this door that I saw a most curious site: an old woman, very grandmotherly, sitting in a chair facing the door, looking like a deer caught in the headlights as she gazed out into the direction of the backyard. I say 'in the direction of the backyard' and not 'at the backyard' only because there was something blocking her view, something between her and the sliding glass doors, and that something was the floating bubble of a large wormhole.

Since I had my WOW stored securely in my official WOW Backpack that Burk gave me—the backpack had a caricature of Mr. Burk's smiling face on the back—I knew that I hadn't accidentally opened the hole. It must have come from some other source and there were only two explanations that I could think of for such a thing.

The first was that it was a wormhole created by the Duo in their unending quest to follow me about and quietly watch me go about my work, occasionally snatching my coworkers and frequently offering no clues as to what they were thinking, feeling, or wanted with me. I had dismissed Martini's journal as the work of a deranged mind with no more truth to it than the Book of Light.

I then decided if it was the Duo, they were planning to come through the hole, have a seat somewhere nearby, and stare at me. They had clearly established that as phase 1 of their plan, and it appeared that they hadn't really thought things all the way through and weren't quite sure what phase 2 would be. They may have had phase 3 all laid out (possibly something involving all three of us cuddling on a hammock), but it was the getting there that was the problem.

The second explanation I thought of was that it was created by Mr. Burk's harassers and that they were going to come through, knock Lily Oh Lily's grandmother senseless (Little Red Riding Hood style), dress up in her clothes, stuff her naked body in the closet, and then take Burk by surprise when he came to the door, shove the broom up his ass, and then click!

Unable to decide which was the case without more information, I crept up to the sliding door for a closer look. I had my finger on the green button just in case, because whether it was the Duo or the Harasser who came through, I was operating under the principal of hog-tie first, ask questions later.

But I saw no one come through. What I did see through that worm-hole, however, was someone's small backyard, featuring a well-kept flower garden and a clean birdbath with two birds happily splashing about in the clear water. There was a middle-aged man down on his knees, pulling weeds and whistling a cheerful tune, and it appeared that the sight of this man was what the grandmother was transfixed by. She rose from the chair, opened her arms, and through teary eyes whispered "Joseph."

I thought I had been spotted and immediately hit the deck. After I realized there was no need for me to feel threatened by an elderly woman, and curious to find out how she knew my name, I got up and went through the sliding doors into the house.

"How do you know me?" I asked her.

"Joseph," she whispered, still looking into the hole.

"Yes?"

"Joseph!"

"What!"

"Oh, Joseph!"

"Oh, stop it! What do you want?"

"Joseph," she whispered, "Joseph." She began to advance toward the wormhole, one arm outstretched, the other making a poor attempt at fixing her hair.

"Where are you going?" I asked.

"Joseph."

"Where are you going?" I whispered back.

As I stood there, frozen by this woman who kept whispering my name without looking at me, I watched her go through the wormhole and over to the other side. There the man in the garden stood up, clearly confused by what he was seeing, and he squinted through the sunlight to get a better look. The grandmother walked right up to the confused man, put her arms around him, jumped up and wrapped her legs around his waist, and squeezed.

I took a seat in the old woman's chair and watched this scene, trying to figure out just what was going on and whether it had anything to do with the mission or me.

While the startled man slowly wrapped his arms around grandma, another woman wearing a large sun hat entered the scene. She was about the same age as the man and about the same size as grandma, and she too had a confused look on her face as she pondered the old woman locked in a four-limb embrace of the man.

Since sound doesn't travel through a wormhole I couldn't hear what these people were saying, but could only watch their lips move like in a silent movie. After the young woman shouted something out, the grandmother eased her embrace, slid down the man back onto her feet, and then turned to look at the younger woman. The two women stared at each other, and when the younger one took off her hat and fell to her knees I saw that she looked exactly like a younger version of the grandmother. And when grandma walked over to the young woman, dropped to her knees as well, ran her fingers through the young woman's hair, and smiled, what I was witnessing became clear to me. And it was horrible.

It got even worse when the wormhole suddenly closed. Leaving grandma trapped in the backyard of her past, in the company of her younger self and Joseph, her husband who must have died some years back.

As I sit here now I often try to imagine what happened after that hole closed. Sometimes I see the younger woman killing her older self and feasting on the meat. Other times it's the other way around. Sometimes the man runs off with the grandma, leaving the younger version of his wife alone in the garden. Sometimes the man loses his marbles and joins the birds in the birdbath. Other times all three of them loose their marbles and join the birds in the birdbath. Sometimes the birds don't mind. Other times they do. Still other times they fly into the house and have tea. The possibilities, as always, are endless.

As I sat in the chair looking out into the unkempt garden, pondering over what I just saw, a door somewhere in the house opened, bringing me back to the situation at hand, especially when I heard a familiar man's voice say, "You're sure it doesn't make me look gift-wrapped?"

9
Hot Pursuit

I made it around to the front of the house and back behind the bushes in time to catch a glimpse of Lily Oh Lily. Confirmation that her name was an apt one came when upon seeing her I whispered to myself, "Oh Lily."

If Mrs. Burk was American cheese, Lily Oh Lily was Havarti. So much so that I reconsidered destroying WOW, followed by saving the girl from whatever tragic death was awaiting her, falling in love with her, moving into the little house together, and letting Burk get the broom shoved up his ass for eternity for all I cared—all this from just one look.

But when Lily Oh Lily disappeared behind her front door, after a sweet little kiss on Burk's forehead, the feeling that had swept over me so quickly and so strongly faded just as quickly, as just one look may be enough for a guy to reconsider the path he's taking, it's not enough for him to go down a new one. If she had perhaps lingered a bit longer, maybe twirled around a couple times, played with her hair, giggled, or bit her lip, giving me more to go ga-ga over than just a look and a peck, then things might have gone differently. And perhaps on some other timeline things did go differently. Perhaps, as I write this, another manifestation of me is kissing Lily Oh Lily's stomach, lying in bed, while she wonders what the hell ever became of grandma. If only we could see all the possible paths in front of us and choose which one we want to take instead of merely stumbling down the first one that comes our way. But we can't. So enough.

After Lily Oh Lily shut the door, Young Mr. Burk did an about-face, sighed, and then marched off down the walkway and onto the sidewalk. I allowed him to get a reasonable distance from me before emerging from the bushes and beginning my hot pursuit. It turned out that the young Mr. Burk was a much faster walker than I had reckoned, and I ended up having to speedwalk to keep up with him.

After tailing him for only two blocks, and as I began to break a sweat, a bicycle built for two pulled up along side me in the street. At first I didn't bother to turn and have a look at the riders, I was too intent on keeping Burk in my sights. But after more than the reasonable time needed for a bicycle to pass a pedestrian went by, I glanced to my left to see what the situation was and found it to be the sort of situation, a familiar one to me, where the Duo is staring at me.

With Nibbles in front acting solely as navigator, since his feet did not reach the peddles, and Boogedy in back acting as motor, they, my old friends, had matched my speed and both of them had their heads turned to stare.

"I don't have time for this," I whispered to them. The strange thing about whispering is that once you start doing it, it's difficult to stop.

They stared at me some more. Then they turned and stared at each other for a bit, possibly exchanging a look that said, "Why is he whispering?" Then, as they returned their stares to me, they increased their speed and passed me, making their way ahead towards Burk.

It was at that moment that it suddenly dawned on me that maybe phase 2 of the Duo's scheme was something along the lines of shoving a broom up Mr. Burk's ass. This dawning caused my eyes to bulge and my legs to pick up the pace quite a bit. I also fumbled around my backpack for WOW as I trotted, wanting to be prepared if it became apparent that I would need to summon Malone.

When the Duo drew even with young Mr. Burk, both of their heads turned and they stared at him as they had done to me, but they also reached out toward Mr. Burk and began to grope about in the air for him. This, understandably, irked young Burk, and he showed it by walking closer to the far edge of the sidewalk and by greatly increasing his pace, so much so that I had to break from trot and shift fully into run. This gave me all sorts of problems getting WOW out, as the backpack was not designed to be a holster. Since it was slowing me down I decided to abandon getting WOW out, and focus on keeping up with Burk instead, who by then had begun to sprint. His sprinting was a very rigid affair, with arms at right angles and pumping, chin up, hands in karate chop position for maximum aerodynamics, knees high, and breathing exaggerated.

As the Duo increased their speed, the old bicycle they rode began to rattle and soon after, wobble. The whole thing didn't look very stable, and by the looks on the Duo's faces, they knew that their situation was desperate. Desperate times call for desperate acts, and for the Duo this meant doing something I hadn't seen them do until then—talk.

Or, I assume they tried to talk. But since I couldn't understand a single sound that came out of their mouths I can't be sure. They moaned, beeped, hissed, screamed, spit, sucked, stuck their tongues out, yawned, grunted, o'd, ah'd, ee'd, la la la'd, and shrieked, all the while waving their arms wildly and causing the bicycle to swerve back and forth.

There was a consistent pattern to their ravings, but that doesn't mean they were speaking. I had an uncle who could belch in a consistent pattern, even to the beat of any song you named, but while he was doing so, no one ever said to me, "You'd better listen to what your Uncle's telling you." Of course he also really wasn't my uncle, we just called him uncle, which in itself is reason enough not to listen to him.

So the Duo made their sounds and waved their arms and before I could get any meaning out of it, young Mr. Burk veered off the sidewalk and headed up a driveway toward a house, while the Duo, watching Burk run off, ran into a parked car at full speed, throwing both of them from the bicycle. Nibbles landed quite violently into a trashcan while Boogedy ended up lying quite awkwardly on top of another parked car on the opposite side of the street.

As I, out of breath, made my way up the driveway, I saw that though Nibbles and Boogedy were not in good shape, they were alive. Boogedy was still on top of the car, but had gotten up on his knees, his head still resting on the car. Nibbles' feet stuck out of the trashcan, and kicked the air.

Meanwhile, Burk had gone into the house and slammed the door shut.

I crept up to one of the house's front windows and peeked through. Young Mr. Burk was being led down a hallway by an older man into what appeared to be a closet. The older man had his back to me so I couldn't identify him. All I saw was his jet black hair and the broom in his hand.

I was actually relieved at that sight since it meant that my work was done and Malone's work had begun. I took out WOW and simply pressed the green button, creating a wormhole a few feet from the front door. And, just as old Mr. Burk promised, through the hole came Malone, a fairly old chimp wearing dark sunglasses, holding a long lassoed rope, and in a rather blasé mood if you ask me.

Leaving the hole open for a quick escape, I opened the front door, moved aside and whispered, "OK Malone, go do it."

He didn't budge.

"Malone. Straight ahead. Go hog-tie."

Nothing.

"Malone? Malone? MALONE!"

I grabbed him by the shoulders and shook him a bit, hoping that would give him a jumpstart. It didn't. He shrugged, sat down, and lit up a cigarette. I gazed at that blind, insubordinate, smoking monkey and tried to make sense of my situation. Couldn't. Sat down next to Malone. Gladly accepted the cigarette offered to me. And smoked.

And I would have been happy sitting there all day, smoking with

Malone, but we were interrupted by the old Mr. Burk, who stuck just his head through the wormhole. He was smoking a pipe, and he took a few puffs while he surveyed the scene. So there we were—me, a monkey, and Mr. Burk's head, all lounging around and having ourselves a nice smoke.

"This won't do, Joe," Burk finally whispered. "You have to lead him. Hold his hand and walk him in. And you can't just say, 'Malone, go do it.' You need to say, 'Malone, *magic time*.' Just like that."

"Hold his hand?" I whispered back. "Well, why don't I just do the hog-tying for him! And why didn't you tell me about *magic time* before?"

"I forgot. Why are you whispering?"

"I don't know."

"Me neither. I think I'm only doing it because you're doing it."

"That's possible."

"Then we're agreed. I'll leave you to it."

Then Burk pulled his head back through the wormhole only to pop it right back out to whisper, "Do you need to use the bathroom?"

I did kind of have to go, but then I thought about Ba Hubba's tea party and decided to hold it.

"No thank you," I said.

"Are you sure? It's not good to hold it in."

"I don't have to go."

"Sometimes people don't even realize they have to go. Take when you go to the doctor's and he has you go in the cup. A lot of times you think there's no way you're going to be able to go in that cup. But somehow you do. The stuff was in there the whole time. Just sitting inside you, a pool of festering sewage, and you had no idea. Totally oblivious."

"I'm fine."

"I just don't see how you can be sure unless you try."

"Leave me alone! I don't want you drinking my pee!"

Mr. Burk's jaw dropped.

"Drink? Your *pee*? Oh that hurts, Joe," whispered Burk, "That was totally uncalled for, and I hate you."

A somber Burk pulled his head back through the wormhole. I can't say I was sorry. I had far too many public run-ins with bodily fluids recently. As if the world was trying to take one of humanity's many dirty secrets and rub it in my face. Frequently reminding me that soap, deodorant, and locked bathroom doors can only hide the truth—that at my most basic level, I am a filth factory. Sucking in everything that this world has to offer and spiting it back out as steaming piles of filth.

Burk's wormhole shut, leaving me alone with Malone. Or so I thought, and was wrong in thinking so, because Malone wasn't sitting next to me anymore. He was down the driveway, enthusiastically hog-tying a rather bloody and somewhat limp Nibbles.

Across the street lay a perfectly tied up Boogedy, looking at me with a rather perplexed expression on his face as if to say, "Just what the fuck did I do to deserve this? Nibbles, yes. I can see why Nibbles. But me, Joe? ME?"

Malone wasn't even breaking a sweat as he put the finishing touches on Nibbles. And when he had finished, Malone took a seat on the hog-tied Nibbles, lit up another cigarette, gave Nibbles a quick drag, and, with his legs crossed, calmly puffed away while I watched, wishing I was as smooth as that monkey, while realizing how unsmooth it was to wish to be a monkey.

10
Magic Time

As I walked back up the driveway, for the first time in many years I thought about my father. What would he think if he saw me now, I thought? Would he approve of his son? Would he be able to look underneath the surface and see something more than just a man walking hand in hand with a monkey? Or would he look past me completely and only see two strange men in the distance, hog-tied and flopping about on the pavement like fish out of water? Could he black out the world around me, place me in a dimly light void, and smile?

As I pondered this, Malone farted and I decided that no, no he probably wouldn't have been able to do that.

Malone and I were still holding hands as we entered the house, and I must admit that if I had closed my eyes I wouldn't have been able to tell the difference between Malone's hand and a man's hand. Not in the texture of the skin, the firmness of the grip, nor the warmth of the blood running through it could I detect a difference. Somehow, I always thought I would be able to detect at least a small difference.

When Malone and I reached the hallway by the kitchen I could hear two distinct but similar voices coming from the closet:

"Couldn't we use something smaller?"

"Like what?"

"Like a pencil or one of those hotdogs we used to stuff up my nose."

"They just don't send the same message you know?"

"I suppose you're right."

"Of course I am. Ready?"

"OK. Nice and easy now, easy, easy, EASY!"

I was only a few feet from the partially opened door to the closet and I was trying to get Malone in position without having to lead him there by hand. I wanted Malone in between me and whoever was in there. So I turned the blind chimp sideways, and using both hands I tried to push him down the hall. But Malone wouldn't budge. He even smacked my hands away and spit on me. So I put my shoulder up against him as if he was a football sled and, using my hips, he slowly began to move. It wasn't easy, especially with Malone pushing against me and then pounding on my back, but I did eventually win out and get him in front of the door. Then I simply stepped back and whispered, "Magic time."

Malone nodded, pushed open the door, strutted in, and then shut the door behind him. After that I thought I would hear all sorts of scuffle sounds mixed in with monkey shrieks and cries for help. But there was none of that. There was only a distressing silence, the kind that settles in when something you had thought was infallible—such as your favorite sports star, your country, your church, or Malone—fails.

Fearing that was the case, I pulled out WOW and slowly backed away from the closet, positioning myself in a better position to make my cowardly escape if need be.

The closet door creped opened, and out came Mr. Burk. Only it wasn't the young Mr. Burk I had followed to the house, and it wasn't the old Mr. Burk who had recently asked me if I needed to use his bathroom. This was a Mr. Burk somewhere in between those two. It was Middle Burk.

"Mr. Burk?" I asked, just in case I was looking at a man that looked remarkably similar to Mr. Burk but was actually merely a Mr. Burk impersonator. He had the same intense green eyes, but something was different about them.

"Hello, Joe."

"What's going on? Why are you here? Where are Malone and young Mr. Burk?"

"They're right here."

Malone came out, followed by young Mr. Burk. The three of them stood next to each other, with Malone smoking, young Mr. Burk leaning on a broom, Middle Burk leaning against the wall, and all three of them looking at me.

I was confused and intimidated by this trio—first The Duo, now, The Trio—and the only thing I felt capable of doing was rubbing my eyes and doing double takes over and over again until they went away.

"Er, right. So this is the part where I scream, is it? Fine then."

I screamed until my lungs gave out while the Trio looked on disinterestedly. I thought that screaming would help. It didn't. So I blinked a few times and then decided to leave.

I pushed the green button on WOW again and the wormhole leading to Mr. Burk's bathroom opened up to my right. I planned on jumping through and shutting the hole behind me, but Old Mr. Burk's head poked out and got in my way.

"Changed your mind did you?" he said, "It's perverse to hold it in, Joe—perverse and foolish."

"I don't have to pee. I have to escape."

"Escape what?"

He followed my outstretched arm to see the two younger Mr. Burks and Malone standing together.

Old Burk's mouth dropped open and his face quickly went from shock to anger. "You!"

"That's right!" Middle Burk shouted back, defiantly sticking out his chest and lifting up his chin.

"How dare you? How? Answer me!" demanded Old Burk.

"How? How do you think? WOW! That's how!" said Middle Burk as he revealed a WOW from behind his back.

Old Burk smacked the top of his head and let his hand run down his face. "I see."

He stepped out of the wormhole. "So that's how it's gonna be, eh boys? Stealing? Betrayal? Cahoots? Fine! Joe, give me WOW."

I did.

Old Burk gave the other two Burks a rather menacing look. "This ends now."

The look was enough to send the Young Burk into hysterics. He karate chopped the air in front of him wildly. "You stay away from me, you maniac. You beast! Stay back! I'm warning you!"

Middle Burk, unfazed, used his WOW to open a wormhole behind them.

Old Burk raised a fist shaking with anger. "I will not stay away. I will hit you!"

"You wouldn't dare!" cried Young Burk, now beet red, sobbing, and still karate chopping the air, though admittedly with less gusto.

Middle Burk grabbed Young Burk by the shoulders and dragged him back toward his wormhole as he said, "See what you've done? You ruin everything! You're the plague!"

"Oh that is IT!" Old Burk was livid by this point. "I am so mad! I can't even think straight! I will hit you BOTH!"

"He's serious!" cried Young Burk.

"I'll protect you," swore Middle Burk.

"You will feel the back of my hand! Charrrrrrge!" trumpeted Old Burk as he went after them.

"Run, you fool!" screamed Middle Burk as he pulled Young Burk through the wormhole.

Old Burk continued screaming with his fist raised as he went through after them. Then, with a shrug directed toward me, Malone followed them through the wormhole, leaving me alone in the hallway.

What I did next baffles me. I had three options. I could have stayed put and courted Lily Oh Lily as I had considered earlier.

I could have gone back to my time through the wormhole into Mr. Burk's bathroom and then joined in with Ba Hubba's and Mrs. Burk's naked games.

Or I could do what I did: closed my eyes, screamed, and charged in after all four of them.

Part 3

Now

1
Butt Tappin'

After stepping through the wormhole I found myself in a very strange place, and very much alone.

As the wormhole diddled away behind me I looked around and saw no trace of the three Burks, of Malone, or of anyone else. My surroundings were unlike anything I had ever seen, both for what I saw and what I didn't see.

There were some plants scattered about, but they were different than the usual types I was used to having scattered about, so they only made feel more lost.

There were also quite a few kinds of birds flying overheard, all unfamiliar to me, and they appeared to rule the skies and land below. They glided around in circles, swooping down every now and then to get a better look at something, with no apparent fears or cares about what other animals might think of them. The fact that they took no notice whatsoever of my presence there, not even a glance in my direction, kind of ticked me off. There I was, watching them in awe for quite some time. Couldn't they in turn at least find me interesting enough for a mere swoop or two? Would it kill them?

I decided that maybe a change of position was needed to get their attention.

I took six steps forward and stopped. Looking back at where I had been, I couldn't see why it was any worse than where I was now. So I took six steps back. Looking around, as far as my eyes could see, there was no place better or worse than where I was right then. I was pretty much in an open field, so the birds couldn't use the excuse that I was in a blind spot.

I considered sitting down, and even went as far as bending my knees a little, but stopped short when it dawned on me that if I sat down the birds might mistake me for a big rock. So I straightened up to my full height and raised my arms high above my head, hoping that the extra inches would make all the difference.

As the minutes went by, and the blood slowly drained out of my arms, I began to think of matters other than getting the birds to acknowledge my existence.

From the looks of things, I decided that I had traveled mind bogglingly far back into the past and was now on an African savannah. This was a rather bold assumption on my part seeing as I'd never been mind bogglingly far back in the past, nor had I ever been anywhere near an African savannah. Oh, I've seen pictures of savannahs, including the documentary at Shamash, but nothing like this. This seemed to go on forever. No fences, buildings, or masses of people anywhere in site.

There was, and still is, a forest of sorts behind me, but that doesn't qualify as a boundary in my mind. The forest will let you come and go as you please, a fact that I've taken advantage of quite a bit since I've been here, but a boundary, such as a brick wall or a fire breathing duck, won't.

Just like with the savannah, calling this a forest is a bold assumption, but it's the only word I can think to describe what I see. I suppose people once had hundreds of words to describe what I'm looking at, people who came in contact with these sorts of places all the time. But those people were long gone when I was born and are a long ways off as I sit here now. So forest and savannah it is.

As I stood there, I began to notice that the savannah was an unnaturally wide open thing, and I soon became nauseous just looking out into it. The flat land stretched out into infinity, and the sky paralleled it overhead. My mind was having serious problems grasping something so vast, so much so that my head started to spin and, despite my earlier fears, I had to sit down and look at the ground to keep from fainting. Luckily, while I did this I happened to notice some dried-out twigs lying around me. This gave me an idea for a project.

Using craft skills I acquired in 3rd grade (thank you, Sister Bernard!) along with the twigs and some grass, I constructed a rectangle, approximately twenty-seven inches along its diagonal. My brain breathed a sigh of relief as I looked up from the ground and out into the savannah, only this time I looked through the rectangle. It was just like looking at a framed painting, or at TV, and that was something I could handle. Handle, that is, until a rather large animal entered my rectangle in the distance.

I suppose it could have been a rhinoceros, although I could have sworn that a guy at the zoo once said that a rhino absolutely, positively would never, *ever* charge a human unless it was provoked through excessive taunting.

This one was charging me before I even had a chance to wave hello to it.

Hoping to scare it away, I threw the twig rectangle in its general direction, and then took off in a mad dash for the forest. I did a lot of zigzagging and stutter stepping as I ran, as if the rhino had a rifle and was trying to keep me in its sights. All this did was allow the rhino to close the gap between us a bit quicker, and before I was even out of breath it was only a few feet behind me.

Strangely, the rhino never got closer than this. It continued to pursue me until I was well into the forest, but it never skewered me with its horn, even though it easily could have. I guess it just wanted me off the savannah, probably so that the birds would have a better chance of acknowledging *his* existence.

As I caught my breath and watched the rhino walk away in a huff, an odd feeling came over me. I felt...normal. Almost as if I was standing on a busy city street. When I looked up I saw why. The trees, boulders, rivers, and general undergrowth of the forest were filling in nicely for the skyscrapers, cars, streets, and people I was used to encountering.

There was, in fact, so much going on around me that I'd have to have the patience and dedication of an entomologist to describe it all. I don't, so why don't I pick one element of the forest and do a real bang-up job on that, and let you fill in the rest using your imagination or, if you want to be really accurate about it, a child's picture book on forests. But even that isn't necessary because I'm sure you know what a forest is, even if you've never seen a proper one in person. When you see the word 'forest' on the page you don't picture a black void in your mind, do you? And when I write 'I'm on a savannah' you don't picture me in your backyard using your grandmother's stomach as a trampoline, do you? Because if you do, then no matter how much I go into detail about what the savannah looks like, it's not going to do much more than confuse you further, so I might as well just say it's a savannah and a forest and leave the rest to you.

Except for the monkeys, they need explaining.

No more than a few minutes after I first entered the forest, as I looked up into the trees, did I come across the monkeys when one shat on my head. This moment, as innocent as it may seem, became the cornerstone of my life here.

When I looked up through the warm feces in my eyes, I saw a small monkey, no bigger than a common cat with arms longer than its body and a tail that curled into a question mark, sitting on a low branch and looking back down at me. And I swear that monkey was laughing.

As if that wasn't enough, it apparently found the sight of me so hilarious that it couldn't contain itself and had to jump up and down and point at me with excitement.

Something happened inside me as I was taunted by that monkey. A haze was lifted from my mind and it was like I woke up from a long sleep that had lasted since I was a child and found that my pajamas, my bed, and my entire bedroom were wet with urine, and the urine wasn't all mine.

The monkey kept laughing and pointing, the feces kept running down my face, and the anger I suddenly had at myself and at almost everybody I had ever met or even seen, quickly consumed me. I grabbed a handful of the crap from my cheek, looked at it for a moment, squeezed it, let it run through my fingers, and promptly lost my mind.

I screamed at the monkey and threw its feces back at it. When I ran out of that, I pulled down my pants and shat right there for the sole reason of getting more ammo. The monkey, however, loved every bit of it, and this caused me to go even further over the edge. I tried to scamper up the tree but my climbing skills weren't up to the task. So I looked around for something more substantial than poo to throw, and that's when I saw one of his friends in a tree a few feet behind me.

This other monkey was hugging the trunk of a tree, tapping the ground with its butt as if testing the water in a hot tub. Up above it, sitting in the branches of the surrounding trees, was a multitude of monkeys, all looking down at the butt tapper in silence.

It felt like I was about to witness something *big*. Whenever a hushed crowd watches one of its own do something, you know one of two things. Either something monumental is about to happen, like man walking on the moon for the first time, or something incredibly stupid, like man doing the moonwalk dance for the first time.

I was curious as to which it was, so I temporarily forgot about my rampage and settled in to watch.

A few more butt taps, and then, as the monkey switched to using one of his toes to test the ground, I realized just what it was that I was witnessing and that it was possibly both the most monumental *and* incredibly stupid thing in the history of the Earth. It was like man stepping onto the surface of the moon for the first time for the sole purpose of doing the moonwalk on it.

I was witnessing a monkey, *the* monkey, the first one to come down

out of the trees. I could draw a line, albeit a rather twisty turny one, directly from him touching his butt to the ground to me standing there watching him do so.

The entire history of mankind, at least what I could remember of it from school and TV, flashed before my eyes. Admittedly, most of what I saw involved me jerking off in the bathroom, but there was also a lot of stuff about wars, scientific achievements, and classic sports bloopers in there as well.

Once again the haze, which had briefly settled back in, was lifted and I promptly re-lost my mind.

There was a hefty stick laying nearby, perfectly suited for wielding, so I picked it up, screamed like a Highlander, and charged at the intrepid monkey. The chimp scurried up the tree well before I got there and I was left with nothing to beat with my stick besides the tree trunk, which I pounded on mercilessly.

As I screamed and beat the tree I swore that none of those monkeys would ever touch the ground. Not on my watch.

When I began this rampage, many months ago, only one or two monkeys would shimmy down each day. It was really quite easy to scare them out of their wits with a good shout or mighty swipe of my stick, which always sent them shooting back up into the canopy. I would see one of them hanging onto the bottom of a tree, tapping the ground with one toe, their butt, sometimes even their head, and off I'd go. I would run toward the monkey, shouting like a father or mother would do as they ran after their child as he peddled his bike into the path of a runaway boulder. It was just enough work for one man to do and still have enough time left over to eat three times a days, to bathe, and to throw things at the rhino from a considerable distance.

But as the weeks went by, more and more monkeys tried to shimmy their way down each day, and often I was confronted with a forest full of toe and butt tapping apes. On those days I was forced to patrol from sunrise to sunset, and I would often spend hours on end running from tree to tree, beating monkeys back with my stick. When I got too tired to run I sat down and threw rocks at them until I caught my breath. Other days only one or two would attempt the descent, giving me a much needed rest.

Overall, the work to be done is far too much for one man, but try as I might I can't bring myself to abandon it. Like an executioner who begins the unsettlingly quick process of putting a man to death, I feel an obligation to see this thing through to the end. Because once you start something like this, even if you have a sudden change of heart when the smell of roasting flesh wafts up your nose, you can't stop until it's finished. If you don't, you'll only leave behind a screaming patty melt for some other poor sap to finish off. And right now I'm the only poor sap around.

At night, while the monkeys sleep under the moonlight, the goats appear. They don't look exactly like any goat I ever saw, and they're certainly much bigger than I thought a goat could get, but they still look like goats to me. They stroll into the forest well after sunset to lick the slime that forms on the tree trunks. After seeing them do this, and do so with gusto, I gave the tree goo a try and found it to be much more disgusting than I imagined possible. It wasn't so much the taste as the texture, which, regrettably, I can only compare to mucus. After gagging a few times, and throwing up in my mouth once, I was able to eventually get the stuff down, and thus ward off starvation.

This is what my life has become. Slime for dinner, and nothing but goats and monkeys to keep me company.

2
Channel Surfing

With my schedule so full, time went by quickly, with no change in my state of mind or daily life until the wormholes started to appear.

At first there was just one. It floated by while I rested against a tree one afternoon, and in it I saw a man and woman, both wearing large white wigs, staring back at me in mouth gaping astonishment. They were Victorian, and I suppose the sight of a man wearing dirty, tattered clothes, holding a large stick, and covered in monkey crap, was quite a shock to them.

Just as the woman fainted and the man gulped back a mouthful of vomit, the wormhole disappeared.

I quickly looked around to see if I could find the source of the hole, expecting to see one or more of the Mr. Burks running about with a WOW in hand. But there was no one.

That night I saw four more wormholes floating around the goats. Through the holes I saw rain falling on a pond, a volcano erupting, wind blowing through a cornfield, and two large turtles humping. There was still no sign of the Burks, or of anything else that could have caused the holes to appear. So I decided that they must be forming on their own, just like the mild blips within localized loop-dee-loops.

Within a few days, just like the monkeys with their tapping, the forest was full of wormholes. There were so many that I had to tiptoe around them to get at the monkeys. And then their numbers went down again, to the point where there are only a few each day.

On days when it's raining, while the monkeys stay under cover of the leaves, I often pass the time by zoning out and gazing through the various holes, if there happen to be any around at the time. When one disappears or becomes too boring, I simply turn my head toward another. It's like watching a parade of televisions march by.

I suppose I could go through one of the holes, find one leading to a more modern time and escape into it. But it's impossible for me to choose one. Most of them are nice to look at, even dream about, but I can't picture myself in any of them. Look, there's a family sitting down to dinner in Italy. What would I do there? Walk right in, push junior out of his chair, sit down, and ask someone to pass the mozzarella? Or look over there, there's a child playing with a poodle. Should I just hop in, pick up the poodle or maybe the child, and run? Just what would I do in those worlds besides muck them up? As my dad once said, "While the grass may often indeed be greener on the other side, it doesn't mean you should go over there and take a crap on it."

So I think I'll stay put. I can take a crap here just fine.

3
No matter where I go, there I am

I actually saw myself come through a wormhole one morning. That was a bit disturbing.

For a brief moment I thought that it was only someone who looked a lot like me and not actually me. The man was at least ten years younger than I am now and, I thought, much uglier than me. His nose was too big for his face, his eyes too far apart, and his ears just looked plain silly. But then he made a facial expression I know for a fact I made quite often because I caught myself in the mirror making that faces countless times. It involves raising one eyebrow, poking the tongue slightly out the corner of the mouth, and bunching up the nostrils. I tend to do that when I'm pondering something, reading a book, and jerking off.

The realization that I was quite hideous came as a bit of a shock. I'd always thought that my facial features were in perfect proportion, forming a Golden Triangle that people immediately found pleasing to look at. But I never spent much time looking at myself in the mirror (vanity, vanity), so I suppose it was really more of an assumption that I was beautiful.

The assumption was terribly wrong. I am quite ugly.

My revolting self cautiously tiptoed out of the wormhole, looked around rather nonchalantly, didn't notice his hideous double sitting under a tree nearby, sniffed the air, sniffed his armpit, sniffed the air again, and then went back through the wormhole, which disintegrated soon after.

So it seems that the random wormholes that have become a part of my environment are also appearing in other times and places that I've been. My past self must have stumbled upon one and gone through to investigate. I'm impressed with myself for having the courage to do such a thing at one time, as I sit here now unable to do so.

As I watched myself tiptoeing back through the wormhole, I considered going through to see what he was up to, but upon quick reflection, decided that chances were my self either wasn't up to anything of interest or was up to no good, and that I was better off on my own.

The wormholes must be causing all sorts of chaos in other times, with some people disappearing through them forever, others proclaiming that the end of the world must be near, and all wondering what could be causing such a thing. That, combined with the mild blips within localized loops, must have many people proclaiming that the world is about to end. Of course, this is only another assumption on my part. But if people nearly lose their minds when the TV goes on the fritz, I think it's a safe assumption to make that things would be worse when space-time gets fuzzy.

The mild blips happen here as well, with both the monkeys and I getting stuck in them from time to time. Once I was stuck in a loop of waking up and going right back to sleep for what seemed like hours and which I hoped would last forever. It was as if reality was playing peek-a-boo with my dreams.

4
Busy, Busy, Busy

The Duo arrived shortly after I saw how ugly I am. Things have changed between us.

They now have little time to sit around staring at me, and the strange thing is that sometimes I wish they would, especially now that I'm doing something that actually merits being stared at.

Look at me, damn you!

I feel like a child whose parents are too busy to watch him do something he feels is monumentally important, such as bend over and smack his own butt from behind.

They're far too busy working on what appears to be a rather ambitious project on the savannah to pay me much attention. This made me think that they're project was more important than mine, so I've begun to pay less attention to the monkeys and more attention to them as of late.

They're building what looks to be a factory or possibly a whole complex of interlocking factories. It's all coming together with astonishing speed, but whatever it is, it's humongous and it looks like it will take many months to complete. And whatever it's for, it must be important. I can't imagine they'd go to all this trouble for a mall.

The materials and supplies for the building have been coming out of the biggest wormhole I've ever seen. You could fit a house through this thing. It only opens for a few seconds every so often—just long enough for it to spit out a junkyard full of materials.

I think that Boogedy and Nibbles are the chief architects of the project, because they seem to do nothing but monitor the work being done, frequently consulting what appear to be elaborate holographic blueprints. The actual manual labor is being done by an army of silver robots.

These robots come in a wide assortment of shapes and sizes and a comprehensive list of them follows. I've broken them up into four categories for classification purposes, and within each category there is some degree of variety in size and disposition:

Humanoids — these stoic tin men are the foremen of the crew. They spend their days monitoring the other robots, making repairs to them as needed, and dishing out beatings when appropriate. Yesterday I saw one chase down a smaller Orb robot, catch it, and then pound it into a smoldering pile of scrap metal with a hammer.

Orbs — these happy-go-lucky robots are pretty much just shiny metal balls with arms. They float around the worksite making pleasant chirping sounds, similar to but not exactly like a bird. Their main purpose seems to be to supply the other robots with tools and materials and to move the stationary Cylinder robots from area to area. The Humanoid that beat the orb yesterday actually got the hammer from another passing Orb. This leads me to believe that the Orbs are not yet unionized.

Cylinders — these diligent robots generally stay put, mainly because they have no legs or wheels to move about with, and they can't fly like the Orbs. They do the actual labor—the welding, screwing, stacking, fitting, and securing, as well as the chopping, cutting, digging, exploding, and imploding. Their tops open up to allow as many as six mechanical arms come out, and the Orbs keep those arms constantly supplied with various tools.

Miniatures — these teeny weenie robots come in all shapes and sizes, and outnumber all of the other robots combined. They hop around the worksite making cute beeping and humming sounds, while flashing their multicolored lights. What purpose they serve—besides adding an air of bubbly insanity to the project—is beyond me.

Desperate for companionship, I tried to befriend one of the Miniatures last week.

It was a triangular little thing with a spring on its bottom and a light bulb at its tip that changed color with its mood. The little guy had hopped off alone near the edge of the forest. He looked lost as he frantically chirped and hopped around in a circle, so I figured he would welcome a friendly face.

I approached it slowly, with both of my hands open and clearly visible. I even said soothing things to it.

"Hey guy. Hey big guy. Are you lost? Don't worry. Joe will take care of you. Joe is your friend. That's right...friend. FFFFFFriend. FFFFFFFFFFFFFFFFFF..."

The encounter ended with the Miniature hopping away chirping bloody murder.

Assuming that Miniatures were simply standoffish by nature, I tried this same approach with an Orb a few days later, hoping that their kind were more open to the idea of making friends.

It smacked me across the face with the back of its hand.

Later, assuming that Orbs were simply assholes by nature, I approached a Cylinder in the same manner.

It threw rocks at me until I was able to run out of its range, which incidentally turns out to be about one hundred yards.

Finally, assuming that Cylinders were afraid of commitment, I went for broke and approached a Humanoid in the same manner described

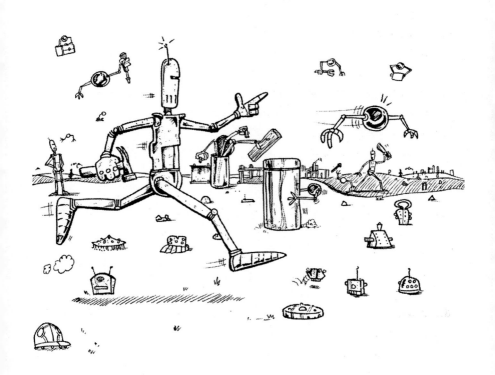

above, hoping that inside its Humanoid form there was some humanoid understanding and emotion.

There wasn't.

My few steps forward quickly turned into a few steps backward when the Humanoid brandished its wrench in what could and should be construed as a threat.

My few steps backward then quickly turned into an all-out sprint when the Humanoid lunged after me. And this, as my lungs gave out on me, quickly turned into defensive fetal position under a tree which certainly would have turned me into a pulp of wrench-bashed flesh if it weren't for the Humanoid suddenly becoming unable to move his arms and legs.

It wasn't an act of God that saved me, it wasn't a power failure, and it certainly wasn't sudden compassion from the Humanoid either.

It was a hog-tying monkey named Malone.

5
Ape Hooky

From the moment he mysteriously arrived, Malone has been a good friend to me. I'd even rank him up there as one of my best friends ever, and seeing as how he can't talk and how he has a tendency to hog-tie anything, animal or robotical, who comes within five feet of my face (regardless of their intentions), that says a lot about what I look for in a friend.

Now, whenever I chase the monkeys he'll lurk around nearby and hog-tie any that get away from me—an occurrence that is becoming more and more frequent as more monkeys join the daily toe-tapping crowd and as I spend less time tending to them.

I really don't know how I ever got on without Malone, and I love him to death, but I'm not sure if his hog-tying method is the best choice for this activity. Because once a monkey is hog-tied, there's the issue of what to do with it. You can't just leave it there, because it'll certainly die within a few days and start to rot. And that would make for an unacceptable work environment.

And you can't simply untie the monkey bundle because it will, without fail, bite you as you're doing the untying. I know this because I tried. And Malone won't untie them because as good as he is at hog-tying he's just as horrible at hog-untying.

To solve this problem I developed a new sport called Ape Hooky.

The object of Ape Hooky is to hook a hog-tied monkey on a tree branch. This is accomplished by repeatedly throwing the bundled monkeys up into the trees until they get hooked on a limb, just like a grappling hook. It usually takes three or four throws, and the less attempts, the more points you get. A hook in one try is called a Popper, in two tries it's a Duce Clip, in three it's just a Hook, and anything over that is a Ba-Cha-Ca-Loop.

Challenges to overcome include, but are in no way limited to, the variable weight of the monkeys, the screaming of the monkeys during the windup and release, sore shoulders, avoiding chimps as they plummet to the ground after a miss, and Malone trying to distract you whenever it's your turn.

The great thing about the game is that once a monkey is hooked on a limb the other monkeys will eventually untie their hog-tied friends, so there's no dead monkeys to worry about.

The untied monkeys are also usually so traumatized by the whole ordeal that they won't attempt to shimmy back down the trees for a good month, preferring instead to spend their days wobbling along the tree limbs, stopping every few feet to gather themselves.

And that does wonders for my workload.

6
Yesterday's Ghosts

"Do you see that, Malone?"

I asked, but of course he didn't. I was hoping that he could at least feel, or sense, what I was seeing, but that's only because at first I thought I was seeing something that could be sensed. I thought that I was looking at two ghosts who were chasing and hog-tying a multitude of ghost monkeys.

The thing that separated these ghosts from the other ghosts I had seen was that one of them looked an awful lot like me, and the other looked an awful lot like Malone.

Now, I knew that I wasn't dead, and Malone looked absolutely robust sitting next to me, so I wondered how this could be. To be sure I felt my pulse—it was still blurping away. I felt Malone's pulse—it too was blurping. I pinched myself—didn't wake up. I pinched Malone— he smacked me.

Clearly we were awake and alive, so what I saw couldn't have been ghosts. Oh sure, they could have been hallucinations. I could see how my steady diet of wild berries and slime could lead to such dementia, but I had been eating the same goop for months without a single hallucination.

I paced back and forth trying to figure this pickle out, and came up with, and debated the merits of the following three theories:

#1: The Parallel Universe Theory

Point — The ghosts are me and Malone's doppelgangers (ghosts of our doppelgangers really) from a parallel Universe, and they traveled here through one of the random wormholes. The fact that they happened upon a wormhole that lead them to us is either divine providence or mere coincidence. Either way they should be pummeled before they eat our brains.

Counterpoint — If they came from a parallel Universe then why the hell are they dead while you two are alive? That doesn't sound too parallel to me. In fact, it's down right perpendicular.

#2: The Unknown Death Theory

Point — Malone and I are indeed dead. I merely wasn't paying attention when it happened and therefore foolishly believe that I'm still very much alive when the truth is that I'm very much dead. It then follows that Malone and I are having out-of-dead-body experiences right now and we're seeing our ghosts do their thing.

Counterpoint — This is death we're talking about. I don't think you can miss it like you miss a bus.

Point — I wouldn't put it past me.

Counterpoint — Even so, if you were having an out-of-dead-body experience right now you wouldn't be seeing your ghosts. You'd be your ghosts and you'd be looking at your dead bodies from the point of view of your ghostly selves.

Point — Look, this is all getting rather complicated. Can't I just run around screaming my head off?

Counterpoint — It's a little late for that.

#3: The Ghostiverse Theory

Point — There exists in another dimension a parallel world of ghosts, where every man, plant, animal, and bug on Earth has a ghost twin that mirrors everything we do, only it does so in a slightly spookier manner. So, for example, whenever I'm picking my nose, my ghost twin is also picking his nose, but while he does so he has a spooky look in his eyes— as if he could, at any moment, use his finger to bore a hole all the way up through his brain. He wouldn't, unless you did so as well, but the look alone is enough to give anyone the heebeegeebees. Or a cat, let's say there's this cat and it's looking at your naked body in a rather condescending way. Now, at that same time, in this parallel ghostiverse, there's a ghost cat looking at a naked ghost you, also in a rather condescending way but with a touch of that faraway misty dead look that ghosts get sometimes. So, therefore, there is no reason to fear the ghosts because while they can always look spooky, they can only do what we do, and we would never do anything to hurt ourselves. Or would we?

Counterpoint — You silly twit.

After turning these theories over in my head for some time, and getting nowhere with them, illumination finally came not from within me, but from an observation. I saw the ghost Malone hog-tie a monkey and then the ghost me throw the ghost bundle up into the trees.

What made this so special was that the bundled ghost monkey landed on top of an alive bundled monkey—a monkey who had been thrown there just yesterday and had yet to be untied by his friends.

I continued to watch the ghosts, and it turned out that every ghost monkey thrown into the trees landed on a real monkey. This, after a few moments of deep thinking, made me realize that what I was looking at weren't ghosts. It was yesterday. The same fluctuations that were causing the time loops must also be causing these images from yesterday to seep into today.

I'm not sure which I'm more afraid of, ghosts or yesterday, but just knowing what I was dealing with put me at some ease. I only wish there was a Bogumil around so I could show him this. I imagine he'd get a kick out of knowing that nothing was left of yesterday's world. Nothing but light.

7
All for company

I saw no less than two, count 'em, two Mr. Burks this morning. It was Old Burk and Middle Burk and the former chased the latter.

This was the first I saw of them since the time when we were all together in Young Burk's house. They looked like they went through quite an ordeal since then. Both were unshaven, wearing the same clothes I saw them in before, only now the clothes were soiled and torn. They lost a considerable amount of weight, so much so that their pants were nearly falling off. I suppose there's little time to wash up and sit down to a good meal while you're being chased (something I'm sure the monkeys could attest to) or while you're doing the chasing (something Malone and I could attest to).

They were both out of breath, completely exhausted really, and the desperate chase degraded to a slow pursuit, like two elderly men racing to the buffet bar to get the last scoop of butterscotch pudding. It appeared that it was all over when Middle Burk, who was in the lead by a good ten yards, collapsed against a tree. At first, Old Burk smiled at this and shuffled forward closing the gap. But his energy quickly faded after a few steps, and he too collapsed against a tree. The two sat there, too focused on each other to notice Malone and I eating just a few feet away. Malone figured out how to lasso tree frogs that day, so we both had frog legs hanging out of our mouths. I looked on with mild interest.

"Let's make a deal," said Old Burk between huffs.

"I'm listening," said his middle self.

"I'll only market WOW for military use."

"Foreign or domestic?"

"Well. Both."

"No dice."

Malone stopped chewing his frog and perked up when he heard their voices. For a moment it looked like he would get up and go over to them, and I was afraid that I would lose my friend. But then he waved them off as if he was dismissing them as something he couldn't be bothered with anymore and returned to eating his share of frogs.

Old Burk's lip started to quiver. "Why do you hate me?"

Middle Burk's lip quivered back. "Because you make me sick! Look at what you've done to yourself. To us! And for what?"

"I did it for us!"

"Ha! Liar! You did it for yourself."

"Same thing! What do you know anyway? You're a child! To you life is no more complicated than a game of Bingo. But when you grow up you find it's more like chess. And you'll make the same moves I made when you realize that you're playing against nothing but jerks and assholes."

"I'd never!"

"Of course you would. I am a product of who you are now. It's like you gave *birth* to me. I came from your spiritual vagina!"

This really got to Middle Burk. It was as if this was the first time he realized he was at least somewhat responsible for the existence of the older man sitting across from him. He looked at the ground for a moment, gathering his thoughts. Then he clenched his fists, rose to his feet, and said through his teeth, "Then I am your mother. And as your mother, I have the God-given right to spank you, even to the point of severe numbness, as I see fit!"

Old Burk stammered to his feet, using the tree for leverage. With ice cold resolve in his eyes he said, "Not if I devolve you first, like the rest of them."

Malone and I raised an eyebrow at each other.

Middle Burk looked concerned after hearing this threat, and he turned to shuffle off on his cramped and tired legs. Old Burk slowly shuffled after him.

The two eventually made their way toward a wormhole. Since there were plenty of natural wormholes floating about for them to choose from, they didn't even have to use their WOWs anymore, which it appeared they had lost anyway.

As Middle Burk inched away from his older self through the wormhole he turned to me, and, without breaking stride, said, as his eyes bulged, "Sic Semper Tyrannis!"

The wormhole stayed open long enough that I could have followed them through, returning to my role in their game, but I didn't see the point in doing so. Either I could go and chase after them through time and space, or I could stay here and chase monkeys. I saw little difference between the two and decided to stay put.

8
Ah, Youth!

The very next day Malone and I came across the young Mr. Burk near the stream where we frequently went to take water breaks. I had briefly wondered what became of him when I saw that he wasn't with his older selves, but I didn't exactly lose any sleep over it.

In the middle of about twelve Miniatures, Young Burk was doing a weird and slightly wonderful dance. It looked like a dance he made up, with a lot of high knee stepping and energetic kicking involved. There wasn't any music playing, but if there were I imagine it would be something with a lot of fast drumming and delirious fiddle playing. It even appeared that the Miniatures were dancing around with him, having a good old time with their lights flashing blue, green, and yellow and their beepers beeping happily along.

Whatever the dance was (perhaps a jig?), it was having an affect on Malone, who must have been able to hear or feel all of the stomping about going on because he started dancing next to me.

"Quick! Join me!" pleaded Young Burk, as if he was asking us to help him pull children out of a burning building.

"I can't dance. I tried once, and I ended up puncturing my date's retina. There was blood and some kind of white goo everywhere. And the screaming...dear Lord, the screaming," I said, while Malone did a remarkable job mimicking Burk's jig.

"Now's not the time for self-doubt, Joe."

"What's it time for then? Dancing?"

"Action!"

"OK I'll try. But you should cover your nose just in case."

"I'm not dancing, you idiot. I'm trying to crush these little robots."

"Why?"

"Why? Why?" He was searching for an answer. "Well, why not?"

He had me there. I ask myself that same question thousands of times each day. I wake up in the morning and before I even open my eyes I ask: why? And the answer I always come up with is: well, why not? I go through this question and answer in almost every action I take, from eating slime to chasing monkeys.

So why should I join Young Burk in stomping the Miniatures? Well, why not.

If they were nicer to me when I tried to make friends with them earlier, then maybe I wouldn't have said why not. But they weren't. Not only did they run away from me, reacting to me like the monkeys react to me (the only difference being that the monkeys have a damn good reason to run, while the Miniatures have nothing but my smile and a warm hello) they also didn't even have the common courtesy to offer to find or make me someone or something else to be my friend—something more suitable.

They are robots, and I'm sure they could make me a robot friend, something small enough that I could carry about with me in my pocket. Something smooth I could stroke with my finger. How easy would that have been for them to make? But no, no, no, they treated me like a monster and ran off in red-blinking-light fear. And for that alone, they deserved to taste my wrath.

I had my stick in hand and, instead of doing a jig, I went at them with that, smacking at the ground in a rapid-fire motion that I had learned from weeks of monkey chasing.

Malone decided to stick with the dance and kick hopped over behind me. I don't think he was interested in smashing the Miniatures because he frequently strayed away from Burk and I, dancing on both sides of, and even in, the water. But the robots were scooting around so wildly that he couldn't help but crush a few of them, if accidentally.

Meanwhile, I was kicking ass. My stick method was far superior to the jig, and I quickly had scored several kills to Burk's one—and that one had been injured by an earlier blow from my stick, so credit me with an assist there.

With each raise of my stick I'd ask why, and with each smash down I'd answer why not.

It didn't take long for the Miniatures to realize that it wasn't all fun and games anymore and that there was a new Sheriff in town—not the "Now take it easy, boys" reluctant lawman, but the shining-his-star-with-tobacco-spit kind. The Miniatures' lights turned red, their beeps turned into sirens of terror, and they tried to flee. But my stick's reach was too long, their hops too short, and Burk and I quickly had them backed up against the river. Within a few minutes it was all over.

This was something new for me. With the monkeys it's never over, and I never have to step back, look at what I've done, and make sense of it all. There's just the endless chase, going from one monkey to the next. But with the Miniatures Massacre there was a definite end, and it came as I watched Burk turn the last tiny robot into a small pile of smoking bits and pieces.

"Now what?" I asked.

"Now we go find some more! And smash them too!"

"YES! BRING THEM ON!" I declared, with my stick raised high. Then the part of my brain that often says things like "You know, Joe, what you're doing doesn't make a lick of sense" kicked in and I had to ask Burk, "But why?"

He should have just said "Well, why not" again but he didn't. Instead he ruined it by saying, "Because we're the only ones who can stop them."

"From what? Being cute?"

"Cute? Look at them, Joe. They're up to something."

"Like what?"

"What do you think they're building over there?"

"A factory."

"A factory? Ha! Why would they build a factory here?"

"Why wouldn't they? Ah-ha!"

Burk shook his head and walked off into the brush, motioning for me to follow. I grabbed Malone by the hand.

Young Burk led us to the edge of the forest where he climbed up a tree and sat on one of the more sturdy branches. We went up after him, the irony of the whole situation of us climbing up a tree was not lost on Malone and I. We exchanged smiles.

As we looked over the savannah toward the construction site, Young Burk said that the whole thing seemed fishy.

We were all quiet for a moment as we pondered this.

"I fear all this has something to do with what's happened to space-time," he said. "And I suppose it's mostly my fault. Not me me, but the two older me's really. But still, eventually it all goes back to me, doesn't it? And I suppose you can't blame those little robots, because whatever it is they're doing, they're just following orders."

"Maybe you could have come to this conclusion before we smashed them."

"Maybe. But who has time to think before acting? Hey, did I ever tell you about the first time I met myself?"

"This is the first conversation we've ever had."

"Oh right. Well, here's how it happened. I was on the toilet one evening, dealing with a nasty bit of diarrhea. The stuff was coming out orange, *bright* orange, so you can imagine my state of mind. There I am, pants around my ankles, and in walks me. Well, not me exactly. More of a middle-aged me.

"He comes in and right off says, 'You're either with me or against me.' And I say, 'Well, who are you?' And he says, 'I'm you.' So I say, 'Then I guess I'm with you.'

"Then he goes on to tell me the whole sad story about how I go on to discover time travel. And how I abuse it. He says I know that it's damaging the very fabric of space-time, and yet I keep on doing it because of greed.

"He sat down on my naked lap and said, with tears in his eyes, that we owed it to ourselves and to humanity to stop him. How could I say no to that?"

"How did he know all this?" I asked.

"Old Burk, your boss, went back in time and brought him into the present. He brought a lot of different aged hims back."

"Why would he do that?"

"Because he needed help. He figured he couldn't trust anyone else to work for him, because sooner or later they'd find out the secret and blow the whistle. So he got himself to work for him. They did all of the research, the accounting, the designing—everything behind the scenes. He built an underground complex for them all, right under his house. It had a kitchen, bedrooms, lab, and office space for them all. He put them to work, said that everything they we're doing was the greater good of Burk, and locked them in. After a few weeks they started to get wise, realizing from their research that the amount of time travel going on was clearly too much for the Universe to handle, and that Old Burk had no intention of downsizing things. So they revolted. That's when Old Burk went over the edge. He rounded them up and did something horrible to all of them. All of them except for the Burk who got me. He escaped."

"What's the horrible thing he did to them?" I asked.

"He devolved them. The bastard devolved them all into monkeys. Malone here is one of them."

"Malone is a Burk?"

"Yep. That's why he's so good with that lasso. Did you know I was Junior State Rodeo Champion three years running?"

"I did. Which reminds me, what's the Texas skip?"

"That's funny. Your friend asked the same thing."

"What friend?"

"Martini."

"When did you see him?"

"A few days ago, over at the worksite. He works there."

"What! How can that be?"

"He said something about an interview, and references, but he didn't go into much detail. He also offered me a cushy office job in his office, but I declined when he wouldn't tell me what they're building."

"Where can I find him? Maybe I can get him to talk."

"Here," he said, handing me a small, oval plastic card. It was white with a blue circle on it. "You just push the button on the back there."

"What is this?"

"It's his business card."

9
The Trio

I climbed down the tree after Young Burk and Malone showed me the Texas skip, which turned out to be a vertical lasso loop that is repeatedly pulled from one side of the body to the other with the roper skipping through the center of the loop with each pass. Hopscotch and chaps apparently had nothing to do with it.

When I hit the ground I looked back up and saw a few of the other monkeys, the ones I had been chasing, join them. They bummed cigarettes off Burk and all of them sat around smoking in silence.

"I'm staying here, Joe," Burk told me, "this is one Robert Burk who has given up. And I'm keeping this guy with me," he said, putting an arm around Malone. "He's the only one who understands me."

I pushed the button on Martini's card. I had never seen a calling card with a button before, so I didn't know what to expect.

The button lit up and a blue laser beam shot out from it, winding its way out of the forest and into the project site. I never knew that light could bend and create a path on its own, without anything reflecting it.

Not knowing if the beam was meant to lead Martini to me or me to Martini, I went ahead and began to follow it, figuring that either way it didn't do me any good to stay put.

As I emerged from the forest, and began my walk through the work site, I got a lot of snippy looks from the Humanoids, Orbs, Cylinders, and Miniatures I passed. Many of them stopped what they were doing to watch me, and I feared, from the hatred in their eyes, that they would all attack me in unison, leaving me with no choice but to fight for my life. I practiced clenching my fist and punching the air just in case.

But they didn't attack, and I think it was the blue light that protected me. It must be a signal to them that I am on official business and that they should fuck off.

The beam led me to a small office building, only five stories high, that stood in the middle of a circular patch of grass that stood apart from the chaos of the worksite. All around the grass the work raged on, with power tools and heavy machinery creating a terrible racket, but inside the circle there was a strange quiet that I noticed with the first step I took into it. It was like stepping into a bubble, or even a wormhole. I played with this for a while, hopping back and forth, on and off the grass, and laughing like a child as my ears alternately took in the peace and quiet and grinding and pounding noises.

The light from Martini's calling card shined directly on one of the buzzers on the front door to the building. There were five buzzers in all, labeled as follows:

1. ♦⤢
2. &⃕)(eᴛ⤢♎❖■eᴛ♦♎≋•)(⤢)(•
3. Hot Yoga by Ba Hubba
4. •♏⊠)(□●&⃕eᴛ≋♑♋•⤢♎⊟○■
5. Tullio Martini, RR Manager

The labels for floors 1, 2, and 4 didn't make a lick of sense to me, and did little more than highlight numbers 3 and 5, making them seem even more out of place. I assumed that the stuff I couldn't understand was written in an alien, or perhaps robot, language and that those floors contained little for me besides further confusion and probable molestation.

The discovery that Ba Hubba Tree Bob was running a hot yoga studio in the building did make me do a double take. I know that it only said "Ba Hubba" and not "Ba Hubba Tree Bob," but really now, how many Ba Hubbas do you think are running around out there.

I took a good look at the hot yoga label, convinced myself it was real, and then quickly forgot about it so I could do what I came there to do—have a chat with Martini.

If I had dealt with the Ba Hubba issue just then, I would sit down and smack my face back and forth for a bit before going on. And I just didn't have time for that.

I pushed the fifth-floor buzzer and the door immediately opened, revealing a flight of stairs. I was hoping that there would be an elevator so that I could bypass floors 1, 2, 3 (especially three), and 4 and not deal with whatever flapdoodle they held. But there wasn't, so I did the next-best thing.

I put my head down and bounded up all four flights without taking my eyes off my feet and belting out "CHARGE!" (drawing out the 'r' for most of the journey) until I reached the top. There I found a door with Martini's name printed on it, and under that a request, in quotes: "Stop. Take a deep breath. Exhale. Repeat. Do the Charleston. Now you may enter."

I did the breathing just because the run up the stairs had me winded, but dancing the Charleston was out of the question. If Martini wanted people to do a dance before entering his office he could at least provide some music. But he didn't, so I went in, and there I found Martini and a Miniature doing yoga by one of the many large windows in his office. Actually, Martini was definitely doing yoga, while the little robot was bopping around next to him and could have, in its own wired mind, been doing a number of different things. I only say that it was doing yoga because it wore a tiny sweatband around its body.

Martini, also wearing a sweatband, looked, for the first time since I've known him, happy. Something had gone awry.

"Joe! What are you doing here?" he asked as if we had bumped into each other in a mall.

He held both his legs behind his head and his butt was, somehow, slightly off the floor. What I'm saying here is that he was, in a way, levitating.

"Joe, this is *so* crazy," he continued, "I was just talking about you. Weren't we just talking about Joe?" He addressed this last question to the Miniature who responded with a blink and a chirp which I suppose could have stood for "Oh yes, we sure were!"

"What's with the robots?" I asked while I squinted to see if a string or something was holding him up. There wasn't anything. The bastard really was floating.

"Oh these little guys?" He said, "Well, you know. Ba Hubba always says one should never meditate, or do anything, EVER, alone."

"What about going to the bathroom? Can you do that alone?"

"I think that's OK...but only if you leave the door open."

"Martini, what are you doing here?"

"What am I doing in this office, in this time, or in this position?"

"Time and office."

"Oh," he was disappointed, "So you're saying that you know that this is the incredibly difficult, and *highly* advanced, Da Love Booty position? I've been working on it for quite some time now, and for awhile I could only get one leg up, but now, NOW, just look at me, Joe," he was joyfully bobbing from side to side, "look at what I've accomplished. You go through your whole life wondering 'Will I ever do anything grand?' And then you finally do, and let me tell you something, it is *so* worth it."

The veins in my necked popped out. "DAMMIT, MARTINI, WHAT ARE YOU DOING HERE!"

The happiness drained from his face as his butt softly returned to the ground. I had grounded him.

"Excuse us, won't you," he calmly asked the Miniature who chirped a "sure thing," and hopped out of the office.

"Well Joe, since you're so set on knowing, I'm the RR manager."

"RR?"

"Robot Resources."

"You're the HR guy?"

"Yeah, but for all the robots. *All* of them, Joe."

The pride radiating out from him led me to think that maybe Burk's suspicions where wrong. Because how could Martini be so proud of his job if the Duo truly was up to no good?

"What are they building out there, Martini?"

"Well, that's the thing. You see—" A buzzer rang. "Oh, hang on a minute, I have an appointment."

An Orb slowly floated into the office, and as much as a shiny silver ball can look like he was a kid going to see the principal, this Orb did.

"Come in, come in," said Martini, who instantly chippered up again as he stood to meet the Orb.

"Look, uh, this is never easy," he said to the Orb, "so I'm not going to beat around the bush. It's not working out, buddy. We're letting you go."

The Orb, who at first looked like it would take the news remarkably well as it gently floated in place, suddenly lost it and began to spin and jerk about.

Martini disapprovingly shook his head. "Now, now. There's no need for that. Look, there are plenty of other jobs out there for a robot like you. You're young, you had a chance to get some good work experience here, and you'll bounce back. I'm sure of it."

Martini gave the robot a thumbs-up, which only caused the Orb to fall deeper into despair. After a moment rocking gently back and forth, trying to figure out what to do with itself, the Orb rammed itself into the wall, leaving a sizable dent. Then it began to violently pound the wall with one of its arms, shaking the entire room.

Martini shook his finger at the robot. "Stop that. That's company property. Don't do this. Don't. No. Come on now. No. NO! OK look here, you. Hey! No. No. No. Whoa! OK, that does it."

As the Orb repeatedly head butted the coat rack (this after slapping itself a good ten or so times), Martini went over to his desk and pushed a yellow button.

"Now you've done it, mister," he said, "You brought this on yourself!"

A Humanoid came into the room and immediately was on the Orb, bashing it with what appeared to be a disembodied arm of another Humanoid. It held the arm by its hand and did the bashing with the shoulder region, which was leaving some rather deep dents in the Orb.

The Orb, shaken, took three more blows before gathering its wits enough to haul ass out of the room. The Humanoid left in pursuit, and Martini and I were alone again.

Martini straightened his tie and took a deep breath. "OK, sorry about that. Busy, busy, busy. So, Joe, I'm just going to need your resume and at least three references."

"I'm not here for a job, Martini. I want some answers."

"Oh right, right, right. What kind of answers?"

"What are they building out there?"

"Oh gee, wow, that's so not my department. Someone on the 1st floor should be able to answer that."

"They're not going to, well, do something fishy are they?"

He was shocked. "Fishy? Oh, come on now. Us? Do something fishy?"

"It's just that Burk—"

"Oh Burk? Burk, eh? *That* guy? He's crazy, Joe. You can't trust him. Completely bonkers."

Martini's right eye twitched, and with the strange tone his voice suddenly took on, led me to suspect that he was fibbing. But before I could call him a fibber to his face I needed more proof.

"OK. How about this: why are they building that thing, whatever it may be, here and now?"

"Well, these guys are professionals, Joe, so I'm sure they did an *exhaustive* study and determined that this was the most ideal, cost-effective, hassle-free time/location for the, uh, thing."

"Right. Do you even know how you got here?" I asked.

"I'm not sure. I went to sleep one night in my own bed and woke up in this office."

"And who made you the RR manager?"

"Beats me. I saw these business cards with that title on my desk, and that name plate on the door and all, and I just sort of went with it."

"You didn't think all this was a bit odd?"

"Well...no."

"What about the hot yoga by Ba Hubba studio on the third floor? Don't tell me that's not odd."

"It's not odd. It's grand." There was a far away, dreamy look in his eyes as he said this, as if he was thinking of a time when he skipped naked through a field of poppies.

"No, it's odd, Martini. Peculiar even. I'd even go as far as saying it's completely stupid."

It was as if I had said that skipping naked through a field of poppies was for kneebiters.

He stood up. "I won't let you say that."

"What are you going to do? Use your yoga to silence me? Unlikely! I'm going to say my piece and you're going to listen, you fibbing dippy little twit."

Martini's eyes bulged as if I had just called him a fibbing dippy little twit.

"You can't talk to me like that anymore. I'm the RR Manager. And you, you're nothing. You come in here, into my office, into my life again, and you do nothing but put me down and call me fat. How dare you. You're the dippy one! And I don't wish to have dealings with you anymore. So get out of my face you, you, you dibbing...fippy little tit!"

I grabbed him by his collar. "This is all really strange, Martini. And you know it." As soon as I said this he put his hands over his ears and began to sing his pancakes song.

"Mixin' pancakes! Stirrin' pancakes!"

"And you're just going along with it!"

"Pop 'em in the pan!"

"I KNOW YOU CAN HEAR ME!"

"Fryin' pancakes! Flippin' pancakes!"

"MARTINI!"

"Catch 'em if you can!"

"I READ YOUR JOUNRAL, MARTINI! I READ THE WHOLE THING! AND YOU KNOW WHAT I DID WHILE I READ IT? I LAUGHED, MARTINI! I LAUGHED AT YOUR GIRLIE, GAY THOUGHTS!"

That, he heard. He stopped singing and slowly removed his hands from his ears, shock all over his face. His lower lip quivered, his nose sniffed, his fists clenched, and then:

"How dare you! I hate you, Joe. I HATE YOU! I HATE YOU! I HATE YOU! AND...I'M TELLING!"

He ran over to his desk and, before I could catch him, pushed the yellow button on his desk once again.

It was in this position—with one finger pressing a button that promised to bring me nothing but pain, and a look of utter defiance and triumph on his face—that I last saw Martini.

Another Humanoid, this time swinging a metal arm at me, came through the door.

I bobbed and weaved to avoid the initial attacks, but knew it was only a matter of swings before my noggin received a floggin'. So I did what the Orb did earlier and took off out of the office and into the stairwell.

The Humanoid followed me out, and was about to overtake me as I reached the third floor. With no other options outside of getting my head kicked in, I flung open the 3rd floor door, ducked in, and slammed the door behind me.

With the Humanoid banging on the door (he tried to trick me with the shave and a haircut bit before going into the straight up pounding) I looked around the 3rd floor room. To my right an Orb floated with quite a few good dents in it. I assumed it was the recently fired Orb from Martini's office. It looked to be at its wits end, and when the Orb saw me it went into a wild frenzy of bobbing and smacking itself, which only stopped after I slapped the foolish thing.

After a pause, the Orb slapped me back, and I was about to karate chop the little bugger into oblivion when a familiar voice from the center of the room stopped me short.

"Hello, little speck!"

10
The Whole Shebang

Ba Hubba was in the same position I found Martini in earlier: floating with his legs behind his head. The only difference was that instead of having one Miniature bopping around him, Ba Hubba had two *floating* around him.

There was a wormhole in the corner of the room, and out from it came a man in a light yellow robe—a Bogumil. He ignored me, walked over to Ba Hubba, looked at a calculator he had in his hand, whispered something in Ba Hubba's ear, which made Be Hubba smile, and then he went back through the hole.

When the man was gone, Be Hubba opened his eyes. He was happy to see me. "Our beams cross again!"

For a second I thought by 'our beams' he meant 'our dicks,' and the trickle of testosterone left in me was about to give Ba Hubba a high-five for the raunchy macho remark. But then I remembered the whole "beams of light" bit, to which all the trickle could do was sigh.

"My, my, my," he said, "What interesting roads our beams have taken. Twisty and turny, one minute here, another there. Zip! Zip! Zip! Never stopping, always shooting forward, sometimes out of control, other times in. But of late, out. Yes, yes? Whoooosh! What a ride! Wouldn't you say so?"

"Well, I guess. Maybe not in those exact words. Except for zip. I actually think I'd just say zip and leave it at that."

"Delightful! Since we're so in tune with each other, don't you think it would be wise for you to meditate with me and these fine robots?"

"Thanks, but I'm not in the mood to mediate on things right now. I'd rather forget. Do you know any forgetation techniques?"

"Your life has taken some unexpected turns lately, yes? And now you feel lost. Yes, yes?"

"Yes, yes."

"Well, how will you ever figure out how you got *here* and how you're going to get your toosh back *there* if you don't sit still for some time and retrace?"

"I'll have you know that I've been doing more than thinking about how I got here. I've been writing about it."

"Oh yes? How far have you gotten?"

"I've gotten to now."

"No, I mean how far *back* have you gotten?"

"Back? Well, er, I started out with this nice little bit about the time I went to the zoo with my family when I was just a kid. But that was too far back, so I kind of jumped forward a bit to when I shot Lincoln. What does it matter? I'm here now and I know how I got here."

"But Joe, how did you get from going to the zoo to shooting Lincoln? Or how did you even get from your mother's womb to a zoo of all places?"

"Oh I don't know. Anyone could fill in the blanks. I was born. I spit up, cried, and shat myself for awhile. Then I learned how to keep my food down, talk, and use the toilet. A bit later I shot Lincoln. There, big deal."

"Joe. Joe, Joe, Joe. Oh Joe. Joe, Joe, Joe. Joe, da doe, doe, doe. Joe. Joe, Joe, J—"

"What!"

"No wonder you're so lost. Life is a puzzle, Joe. One long puzzle.

And there is no such thing as an extra piece that you can toss aside. Your problem is that you're not working with a complete set of pieces."

"How could I possibly remember *all* of the pieces?"

"By sitting down here with me, closing your eyes, envisioning your life as if it was a continuous beam of light, traveling back along that beam, recalling every moment, until you make it all the way back to your mother's womb."

"I'm not sure I want to go back there. I mean, I must have left for a good reason, right?"

"Just because you left the womb doesn't mean you shouldn't revisit it in your mind," he said as he lifted up his shirt to reveal his potbelly and the huge outie-bellybutton on it. "The feeling of warmth and connectedness to another person you had there was stronger than anything you could imagine. Nothing, not sex or even love come close."

The graphic image of my mother's womb that popped into my mind and the image of Ba Hubba's outie in my eyes were combining in my guts to make me nauseous. He must have seen this in my face because he quickly pulled his shirt back down and thankfully changed the subject.

"But there's more to it than that," he said. "You'll be able to go *beyond* the womb, beyond this world, this dimension, back to the very source of all life! To fundamental connectedness! It will take a lifetime to get there, and not all of us will make it, but we must try. It's what everybody wants, Joe. They just don't know it."

"What do they want?"

"To have something in common. Not just with their family or a few friends, but with everything. With the entire Universe! From the bug in your soup to the woman in your arms, imagine how wonderful life would be if you felt an unbreakable connection to everything that has ever lived or will ever live. Every particle joined at the hip!"

Maybe the overwhelming heat in the room got to me—it must have been close to 100 degrees in there—because I found myself able to look past the corniness of what he was saying, and I actually yearned for the feeling of connectedness he described. The more he talked about it—and he went on for quite some time—the more I wanted it. To feel, at some fundamental level, linked to all the people I bump into and stand in line with everyday, to my co-workers, my dead parents, the people I see in the past, Mr. Puss, the Duo, the monkeys, some girl half way around the world who just yawned ...

If I felt that, I thought, my life wouldn't be so detached, and I wouldn't feel as if I was bouncing around in someone else's perverted pinball machine. If I ever felt lost I could just find the nearest living creature, look into its beady little eyes, see the faint glimmer of the spark that is the fundamental connection that binds us all, and feel like I was home.

If Ba Hubba could give me that, I would flap my arms like a duck and fly around the room with those little robots until I was wearing diapers again.

"And all it will cost you," Ba Hubba continued, folding his hands and closing his eyes, "Is just $49.95 a month."

My heart slammed on the breaks while my brain yelled, "Watch where you're going!"

"What?"

"$49.95," he repeated, "It's a bargain. Who can't afford $49.95 a month to achieve Whole Shebang Oneness? If these little robots can afford it, you can too."

"The Miniatures are *paying* you? My God, you're a crook!" I shot him an accusatory finger my mom would have been proud of. "A flim-flam man!"

"Would a flim-flam man cut you such a square deal? Look, if you don't like the monthly payment plan, you can just buy something from the ongoing auction of my personal items. You can really feel My Blessing in each piece. I just added a pair of hot pink terry shorts that I've worn *several* times."

"And how much are they?"

He didn't even blink before saying, "Opening bids start at 4,000 dollars. Winning bid automatically gets a *very* light yellow robe."

I did blink. Then I took a minute to calm down.

"Those robots aren't even alive," I said, "What the hell do they care about Whole Shebang Oneness?"

"Everything cares about it. Plants, bugs, stars. We're all connected to the same thing, Joe."

"And what is that thing? What are we all connected to? A ball of light? Couldn't you think of something better than that? Huh? Jerk!"

"There is something much better than that."

"Well then what is it? Do you even know?"

"Of course."

"What is it then? What are we all connected to?"

"Do you really want to know?"

"Yes."

"Are you sure your unprepared mind can handle it?"

"Just tell me before I slap your fat face!"

"Fine! You asked for it. We are all connected To The Spiritual Master, The Great Transmitter, The Love-Delight, The Ever-Bright Sun, to Me. ME, ME, MEEEEEEEEEEEEEE!"

Then the bastard stuck his tongue out and gave me the longest, juiciest, most disgusting raspberry ever.

11
No Vacancy

Ba Hubba closed his eyes and went into a deep meditation after he finally ran out of raspberry juice. I assume he went back to rolling around in his bloated delusions of grandeur like a pig in shit.

I wanted to ask him how he got here and if he knew anything about the building project, so I tried to get his attention by whistling, clearing my throat, and throwing things at the Miniatures. Nothing worked.

Feeling that world had finally lost the little sense it once had, and finally getting sick of the holier-than-thou looks I was getting from the floating Miniatures, I left the room. In the stairwell, the Humanoid that chased me earlier didn't even notice me this time. It was too preoccupied trying to swat down a Miniature that floated around its head like a fly.

I made my way out of the building, and then the work site, ending up back by the tree that housed Burk and Malone. Once there I saw that the dented Orb had followed me.

"Shoo, Orb. Don't bother me."

The robot sunk low to the ground and made a sad, powering-down sound. It wasn't much but it was enough to make me feel bad for the thing.

"Fine. Stay."

The Orb popped back up to eye level with me and made an uplifting powering-up sound, which was almost enough for me to tell it to shove off again. But I didn't. I realized that the thing, along with Malone, were the only friends I had.

On my way back to the tree I considered climbing back up and re-joining Burk and Malone, but once I got there I found that wasn't even an option. Someone had posted a "No vacancy" sign on the tree trunk.

At first I thought that maybe the sign was only meant for the other monkeys, but then I realized that monkeys can't read and the only way to inform them that there's no vacancy would be to beat them out of the tree with a stick.

So the sign must have been for people, or possibly robots, but just to make sure I decided to yell up into the tree and ask.

"Does this apply to me as well?"

"Does what apply to you?" called back Burk, who stuck his head out from behind a thick cluster of leaves.

"This 'No vacancy' business."

"Oh that. Yes."

"What about him?" I asked, pointing to the Orb.

"Um, hold on." He popped his head back behind the branch for a few seconds and then came back and said, "He can come up."

"Now wait just a minute!"

The Orb floated up past me and into the tree, leaving me once again alone and abandoned.

Feeling tired and with nowhere else to go, I walked over to the next closest tree and collapsed against it. It didn't take long for me to fall asleep.

12
Toodle Loo!

When I awoke the following morning I had a visitor standing above me. It was Boogedy. But I wasn't sure it was him because he wore a plaid suit and did something I never saw him do before: smile.

"Good morning," he said (yes, said) in a voice that would have put many professional voice-over artists to shame. And he was even chipper.

"Good morning," I replied, somewhat unsure if I was dreaming this.

"Now that you're awake, we can start. Are you guys up there ready?" He shouted up into the tree.

"Go ahead," Burk shouted back. Only his head was visible, and next to it was Malone's head. The Orb floated slightly above them.

"What is all this?" I asked.

"I have a very important message for everybody."

"You speak English?"

"I speak beautiful English. And in the proper frequency range at that. We just figured out how to do it right. Oh! And I sing! La, la, la, la, la, la, la. Lo, lo, lo, lo, lo, lo, lo. De, de, de, de, de, de, de. I've been taking lessons for months now."

"It shows."

"Doesn't it? Now, ready to listen?

"To what?"

"To an important message from the people and leaders of Aucky Spinsty."

I looked confused.

"It's my home planet," he said.

"Ah, I see."

"OK then. I wrote the message down so I wouldn't muck it up," he said as he pulled out a crumbled-up piece of paper from his pocket. He then sprayed something into his throat from a small canister.

"Here it goes."

Dear Mr. or Mrs. Human,

Events on Earth have reached the final days of decision. For more than a week, Aucky Spinsty and other planets have pursued patient and praiseworthy labors to neutralize the human race without violence.

We have passed more than three decrees in the Cohesive Planets Union (CPU). We have sent two inspectors to try and warn you. Our good faith has not been returned.

The human race has used foolishness as a ploy to gain time and advantage. It has consistently dodged CPU decrees demanding full neutralization. Over the past few weeks, CPU inspectors have been threatened by a human with a flashlight, hog-tied by that same human's monkey sidekick, and thoroughly deceived. Peaceful efforts to neutralize the human race have failed again and again and again.

Intelligence gathered by this and other planets leaves no doubt that the human race continues to possess and overuse some of the most ridiculous contraptions ever devised. Humans have already used these contraptions to seriously degrade the space-time continuum around their own planet.

The human race has a history of reckless aggression. It has a deep hatred of the unknown. The danger is clear: using ridiculous contraptions, you humans could eventually destroy the entire known Universe.

Aucky Spinsty and other planets did nothing to deserve or invite this threat. But we will do everything to defeat it. Instead of drifting along toward tragedy, we will set a course toward stability. Before the day of awfulness can come, before it is too late to act, this peril will be erased.

The Walloping Weapon of Harmony is currently being built on Earth at a time before the dawn of humans, and it will ultimately destroy the planet. Since the Earth is a living thing, in destroying it we will also wipe out any trace of its existence from this point forward. We regret to inform you that this will cause the Earth to, in effect, be pulled right out from under all of its inhabitants across time.

But not to fear! After wiping away Earth we plan to build a new planet in its place. This planet will be called Farth, and will be an exact replica of Earth. The only difference being that there won't be any humans nor, as an evolutionary precaution measure, any primates either. In your place, we will establish the Californian Sea Lion, Zalophus califonianus, as the most dominant species on the planet, an animal which recently won the "Earth's Most Agreeable Disposition Contest" held on our planet. It narrowly beat out the panda bear's enlightened apathy with its playful exuberance. These sea lions look just like the ones you remember from the

circus, the only differences being that they are slightly more intel-
ligent and their flippers are much stronger and can be used to
better walk on land.

Oh yes, and they have wings. That was the prize for winning the
contest. This way, along with their natural high adaptability, they'll
be able to thoroughly enjoy all that Farth has to offer—land, sea,
and air—and will thus be forever distracted from evolving into
deadly, contraption-building lunatics.

If you would like to see what these sea lions look like, just ask one
of our ambassadors who will be more than happy to show you.

We urge every member of the human race: do not fight for a dying
planet that is not worth your own life. It is too late for humans to
remain in existence. It is not too late for individual humans to act
with honor and protect your Universe by permitting or even aiding
in the peaceful construction of The Walloping Weapon of Harmony to eliminate you and your ridiculous contraptions.

Toodle loo, and thanks in advance for going softly into that deep
dark night.

I was disappointed in myself after hearing that because I didn't
quite react the way I felt one should react when he hears such an awful
thing. I thought I should cry, or sing God Bless America, or at least
perform an act of senseless violence on Boogedy. But I didn't. I just
sat there, staring off into the forest for quite some time. I didn't see
them, but from the sound of it I suspect that Burk, Malone, and the Orb
did the same thing.

It was Boogedy who finally broke the silence.

"Well?" he asked, tapping his foot. "Do you want to see it, or
what?"

"See what?" I asked.

"The sea lion."

"Oh, that. Sure, why not."

"Right."

I thought he was going to whip out a photo, or maybe project a hologram of the sea lion. But he didn't. Instead he pulled out a herring, held it above his head, and whistled.

Out from behind a tree flew an animal that scared the crap out of me. I screamed at what I thought was a barking baby dragon as it flew toward the herring. Burk and the monkeys also screamed as they retreated further into the trees, abandoning me much as I abandoned Mr. Puss not so long ago.

As I watched the creature hover around Boogedy and the fish, I saw that it was in fact a sea lion with wings, and not a dragon. While I no longer feared for my life, I still didn't want the hideous thing anywhere near me.

Boogedy threw the herring high into the air, and the sea lion flew after it with a gentle grace I was amazed to see come from something so disturbing. The sea lion easily caught the fish, gently glided to the ground, and then gave itself a nice round of applause with its flippers as it happily gulped down the fish.

"There," said Boogedy, "That's that. Any questions up there in the tree? No? Good. How about you? Well? Speak up!"

"Um, are you the guy who's been following me?" I asked, keeping an eye on the sea lion which was rocking back and forth like a madman.

"Following you? Oh no. Not me. Must have been one of our inspector teams. They had the fool idea that they could solve all this mess by warning some of you. Ha! Of course, that was before we learned how to speak your languages...oh well, doesn't matter. Me, I'm just an ambassador. I don't follow, I bring messages. And I sing. Now, if you'll excuse me I have separate letters for all of the other animals, plants, and bugs telling them about the sea lion and that it's not

their fault. Wouldn't want them to give up the ghost with *that* on their conscience. I mean, wow!"

"But whose fault is it then?"

He didn't even pause to think about it. "Yours."

"Mine?"

"Well not you specifically. Everybody really. Oh, some more than others, that's for sure. But we've determined it's really all of you. And I *really* need to get going. Busy, busy, busy. Toodle loo!"

And he dashed off into the woods, probably on his way to read a letter to the monkeys I used to chase. I was left staring at the rocking sea lion.

We sat there looking at each other from a distance for a moment before the sea lion hopped over to where I sat. I thought about getting up and running like hell, but I figured that anything with wings could catch me rather easily.

The thing came right up to me, reached out with one of its flippers, and touched my chest as if it was pointing at something. I slowly looked down to see what it was pointing to (perhaps a stain?) and the sea lion immediately flicked its flipper up and slapped my nose. It took me a second to realize what happened—I had fallen for that classic "nose flick" gag.

The sea lion was very pleased with itself and clapped and grinned to show it. Thankfully—or else I suspect I was in for a wedgie—the sound of the Ambassador's whistle in the distance caused the creature to fly away, giving me a wink as it took off, and taking the time to do a few loop-de-loops and mid-air pirouettes along its merry way.

13
Poof

Last night I had a dream that I was swimming through outer space as if it was an ocean. I wasn't alone. It was like a community pool on a hot day, overflowing with people of all colors and ages splashing about. Every animal I could imagine was also there, paddling about as if Noah's Ark had sunk.

As I doggy paddled in place, Mr. Puss swam up to me and looked me right in the eyes with utter contempt. Then he just swam off.

Then Ba Hubba Tree Bob and Mrs. Burk passed by, both naked and doing the backstroke.

In the distance I saw Malone and Watt doing some inspired synchronized swimming and not too far from them was Old and Middle Burk. They were chasing each other in circles.

May swam over and tried to kiss me, but we barely missed each other's lips over and over. Actually, our lips never even made contact with any skin at all as they passed by untouched and smooched empty space. We could have had more success with our eyes open like fish, but we both really wanted to do things right for once. So we kept on trying, and we kept on missing.

We would've gone on like that forever if a Qualcon hadn't finally grabbed May and swam away with her. I hoped she would have struggled more to get back to me, but she let her body go limp. I suppose I can't complain since I didn't even consider swimming after her.

Then a determined Abraham Lincoln floated by. He had a small pistol and was taking shots at me, missing wildly, and shaking his fist with each miss. After awhile he drifted out of range, but I could still hear the shots in the distance.

Finally came Martini, who swam up to me like a frog and actually did kiss me on the lips. I slapped him for it, and he drifted away looking quite crushed.

His was the last familiar face I saw. Everybody else was a stranger, from the family of four holding hands and swimming after what must have been their dog, to the old man chuckling to himself as he spun by like a top.

When I woke up, I decided my life needed a change.

In a few minutes, I'm going to use my belt to tie these pages I've written into a bundle and then throw it through one of these random wormholes. Maybe someone else in a different time and with a firmer mind will be able to make better sense of it all.

Then I'll walk back over to Martini's office, where I intend to apply for a job. I think I'd make a decent Humanoid, if they'll have me. And I hope they will, because it seems like good, honest work.

Hopefully, Burk, Malone and the Orb will soon see me at work, among the other Humanoids. I'll be doing what I do best: focusing on the simple task in front of me, on the how and the now, and letting someone else worry about the why.

And every now and then the other Humanoids will see me step back from my work, and close my eyes. That's when I'll think about last night's dream—about the darkness full of billions of swimming people and animals, stretched out over millions of years, all floating around in empty space. All of them look incredibly surprised and are wondering who or what they can blame for the pickle they're in. Maybe they'll all blame me.

Because chances are they'll feel they haven't done anything to justify their homes and history vanishing on them. Or maybe I'm wrong. Maybe, like a mongrel dog that's shot in the head before it has the chance to maul its owner's son, the swimmers, with their cheeks puffed out and their bodies rotating in the cold shadows of space, will be able to look into themselves, see the potential for each one of them to bring all sorts of horrible things into this world and even into this Universe, and say, before their heads implode, "Maybe we didn't deserve it. But I guess that has nothing to do with it."

More likely though, they'll be pissed off beyond belief. They'll quickly look back down the path of their lives, or possibly like me, only at the most recent pieces in the puzzle, and find nothing to warrant such a thing happening to them. Instead of accepting it, they'll be furious. They'll kick and punch the air, pull their hair, throttle the first person they can get their hands on, some will even cry at the injustice of it all.

But they'll be wrong. Because chances are somewhere along the way, if not multiple times along the way, whether they were aware of it or not, they all played a role in certain a-goings on both in the deep dark night and in the shallow bright day. For most it was only a piddling Rosencrantz or Guildenstern role. Only for a chosen few was it a whopping Hamlet role. Either way it doesn't matter, because in the end whether you deserve it or not has nothing to do with it. There's never enough time to pick out the piddling from the whopping, the brawn from the brains, the Joes from the Burks.

There will only be a few seconds for us all to hold our breath and look childish and foolish one last time.

I wish I could capture that moment on a postcard. I'd mail it to that tender and savage Gawd of Light, with the note on the back reading, "Wish You Were Here."

I kneel down every night and thank Ba Hubba for the artistic powers of Chris Daily, the mad editing skills of Richard SanFilippo, the web design moxie of Beth Cherry, and the big brass balls of Carlton Mellick III.

My writing wouldn't be the same if there wasn't music out there to keep me bouncing in my seat. And no one made me bounce while I wrote *Foop!* like The Flaming Lips, Neutral Milk Hotel, David Byrne, De La Soul, The Magnetic Fields, and Tiny Tim.

For reading an advance copy of the book and giving me some much-needed words of encouragement, I tip my hat to Nick Sagan, Christopher Moore, Neal Pollack, James Morrow, and Tony Vigorito.

Above all, thank you Sara, Mom & Dad, Gina, Mark, the Crisanti's, and the Schaefer's for always having my back, even when I'm acting like a lunatic.

ABOUT THE AUTHOR

Chris Genoa was born in Philadelphia,
went to college in Virginia and London,
and has a special place in his heart for
New Orleans. Foop! is his first novel.
He lives in Brooklyn where he is at work
on his second novel.

Visit him online at **www.chrisgenoa.com**

ABOUT THE ILLUSTRATOR

Chris Daily has no recollection of where he got his artistic powers, nor what any of you are talking about. You can read his online comic *Striptease*, at http://www.stripteasecomic.com.

He lives in Santa Clara, California with his dog.

ABOUT THE COVER ARTIST

Lori Phillips (aka Throw-a-bomb) is 20 years old, from Cincinnati OH, and currently a sophmore in college where she is majoring in ceramics. She plans to add photography as a second major and get my masters degree in both. After school she plans to teach ceramics or photography on the college level, and also be an artist in her my own time. She also hopes to travel the world and maybe one day do photography for National Geographic magazine.

Check out her online at
http://throw-a-bomb.deviantart.com/

NEW TITLES FROM ERASERHEAD PRESS

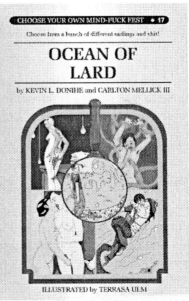

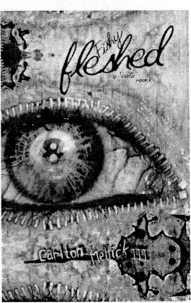

ERASERHEAD PRESS

www.eraserheadpress.com

Books of the surreal, absurd, and utterly strange

WWW.AVANTPUNK.COM

A New Imprint From Eraserhead Press

BIZARRE NOVELS BY
CARLTON MELLICK III

RAZOR WIRE PUBIC HAIR * STEEL BREAKFAST ERA
BABY JESUS BUTT PLUG * OCEAN OF LARD
SATAN BURGER * ELECTRIC JESUS CORPSE
TEETH AND TONGUE LANDSCAPE * FISHY-FLESHED

Printed in the United States
34382LVS00002B/46-48

9 780972 959896